WITHDRAWN
50p

The
Patchwork Quilt

The
Midwest
Patchwork Quilt

Rose Bowden

The Patchwork Quilt

Rose Boucheron

PIATKUS

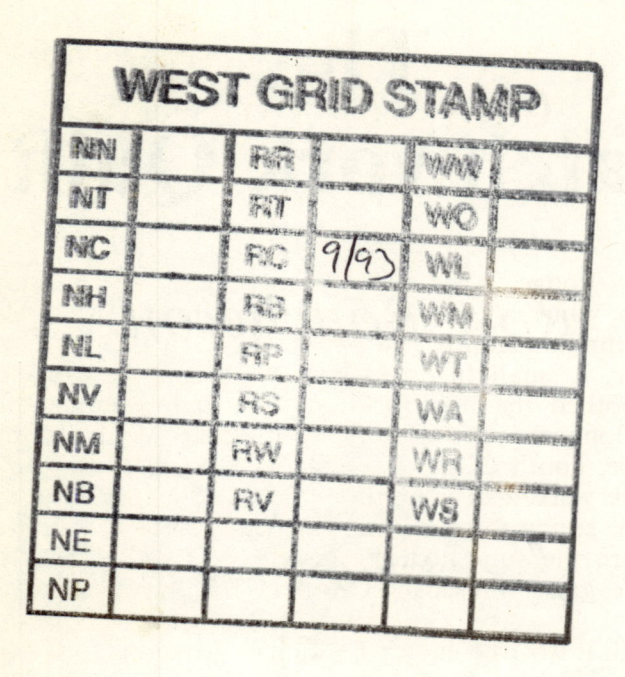

Copyright © 1993 by Rose Boucheron

First published in Great Britain in 1993 by
Judy Piatkus (Publishers) Ltd of
5 Windmill Street, London W1

**The moral right of the author
has been asserted**

*A catalogue record for this book is available
from the British Library*

ISBN 0 7499 0200 0

Phototypeset in 11/12pt Compugraphic Times by
Action Typesetting Limited, Gloucester
Printed and bound in Great Britain by
Bookcraft Ltd, Avon

Chapter One

In Chantry Lodge, Alice Amber was putting the finishing touches to Vanessa's homecoming from India. The teddy bear sat upright against the pillows next to the battered koala bear, a small jug held newly gathered snowdrops. Alice smoothed the bedspread of blue and white cotton with its flounced edge and frills, a small smile playing around her mouth at the thought of her granddaughter's return. She walked over to the window which overlooked the garden, seeing the lawn cut diagonally in two, a bright green where the sun shone now clear of frost, while the rest of the grass was covered with a fine layer of white crystals.

Although it was the end of February, the snowdrops had made a welcome appearance, and the yellow winter aconites shone brightly beneath the window. Vanessa would find a change in temperature after a year in India, she would feel the cold terribly. Alice's mind harked back to her own stay in India as a young married woman. It was difficult to remember now how hot it had been and how listless one felt. It is like pain, she thought, only a remembered thing.

She hoped Vanessa had not been disappointed in her visit, but thought not, judging by the letters she had sent home. She had had another birthday since then, having been away a full year, so that now she was twenty-two, Alice wondered what the experience would have done for her.

She peered through the window at the shrub below, her precious Daphne odora marginata – she hoped to goodness it had not caught the frost. Grown from a sprig no bigger than her hand from someone's garden, she had planted it where it thrived and grew to a bush four feet high, massed with tiny buds that would open and scent the air with their perfume. But it was not all that hardy, as she well knew, and now it looked saddened and pinched with cold. With gardening there were many disappointments as well as joys.

Sometimes she thought she had two faces. Granny Amber, the woman she had become when she had taken Vanessa under her wing all those years ago, and Alice Amber, the woman she really was.

For she had been mother and grandmother to Vanessa, the daughter of her son James and his wife Amanda, that wilful, beautiful, wild creature who had run away with another man when Vanessa was only ten years old.

How could she have done such a thing? The question had been on everyone's lips, but Alice had known no man could have ensnared Amanda for long. She was like a captured butterfly struggling in the net. The question uppermost in Alice's mind had been, how could Amanda have stayed as long as she had? Now Alice was Granny Amber once again to Edouard, six-month-old son of James and his new French wife, Odile. He had been born while Vanessa was in India.

Alice was who she really was. In her sixties, widowed for so long that she almost forgot what her dear husband had looked like. The young man whose photograph stood in a silver frame on her bedside table resembled someone from another age, which indeed he was. Their life together, however idyllic, had been brief. They'd had one son, named after his father – there had been no time for more when James was cruelly taken from her and she had to face early widowhood.

But she was a survivor, with her love of antiques and wild birds. Her main passion was for gardening, as her own garden testified. There'd been years of voluntary work too, everyone knew you could go to Alice Amber if you wanted help or advice. Yet she was a private person who loved to be alone. Her patience and serenity she put down to her stay in India whence she and James had gone as a newly married couple. It was owing to her tales of the sub-continent that Vanessa had taken herself off there.

Fair, willowy, blue-eyed Vanessa was nothing like her exotic glamorous mother — thank God, Alice thought fervently. Hopefully she would find a good husband and settle down. Alice could never get to grips with career women who thought the world was their oyster and that they could live like men. There was nothing as good as a happy marriage, in her opinion.

With a last glance around Vanessa's room, her eye fell on the silver-framed photographs, one of James and one of Vanessa taken on her twenty-first birthday. There were no pictures of Amanda.

Closing the door behind her she made her way to the little sewing room. Thursday was the day of the Red Cross sewing bee, and from the corner cupboard Alice took a large box filled with cotton squares then made her way to the dining room where Gina had covered the table with a cloth. She tipped out a heap of coloured squares in the centre of the table and put out a large basket of assorted cottons and needles. In her spare time she had sewn six-inch squares together and filled them with a polyester stuffing, leaving them open for the sewing circle to sew up and join to each other. The six-foot lengths were then joined sideways and made into wide blankets for the Red Cross. Alice had been doing this for the last twenty years, had indeed instigated the whole idea, and at one time there had been ten or more ladies around the table; now there were only three or four, depending on who had spare time.

Alice sighed contentedly. She always enjoyed these sewing bees.

She ushered in the sewing party when they arrived, noticing that Sheila and Joanna had come in Joanna's car, Ann in her pale blue Mercedes Sports, no sign of Maggie. They hardly ever saw her these days.

They left coats in the hall on the chair, and followed Alice into the dining room.

'Oh, this is nice. I shall look forward to my coffee this morning.'

'Alice — you have a fire. How nice.'

The flames cast a rosy glow on the legs of the old oak table and the red Turkey carpet. They dragged out chairs and sat down.

'More pieces,' Sheila said, diving into her basket. 'I was in Laura Ashley the other day and thought I'd grab these — aren't the colours pretty?'

'Lovely,' Alice said appreciatively. She was always pleased when someone made a spontaneous gesture towards Red Cross funds.

They sat down and raided the workbasket for needles and cotton. 'Where were we?' Joanna asked.

'I filled these the other evening, so now it's joining together,' Alice said as Sheila picked out the brightest coloured squares. It interested her that Sheila always did that, while Joanna picked out the pastels. Ann, who had no idea of colour at all, and never tried to match, always picked up whichever piece was nearest to her.

'No Maggie again,' Joanna said, licking her thread and trying to get it through the eye of the needle.

'She's in California,' Alice said.

'Lucky her.'

'Did I tell you we're going to lose the supply of this filling — apparently Archie Bignold's firm has folded, so no more for us ...'

'Oh, dear.'

'You know, years ago we used to fill them with old nylons, cut into pieces.'

'Perhaps we should do that again?' Ann said.

'Yes. Although we've enough to go on with.'

They settled into a steady sewing routine.

'I expect you're excited — Vanessa coming home tomorrow?'

Ann looked up. 'Oh, is she due home? It only seems like yesterday that she left.'

Sheila closed her eyes then, opening them, smiled at Alice.

'You're going to the airport, of course — when's the plane due?'

'I'm not sure, James will take me. I can't wait to see her again.'

'Of course you can't,' Sheila said sympathetically. 'You've been like a mother to that girl.'

'I wonder what she'll think of the new baby brother?' Joanna said. 'It will seem strange, won't it?'

'She wrote back to say she was delighted, for both of them,' Alice said. 'I expect now, though, she'll make up her mind to get a place of her own in London. There's not much for her round here — I'm not expecting her to make her home with an old woman. She needs to be somewhere where there are other young people.'

'I wonder what she thought of India?' Joanna asked. 'I think she was awfully plucky to go at all.' She shuddered. 'I couldn't bear it. The beggars, the poverty — '

Alice smiled. 'There's more to India than that,' she said.

Joanna took another square. 'I keep forgetting that you were there — how long ago, Alice?'

'Forty years,' she said without looking up. 'It's a long time. A lot has happened since then.'

Ann's long scarlet nails, her fingers much beringed, took another square, her bright little monkey face pulled into an expression of distaste.

'Ugh!' she said. 'The thought of India makes me go quite cold.' And she resumed her sewing while Sheila Barrowby threw her a swift glance of impatience.

Sheila was a widow with two grown up daughters, Alison, who had been married for seven years with no sign of the baby which she passionately wanted, and her clever daughter, as she called her, Gillian, who had worked her way through university reading Oriental languages, and now had a teaching post in Dubai.

'What news of Alison? How did she get on at Cambridge?'

They were all well aware that she had embarked on the new fertility treatment there.

'Costs an arm and a leg,' Sheila said. 'Still, if it's successful there'll be no one more pleased than me.'

Ann was absorbed in her sewing, small pink tongue held between her teeth. She looked up with a puzzled frown. 'I don't understand any of it, ' she said, almost grumbling as though someone was holding out on her. 'I mean, you said they froze three eggs — '

'That's right,' Sheila said shortly. Ann was not one of her favourite people. Ann was one of the lucky ones who appeared to have everything — two sons, three grandsons at Eton. Not for her the worry of a childless daughter.

'It's beyond me,' Ann sighed, dismissing the rest of the subject. 'I mean, you do wonder sometimes if it's right to interfere with nature.'

'It's wonderful what they can do nowadays,' Alice said gently in order to mollify Sheila. 'I always feel desperately sorry for women who want babies and can't have them.'

'I so long for a grandchild,' Sheila said. 'So far the only sign is in the freezer.' And they didn't know whether to laugh or cry, it sounded so bizarre. 'Anyway, Alison is going up to the hospital next week so we'll have to see what happens.'

'Sheila, my dear, Alison will have her baby — you'll see,' her friend assured her.

'Alice, you're always to confident!' she wailed.

Joanna Simpson sat and listened. She had one daughter, Sally, recently started with a Knightsbridge interior decorator, and was removed from ordinary day to day troubles since she and her husband Donald ran the exclusive hotel nearby, although Joanna was more of a chatelaine really. The hotel was luxurious, with a wealthy clientele, and consequently well staffed.

'How's Sally getting on?'

Joanna looked up, her beautiful eyes serene behind her sewing glasses. Her long pink nails were as perfect as ever, her gold bracelets jangling.

'She loves it, I'm glad to say. You said she would, Alice, and you're quite right. She can't wait to set off in the mornings so she must enjoy it. After all, if she's successful at it, perhaps she could start her own business one day — who knows?'

'Who indeed?' murmured Alice, seeing the look on Sheila's face, and her own brightened. 'My grandson is six months old today!' she said triumphantly.

There were cries of pleasure and good wishes.

'James must be delighted,' Joanna said. 'A boy, after all this time.'

'He is,' Alice said. 'I'm not too sure how Odile is settling down to motherhood though. She can't stand the idea of an English nanny, poor dear.' And they all joined in the laughter.

'Well, she *is* French,' Sheila said, taking another square.

'Don't they have nannies in France?' Joanna asked.

'Yes, dear, but there's all the difference between an English nanny and the so-called au pair,' Alice said. 'Ah, here's Gina.'

Her Italian weekly help worked at the local hospital as a dining-room maid, and on her day off, which was Thursday, regularly gave Alice a hand with the chores of Chantry Lodge.

They all liked Gina who was a character, her accent still markedly Italian, her mode of dress quite eccentric for she wore mostly cast offs from Alice's friends. She was of indeterminate age, small and dark-skinned with small black eyes, almost Japanese in appearance, an unlikely ex-philosophy student from Rome, who called everyone 'Madama'.

'Goo' morning – you' coffee, Madama.'

'Ah, Gina. Put it down here, thank you.'

'Thank you, Madama.' And she went out, the navy kerchief tied round her head adding somehow to her dignity.

Joanna looked up. 'I wish I could wear a headscarf like that.'

'I know what you mean,' said Alice. 'Some of us look like peasants, while others ...'

'Princess Anne wears a headscarf well.'

'And the Queen,' Ann said.

Handing round the coffee and biscuits, Alice sat back and looked at them thoughtfully, iron grey hair framing her face and gathered loosely into a centre knot on top of her head, the honest blue eyes in her craggy face one of her most appealing characteristics.

'I had an idea the other day,' she said, stirring her coffee. They looked up expectantly.

'Why don't we make a patchwork quilt – a real one?'

she asked. 'We could raffle it when it's finished, probably make quite a bit of money, and it would be a change from these endless squares.'

Ann frowned. 'I don't think I could do that. Isn't it difficult, real patchwork? A bit pernickety?'

'Nonsense,' Alice said firmly. 'There's nothing to it — if you can sew you can do patchwork. What do you think?'

There were murmurs of approval as they warmed to the idea.

'I thought in pastel shades — we might have to buy some material, but it would be worth it. Octagons, or diamond shapes.'

'Anything but squares!' laughed Joanna.

'You're right,' Alice agreed. 'Perhaps octagonal — we could buy the templates — don't you think it a good idea?'

'Excellent,' Sheila said. 'When would we start?'

'When we've finished this one. With all these strips ready, I'll spend one evening joining them, then we could embark on our new project.'

'You are good,' Sheila said. 'You give so much time to all these things.'

'Nonsense,' Alice said firmly. 'We have to keep busy, don't we?'

Joanna glanced at her watch. 'Goodness, I have to be going.'

She placed her strip of material on the table, and pushed the needle into its case. 'I have to be back at eleven-thirty.'

'My dear, we're glad that you came at all, with all you have to do,' Alice said gratefully. 'So few of us now find the time.'

'I enjoy the break,' Joanna said, pushing in her chair. 'Don't come to the door, Alice dear, I can see myself out.' And she bent and kissed her briefly. 'Stay well,' she said, and was gone.

As the door closed behind her, Ann looked up from her sewing.

'I can give you a lift home, Sheila.'

'Thanks all the same but I'd like the walk,' she said.

'Anyone like some more coffee?' Alice asked.

'No, thank you, my dear,' Ann replied. 'Tell me about the baby. Who does he look like?'

'Dark like Odile,' Alice said. 'He's a real poppet, smiles all the time, with two bottom teeth just showing through — '

'Oh, I love that stage!' Ann cried. 'I remember when the boys were small . . .'

'Yes, he's fat and bouncy, and not a pallid baby — something of Odile's French skin, darkish, and his eyes are enormous with long lashes. I'm hoping she'll bring him to see us one coffee morning.'

'Why doesn't she approve of Phillips?' Sheila asked.

'Oh, I think it's English nannies generally, but as you know, Phillips can be a bit of a tartar — after all, she's been around long enough.'

'I had her for Gillian,' Sheila said, ' and she frightened me to death — she was so strict. Don really hated her.'

'I wasn't in the Park then,' Ann said. 'Who is this Phillips?'

'You may well ask!' Alice laughed. 'Nurse Phillips has been working as a nanny in the Park for donkey's years — she's an excellent nurse, but quite terrifying. What Nanny Phillips doesn't know about babies isn't worth knowing. Am I right, Sheila?' She re-threaded her needle.

'Quite right,' she said. 'I suppose she must be due for retirement soon?'

'She'll die in harness,' Alice said.

'Your poor daughter-in-law,' Ann observed quietly. 'It must be frightful to live in a strange country and have their rules and regs imposed on you . . . and she is very young, isn't she?'

'Yes,' Alice agreed slowly. 'It *is* hard on her, she's a great deal younger than James, but my son — well, as you know, he's quite resolute. I think he wants to avoid any sign of the baby's being brought up as a French child.'

'Yet he married a Frenchwoman!' Ann cried.

'Well, that's just like a man,' Alice laughed. 'They have one law for themselves . . .'

'Oh, I know what you mean.'

Gina came teetering in to collect the cups, just a little bit unsteady on her very high heels.

'Finish, Madama?'

'Yes, thank you, Gina.'

Sheila looked down as she left the room, biting her lip to prevent a smile.

'How does she do it? Walk on these polished floors with those heels?'

'My dear, she adores them. The higher the heel and the more patent, the better she likes it,' Alice whispered. 'They were Joanna's — she loves Joanna's things.'

'I couldn't wear heels like that nowadays, yet we used to, didn't we, Alice?'

'I should say so,' she said staunchly. Ann glanced at her watch and put down her sewing. 'Well, that's enough for today, I think. I'm meeting Gerald this afternoon — we're going to the theatre this evening. Taking American friends to see Les Miserables.' She sighed. 'This will be the fourth time, and even a show as good as that palls a bit.'

'Poor you,' Sheila said wickedly, not daring to look up at Alice.

'Are you sure you don't want a lift?' Ann asked.

'No, thank you, dear,' Sheila said. 'Kind of you to offer.'

'Oh, you are awful to her,' Alice said when she came back from seeing Ann off.

'Not half as bad as I'd like to be,' Sheila said. 'She really makes me tired — she has so much and is so spoiled, with no idea what life is like for some people.'

'Now, you really wouldn't want to change places with her, would you?' Alice asked.

'Alice, you're a saint. You see good in everybody.'

'Not really,' she said equably. 'I just think life balances out in the end.'

'Oh, you can't think that!' Sheila cried. 'For some people life is really hard, they have one catastrophe after another.'

'Yes, it's hard,' Alice said smoothly, seeing that Sheila was het up about something and not in a mood to be reasonable. She had been like this ever since Don, her husband, had died two years ago.

She began to fold the strips which had been sewn. 'One

more of these and we'll have a finished blanket,' she said. 'It'll be a pretty one. They're not all as attractive.'

She glanced at Sheila who was putting needles and cottons back in the basket.

'So what is it?' she asked. 'You've heard from Gillian?'

Sheila's shoulders sagged. 'I had a letter yesterday. Alice, I didn't want to say anything in front of Ann...'

She looked compassionately at her friend, knowing that Sheila was worried.

'She's coming home in April for an Easter break.' She stopped.

'Well, that's nice,' Alice prompted. 'And?'

'She's bringing her friend — and hopes he can stay. Oh, Alice!'

'What's wrong with that?'

'His name is Abdul. Imagine — Abdul!' Sheila's eyes filled with tears. 'Oh, Alice, why has everything gone so wrong? First Alison, and now Gillian.'

'But what are you afraid of?'

'I can read between the lines,' Sheila said miserably. 'He's a boy friend, she'll probably end up marrying him — Alice, I couldn't bear it!'

'You goose — aren't you jumping the gun a bit?' Although common sense told Alice that her friend was probably right.

'If only Don was alive — '

'Yes, life can be very cruel,' Alice said matter-of-factly. 'I felt like that when my husband died — and also when Amanda ran away.'

Sheila took the reprimand gracefully, drying her eyes and blowing her nose.

'You're right. I'm turning into a real old misery,' she said, standing up and pushing her chair in. Then she took off the cloth and began to fold it. 'You're a good friend, Alice.'

She glanced at her watch. 'It's almost twelve. Tell you what, let's go out and have a pub lunch — cheer ourselves up, shall we? Are you doing anything?'

'Only the ironing,' Sheila grinned.

'Then that's settled. I'll get the car out.'

Sheila looked contrite. 'You must have plenty to do with Vanessa coming home tomorrow.'

'No, I'm all ready. Sit down with a magazine while I go and have a word with Gina.'

I've a lot to be thankful for, she thought, on her way to the garage. A new daughter-in-law, a new grandchild, and Vanessa — then stopped as by the front door she saw masses of tiny spears which had pushed through the cold earth.

Daffodils! she thought. Oh, come on spring.

Chapter Two

When the plane touched down in Dubai, Vanessa Amber stayed on board. On the journey out to India she had left the plane at this stop, full of excitement, walking out into the dazzlingly white sun-baked airport with the other passengers, eager to absorb everything that this trip had to offer. The sun had burned down fiercely on her back; it seemed hardly possible that she had left home but a few hours before in freezing cold weather.

Now she was on her way home, back to London, almost a year to the day since she had left. Her eyes suddenly filled with tears and she searched for a hankie, glancing round to see how many other people were on the plane. Well, what did it matter who saw her tears? Hadn't she learned anything at all in the last twelve months?

She blew her nose and stuffed her hankie into her jeans. She leaned back, closing her eyes, re-living the outward journey.

It had been a bitterly cold February morning, the bare trees white with hoar frost, when her father had driven her to the airport. It was five o'clock in the morning. Her father's jaw clenched and unclenched — oh, he hadn't wanted her to go — but there she was. Having had the jabs and the injections and carrying in her meagre luggage the tablets and pills against any number of dreadful scourges, with admonitions not to drink the water, not even to clean her teeth in it, and certainly no salads, no meat, no unwashed fruit.

'Yes, yes, I promise,' she had told him, and he had

waved, and she had made her way to the boarding gate.

The plane lifted up into the sky and she felt a powerful surge of adrenalin. Freedom and India — a place she had wanted to visit ever since she could remember.

In less than half a day, she would be in Delhi in a temperature of ninety degrees.

Then there was the girl — what was her name, Angie? — she had met in the airport lounge, who had been so helpful and given her so much useful information, and any number of tips on what to eat, what to buy, where to stay. What would she have done without her?

It was Angie's third trip. She explained that each time she went back to England for good, she couldn't stop thinking about India — and made plans to return.

Kindred spirits, Vanessa thought, although why she had this obsession with India, she had no idea. Perhaps it was the memory of the stories Granny Amber had told her about her life out there in the past.

She had contacts, too, from her grandmother — addresses of people whose families she had known, and who still had friends or relatives in India — that is, if Vanessa needed them. And Angie had given her some, too — they might meet up later. It was surprising, Angie had said, how you came across people in India — people that you had met or knew back home. Meanwhile, Vanessa was to spend two nights in Delhi in a luxury hotel that her father had insisted she stayed in, in order to settle in in a civilized way before being exposed to the horrors they expected her to find. She had promised to telephone them as soon as she arrived.

And then — Delhi. At five in the morning, it was fiercely hot, and once free of the regulations queue she had gone outside to board the coach. Lots of pretty girls in brightly coloured saris came to hang marigold garlands around the travellers' necks, and on the roof of the airport building it seemed as if all of India had gathered to give the new arrivals a welcome.

When had it started? When had she met him, the boy? That luxury hotel in Delhi — the swimming pool — then Jaipur and the elephant ride, the hostel in Agra — the peacocks on the lawn — no, that was Jaipur, and the Taj Mahal where she had wept to see such beauty, that incredible walk down the edge of the River Ganges where she could see the palaces and temples rising out of the mist, the hundreds of people bathing in the water, washerwomen, the burning ghats. How simple it seemed when you were there — and civilized. Then the hostel in Khatmandu — she hadn't liked Khatmandu. The hostel was overrun with climbers and everything was very commercial. It was depressing too to see the British dropouts begging at every corner.

She had walked with a young student from Bradford and had said, 'Just look at those white roses down there over the tree.' And from out of nowhere a dirty little urchin had appeared at her side and presented her with one, begging for money.

'The children are everywhere,' the student had said. 'Sometimes they seem to appear from under your feet.' He stood still and pointed across the cultivated hillsides with their rows and rows of vegetation. 'Only thirty miles to Tibet — you can almost see it.'

But she couldn't wait to get back into India, back to its jewel colours. Even the beggars, deformed children, legless men and women, whole families on one bicycle, the cows, the sacred cows, the crowded buses with everyone hanging out of the windows and on the roof — that was where she wanted to be.

She took a plane from Khatmandu to Varanasi where she met up with some English girls, three of them, who were staying in an ashram and who suggested she join them.

She had been pleased to do so for a few days, but grew tired of hearing about their everlasting experiences and decided to take a train to Agra... That was where she had met Gopal. Everything was going through her mind at such a fantastic rate — now it was all coming back. Gopal — the holy man she had met on the train.

She could see him now: a big man with a full black beard, his beautiful lustrous dark eyes warm with kindness and understanding and friendship. He had introduced himself, and his English was excellent — not surprising since he had been educated at Oxford. They had talked all through the long train journey, and she learned that he wished to follow in Mahatma Ghandhi's footsteps as a holy man; that ever since he could remember he had known what he wished to do with his life: to travel throughout India, preaching and trying to improve the lives of the people who lived in such poverty.

This was meat and drink to Vanessa, just the sort of person she had hoped to meet, and when Gopal told her that he had a room that he always kept in Agra, and that the landlord was a kind man who would understand her need for a temporary home, she realised how fortunate she had been to meet him.

When they arrived in Agra she followed him down back alleys and colourful streets until he came to a small house where he stopped. Going up the stairs to the first floor, he introduced her to the landlord, himself a kindly man who obviously held Gopal in great esteem, almost bowing to the floor when he saw him.

After they talked, Gopal led the way downstairs to a back room, divided in two, which held a sink in one corner although the running water was outside.

'If you wish,' he said, 'you may use this room. I shall not be here all the time – but you are welcome.'

Both rooms held the usual truckle bed and Vanessa guessed that he was used to helping people out who had nowhere to go. Outside at night the pavements or dirt paths would be full of Indians lying on such beds or else on the ground, totally oblivious to anything going on around them. With darkness a stillness crept over the city. The air was filled with the smell of cooking oil, and by the dimly lit flares whose smoke wafted gently up into the sky you could just see the outline of squatting figures silhouetted against dark, clear sky which always seemed to be full of huge stars. It was a scene Vanessa never tired of looking at, and she often thought that India seemed closer to what life was all about than anywhere else she had been in her young life.

So she had settled in Gopal's spare bit of room, only the hanging curtain of bright cotton separating them, feeling safe with him nearby. She explored the markets and the nearby villages, shopping for food, sometimes cooking for

Gopal as well as herself after he had shown her how. She washed her linen under the outside tap as any native woman, conscious that they regarded her if not as insane, then as a strange and probably depraved Westerner.

Gopal never questioned her reasons for staying there.

'I suppose you think I'm mad?' she said once as they sat talking about religion.

He shook his head and smiled. 'Then the world is full of mad people,' he said. 'I sometimes worry that you are not getting enough to eat — you hardly eat a thing — but I believe you are intelligent, and curious about life, and that is good.'

Sometimes she thought she seemed to be waiting for something — what, she had no idea — and was determined to stay on until she felt she had found it.

She had been in Gopal's house for two weeks when she first saw the gardener's boy — or at least that was what Gopal said he was.

'Who is he?' she had asked as they watched the handsome young man weeding in the garden of the house next-door. His bearing was regal, as with most Indians, and his looks remarkable. Once or twice he had felt himself watched and had turned round. Those liquid eyes meeting hers sent a thrill down Vanessa's spine.

She found herself looking for him, waiting for him.

'Why is he a gardener?' she asked Gopal. 'He doesn't look like a gardener.' And Gopal had looked at her intently.

'Karim is the son of a wealthy aristocrat who has quarrelled with his father. He is a rebel — a young man with a cause. There are many such men in India.'

'There is nothing wrong with that, is there?'

'It depends what you are rebelling against,' Gopal had said. 'Also he is having expensive education — for in his family no one has ever worked.'

'Then all credit to him!' Vanessa had said.

Sometimes at night she found herself walking past the house next-door, just to see if she could see him in the garden. There was a gardener's hut at the far end of the lawn, and she guessed he slept in there for the light was on sometimes far into the night. What did he do in there — did he study, read?

Gopal grumbled at her interest. 'You are foolish,' he said. 'He is not worth your kind attention.'

Vanessa flushed. 'I am merely interested in him as a person — what makes him tick.'

But still Gopal worried.

By day, Vanessa walked round the market buying food, which she sometimes shared with Gopal and sometimes with the other very poor residents who lived outside the house in a kind of lean-to. She became interested in the different kinds of vegetables and spices she found at the market. The vendors sat behind tables piled with deep bowls of every imaginable colour — orange, deep reds, pale yellows — it must take her forever, she decided, to get to know them all.

Sometimes she visited the holy places and watched as families placed flowers in the temples at shrines to Kali, the fierce-looking goddess with four arms with which to fight evil while her foot trod on a demon to hold him down. Across the courtyard was the figure of Kali's husband, the Destroyer. Families brought garlands of marigolds, and the statue was kept shiny and smooth by being rubbed and kissed by devotees who hoped for fertility or a cure for impotence.

Vanessa had been a month in the village of Prishna when she first spoke to Karim, deliberately waylaying him as he returned from market.

'Hello,' she said. 'I am Vanessa — a friend of Gopal who lives next-door.'

He pressed his hands together, and his dark eyes looked into hers. He seemed so young close to, Vanessa thought.

'I often admire your garden. It is beautiful.'

'It is not my garden,' he said, in slow and careful English. 'I am working there — '

'I know,' Vanessa said, and nodded towards the little hut. 'Do you live there?'

'Yes,' he said shortly. 'It is a temporary arrangement, you understand.'

'Of course,' she said hastily. 'I am from England.'

'I imagined so,' he said courteously. 'I hope you will be enjoying your stay. India is very beautiful.'

'Oh yes!' she breathed.

'You are educated young lady,' he said. 'It is unsuitable for you to be seen talking to me.' And Vanessa blushed. Was he reprimanding her for her forwardness in speaking to him? She knew a well brought up Indian girl would never have done such a thing.

From embarrassment more than anything else, she placed her hands together and turned and walked back into the house.

'You are foolish,' Gopal said. 'I saw you — it is not seemly. That is why Western girls are getting a bad name.'

'How dare you?' Vanessa said, her lips quivering. 'I only wanted to be friendly.'

'Friendship between man and woman is not easy,' Gopal said seriously. 'Especially in India. Especially with someone like Karim. All the young women fall in love with Karim — he is that kind of young man.'

'Well, I'm not about to fall in love with him,' Vanessa said firmly. 'He's so young — how old is he?'

'He is twenty-two years old, and I am in a way responsible for him. His father is asking me to keep an eye on him.'

Vanessa was astonished. 'But why? Isn't he old enough to look after himself at twenty-two?'

Gopal shrugged and went back to his religious studies.

In her own room Vanessa sat on the bed in the corner, knees hunched, arms clasped around her knees. Lately she had taken to wearing Indian attire, because it was so cheap and cool. She wore white cotton trousers and a loose-fitting shirt tied round the middle, and thonged sandals. It was hot, there was no air in the room, and she got up and tied her fair hair away from her forehead, wiping away the perspiration from her face. Nights like this were the worst, when there was no air and you felt the heat up against you, stifling you, while a fan seemed only to make matters worse.

She got up and wandered outside, but it was no cooler. Tying a scarf over her hair, she walked to where the women sat and children played, dark-eyed little beauties, sitting in the dusty soil. She knew by the way the women looked at her that they disapproved of her, yet they were friendly enough. As far as they were concerned, any Western girl who came out to India must be either mad or of dubious morals. Far from resenting this attitude, she accepted it and didn't care.

Walking past the railings of the garden, she kept her eyes averted from the hut where the light burned. Such were her feelings that it was almost as much as she could do not to open the gates and walk inside. Gopal had gone to Delhi and would not be back until tomorrow. She would have given anything for someone to talk to. Perhaps it was time she moved on — back to Jaipur where a doctor and his wife, the son of friends of Granny Amber who were themselves now retired but had chosen to stay in the place where they were both born, were looking forward to meeting her. Granny Amber would be very disappointed if she did not visit them. Yes, perhaps it was time she moved on.

Tomorrow perhaps, when it was cooler . . . but she knew it would be no different then. Slowly, she turned and sauntered back.

Karim was waiting at the gate, and her heart leapt. He was waiting for her, she knew — he had seen her go by.

They greeted each other, Indian fashion.

'It is not wise to walk at night,' he chided her. 'Are you not afraid?'

She shook her head. 'I would be more scared walking in London at night on my own.'

He looked astonished.

'Is this true?'

She nodded. 'Yes, I'm afraid it is. Western cities these days are all the same — young women do not like walking alone. They are not safe from attack.'

He shook his head as if he couldn't comprehend such a thing.

'We must not talk here,' he said. 'Should you be wishing to see my home?'

Vanessa was not quite sure what he meant — the hut where he slept or his real home.

Seeing her hesitation, he turned. 'Come,' he said, leading her inside the gate and closing it firmly.

He took her hand, and the feeling between them was electric — surely he must respond to it? She took a deep breath and followed him in silence.

There was a light on in the hut and he led her inside. She was surprised to find it furnished like a small home. A kerosene lamp burned in one corner where a table was piled high with books and manuscripts of every description.

'What are you studying?' she asked him. 'Gardening?' But he turned to her, those velvety black eyes behind long dark lashes assessing her, as if he wondered what to say to her.

'Not altogether.' He smiled. 'I am working on Indian philosophy, a history of India — '

'Quite an awesome task,' she said.

'Please.' He indicated a chair.

She sat down. 'May I get you a cool drink?' And as she hesitated: 'It is quite all right — it is bottled fruit juice. I drink it myself — one cannot be too careful.'

'I thought the water was all right for natives to drink? It's just that we are not used to it.'

'No, no,' he laughed. 'I think you are told also that after six months in India you may drink anything, but that is not true. Better to be safe than sorry.'

He opened a bottle and poured them a drink, then sat down opposite her.

'Tell me what you are doing here,' he said, and waited.

'Put like that,' Vanessa said, 'I can't think of a good reason except that I so wanted to see India. It's always been a dream of mine.'

'Why?' he asked, studying her.

She thought for a bit. 'Well, I suppose if, like me, you come from a cold northern clime, with grey winters and leaden skies — the thought of India is so romantic.'

He gave a half smile. 'And is that what you think it is now? Romantic?'

She flushed under that steady gaze.

'No, of course not.'

'You are disappointed then?'

'No, it is even more wonderful than I thought it would be.'

'Even with the poverty, the beggars, the sickness – does it not make you angry? Does it not make you wish to do something about it?'

'It would if I stayed here long enough.'

'So – you have not come to India in order to help with our problems, to work in the hospitals or among the beggars with leprosy?'

'I am not a trained nurse,' she said, hot under his intense gaze.

'I am sorry. To do charity work, then?'

'No,' she said shortly. 'I came to look .' And waited for his reply as she stared coolly back at him.

'I am sorry. Forgive me. I have been rude,' he said, getting up and going over to the tiny window, where he looked out from behind the scrap of lace curtain. 'Is Gopal back?'

'No. He returns tomorrow.'

'Ah.' He let the curtain fall. 'And your parents? Are they agreeing with their beautiful daughter's wishes to see the world?'

Her face coloured. 'I have only a stepmother – a new stepmother. The trip was a twenty-first birthday present to me from my father.'

'So you come from monied family?' he said, regarding her seriously. 'Like me. Except that I do not think my father will give me expensive presents – I have left home.'

'That seems a shame,' Vanessa said.

'My father does not understand me or my principles,' he said. 'To know that I am working as a *mali* is more than he can bear.'

Vanessa knew that the word *mali* meant gardener.

'Perhaps he feels with your education you could be doing something more constructive?' she suggested. 'Using your brain?'

He sat looking at her for what seemed like minutes, as though conjecturing, and under that intense scrutiny she began to wish he would come closer to her and take her in his arms. She made herself get up, put down her glass.

'Thank you for the drink. I must be going.'

He was on his feet in an instant. 'I will escort you to the gate.'

In silence they walked out together. As she turned to say goodnight, he placed his hands together and she did likewise.

'Goodnight,' said Vanessa.

'Goodnight.' As she walked by the railings she heard the door of Karim's hut close softly.

For some reason she decided not to tell Gopal where she had been.

Several nights later, Karim was waiting by the gate for her again and in silence she went with him to the hut. As before they talked a little, but it was unbearably hot and soon they fell silent. Vanessa fanned her face with a paper fan, knowing that she had fallen more than a little in love with this handsome Indian. All she wanted was for him to make love to her, but it didn't happen.

At the end of the third week she had not seen him again. Then, out of the blue, one evening he was waiting for her once again.

'I thought you'd gone away,' she said, delighted to see him, feeling she wanted to throw her arms round him. She had done nothing but think of him ever since that first night.

'I have been away – on important business,' he said, and she didn't enquire as to what it might be. This time as they talked he sat on the truckle bed by the wall while she sat on the chair. Presently he beckoned her to sit beside him.

'Come here,' he said. 'It is more comfortable.'

Knowing she was asking for trouble, Vanessa complied. Such were her feelings for him that she no longer cared what happened. This, she thought, was what she had come for – she might have known someone like Karim would be waiting for her in India.

'Tell me about your boyhood,' she said. 'Where you grew up. What your life was like.'

He began to tell her, then his arm went casually round her, and with his other hand he turned her face towards his, and slowly, surely, kissed her. As their lips met, she felt ready to swoon with ecstacy and wished he would never stop. Presently he pushed her down on the pillow, and at that moment sanity returned. She jumped up to face a pair of burning dark eyes.

'I'm sorry,' Vanessa said, startled at the strength of her feelings. She had suddenly got cold feet.

'You did not like it?' he asked.

'Oh, yes – no. I mean – '

'You are a virgin?' he asked, and Vanessa blushed to the roots of her hair.

'I see you are;' he said. 'I thought all Western girls were experienced in lovemaking?'

'Well, I'm not,' Vanessa said, and walked to the door and opened it. He did not call her back.

All night she thought about it. She had egged him on and then, when it came to it, had refused him. What must he think of her? Maybe it was unusual that at her age she had never been with a man, but that's how it was. She had never met one who appealed to her before now – the boys she had gone out with were all friends, men you played tennis or swam with. And that was all. There had not been much romance in her life. And now this – it had been too much for her to take. But he had roused in her feelings she had not known she possessed, and now she knew that more than anything she wanted him to make love to her or she must leave. They could not go on as they were.

Three days went by. Gopal watched her as they sat in his room while she ironed his clothes. She was glad of something to do; this listless way of life was already beginning to pall and if had not been for her passion for Karim she would have travelled on. Now she felt she couldn't leave.

'You are making trouble for yourself,' Gopal said gently. 'You have been seeing Karim.'

She turned startled eyes to him. 'How did you know?'

'That's not important. As I see it, you are heading for disaster if you stay here.'

'Aren't you dramatizing things a little?' she asked coldly.

'I don't think so. When a young girl like you comes to a country like India, in search of romance – '

'I did no such thing!' she said hotly.

'You may not have realized it,' he said. 'You are bound to be impressed, moved, by your surroundings – I can understand that. But Karim is the last man you should become entangled with.'

'I love him,' she said slowly, surprising herself, and Gopal looked at her with such sympathy and affection that she walked towards him.

'You are so kind,' she said. 'I have never met anyone like you before.'

'India is full of young men like me,' he said. 'But Karim is — selfish.'

'So am I,' Vanessa said.

'We all are — to a degree,' he said, and she smiled.

She felt so different since meeting Karim. Her life had a purpose — and, besides, she believed she was good for him. They understood each other.

For a few days he seemed not to be there, then on the next evening he was waiting at the gate. Seeing him, Vanessa threw a fine scarf over her head and went to join him.

'Where did you go?' she asked, but he shook his head.

Inside his room he led her to the truckle bed by the wall, and when he suddenly jumped on her, shocked and surprised, Vanessa submitted to him without a struggle. He was quick to climax, leaving her hurt and frustrated, but then he made love to her again, carefully and gently, and she realized what a practised lover he was and remembered Gopal's warning. Perhaps Karim had had plenty of girls — she was past caring, only giving herself up to the pleasure of him which was almost unbearable. She had never thought it could be like this. It was a night of passion. Sometimes he would be almost brutal with her; at other times he was gentle and considerate, as though protecting her.

Sometime during the hot night he got up out of bed and lit a candle, and by its flickering light she watched as he stripped and filled the plastic bowl with water, soaping his lean brown body all over. When he came back to bed he lay down beside her, asleep in a moment like a baby.

She waited until dawn before leaving the hut, wondering if anyone had seen her. In her own room she flung herself down on the bed. She didn't care now what happened. Even if she had a baby, she didn't care. Karim's baby ... She hugged herself at the thought.

After that first night, she went to the hut whenever Karim was there. They made love ceaselessly, and all thought of leaving him had gone now. Once, when she suspected she might be pregnant, he turned on her in a fury.

'What did you think might happen?' he asked her. 'Do you know nothing about such things?' His eyes blazed. She could only hope she was mistaken — the climate was responsible for many things.

She soon realized that she had to accept Karim on his terms. She never knew when he would be there, but if at times she thought she had placed herself in an invidious position, her passion for him overruled her.

'What is the matter with you?' he asked her once when she was feeling a bit queasy in the heat and wondering if after all she might be pregnant.

'Nothing,' she had said, not wishing for those black eyes to blaze at her in fury again.

'What is that, nothing?' he asked contemptuously.

That night she lay beside him as he slept and knew that she had created a situation for herself which she would not have believed possible a few weeks ago. She was trapped like a fly on sticky paper — and all through her own weakness.

Several days passed and she saw nothing of him. Letters arrived from her father and Granny Amber, and she wept as they brought back England and her home to her so vividly. Was she falling out of love with India if not with Karim?

One night she was sitting outside with Gopal. There was still no sign of Karim and she could see that the hut was unlit as it had been for the past six nights. Presently an army vehicle drew up followed by a police van. Several uniformed men got out and hurried to the hut, their guns drawn.

Vanessa was speechless with horror.

'Come inside!' hissed Gopal. From the window they watched as the men finally withdrew, carrying armfuls of books and papers.

'What is it? What do they want?' she asked. 'Where is Karim?'

He took her hand and sat her on a chair.

'You must leave as soon as possible,' he said. 'Tonight — I shall escort you to the train.'

'But why? What do you mean? Karim — '

'It is as I expected. Karim has obviously been arrested.'

She covered her mouth with her hand. 'Gopal! What are you saying?'

He sighed. 'I did warn you, but I hoped it would not come to this. I had hoped he was merely playing with fire as a young man will. But now — '

His kind eyes looked into hers sadly. Then he got up and went to the window.

'They have gone but there is a sentry placed there. We must hurry.'

'I don't understand, what has he done?'

'He is a revolutionary, plotting against the government.'

'Oh, Gopal! You mean against Rajir Ghandi's government?'

He nodded. 'There has been a plot to kill Ghandi — let us hope it never comes to pass.' And he put his hands over hers and held them within his own.

'I could not tell you without betraying Karim but he is a man who knows what he is doing — or thinks he does, shall we say. Warnings of dire consequences mean nothing to him. Come, my child.'

Vanessa walked slowly to the chair in the corner, where she sat down and cried. Gopal waited until she had finished, then helped her pack her small bag of belongings.

'Through the back way,' he said when she was ready. 'With me you will be safe.'

In the steamy hot night she walked just behind him, as she should, while he led the way. Her thoughts were in turmoil. He took her to the station and waited for the train with her, buying her a ticket and cool drinks at the station buffet and seeing that she had enough food for the train. When it came in, he helped her find a seat, which was difficult enough, then waved to her from the platform, seeing the pale, distraught face at the window, staying until the train was out of sight.

Vanessa watched as wonderful scenery passed by, hour by hour. She saw nothing of the crowds who piled on at every stop, pushing and shoving, surging around her, a mass of dark humanity. The train journey seemed interminable. Finally, in spite of everything, she slept.

The next day she arrived in Jaipur, feeling sick and

tired and weak, and found the hostel which Angie had recommended to her.

The room was small and cramped, but clean, and she washed outside under the tap, rinsing away the dirt of the train journey. What she wouldn't give for a bath! After a few days, if she felt better, she would book in at a hotel for a day or two — she had never been short of money, unlike a lot of the young in India. Her father had seen to that. The first thing she must do was to get a letter home to him and Granny Amber and let them know she was safe and well. They deserved that much at least.

The next morning she made her way back from the post office to the hostel and met one of the three girls she had encountered earlier on her trip.

The girl was excited to see Vanessa again. 'Where have you been? Fancy us meeting again! I've just got back from Kashmir — I left the others in Nepal. I say, you look pretty rotten — are you all right?'

'Yes, thanks, I'm just tired after the train journey,' Vanessa said. Truth to tell, she felt awful. 'I'll be all right as soon as I've had some sleep.'

They walked back to the hostel together, Sandy promising to look in on Vanessa later to see if she was all right.

By then Vanessa had a raging temperature, was in violent pain, and didn't care if she lived or died.

'Dysentery,' the Indian doctor said when Sandy called him in. 'Can you look after her, young lady?' he asked sternly. It was clear he had not much time for English girls who came out to India with no thought or care for possible illness or accidents.

'Yes, of course,' Sandy said. She hadn't bargained for this, but what could you do? An English girl in trouble — it was up to them to stand by each other.

Vanessa was barely aware of the many days that followed — days when she thought she would die, when she grew so thin that Sandy despaired and wondered if she should cable Vanessa's father. But in her moments of lucidity, Vanessa begged her not to.

The first day she sat up and took nourishment was a happy day for Sandy, a kind of victory. She couldn't imagine that the girl lying on the narrow bed was the same Vanessa she had met on first arriving. She was just a shadow of her former self, frail and thin, her lovely fair hair matted on the pillow, blue eyes enormous in her pale face.

'Now we shall have to build you up,' Sandy said without the confidence that her words carried.

But each day Vanessa became a little stronger, eating small amounts, and within two weeks looked more like herself.

She persuaded Sandy to join her in a room in a small hotel where they would be able to bathe and eat fairly presentable food.

'When I feel strong enough I'm going to stay with friends of my grandmother in Jaipur,' she said, 'but I don't want them to see me like this. Then, when I'm well enough, I shall fly home. You could come with me to see them, Sandy, they're not far from here.'

'No thanks all the same,' she said. She had done her bit and was anxious to get back to the life she had chosen. It wasn't for everyone, she knew, but it suited her.

When Vanessa arrived at the Dobsons' house, she was still very thin and pale but much more like her former self.

'Oh, my dear,' said Mrs Dobson, a motherly woman in her sixties. 'It's wonderful to see you. Alice wrote to us that you were coming. You could do with fattening up — but India keeps you thin. And I expect you've been careful what you ate.

The bungalow was as much like home as anywhere she might see in India, Vanessa decided, with its cretonne chairs and pretty curtains. Hard to think this elderly couple had been born out here, and only returned to England from time to time for holidays. They seemed as English as anyone from home.

That night, in her pretty bedroom, in the bed masked with nets and with the overhead fan moving slowly and surely, she thought back over the events of the past few weeks.

It had been like a dream. All of it. And whether or not she had ever become pregnant with Karim's baby, she would never know. She certainly wasn't pregnant now. There had been times in the last few weeks when she thought she had nothing inside her at all.

What had she thought she would do if that happened? And Karim — where was he? What had happened to him? She would never know.

Feeling strengthened after her stay with the Dobson's, she decided to continue her travels, having no desire to go home too early. After three weeks she packed her belongings and set off for Kashmir where she joined the two English girls. It rained almost every day for a fortnight. Then she made her way south to Goa and Bombay where she spent some time working in a children's settlement near Hyderabad. By then fully recovered, she was on the train to Delhi en route for the airport when news came on the assassination of Rajiv Ghandi.

Her first thought was of Karim. Had it been anything to do with him or was he still incarcerated in some filthy Indian gaol? She felt great sadness at Ghandi's death. The country was in deep mourning, and for the first time she was glad she was going home.

When the plane touched down at London Airport, she felt an unexpected surge of excitement. Home! She had never thought she would be so glad to see England again.

Granny Amber was there, and her father — never had their familiar faces looked more dear. She threw her arms round Granny Amber then James whose pleasure at seeing her again could not be doubted.

In the car she sat and chatted nineteen to the dozen to Granny Amber who, while saying nothing, knew that Vanessa was not the same girl who had left a year before. Something had happened to her in India — it had affected her as it did everyone who ever visited that country. They were never the same again. In the fullness of time she might learn what it was.

'Well — ' James said from the driving seat in a slightly self-conscious voice — 'what do you think about having a new baby brother?'

'Oh, yes, the baby. Great!' Vanessa said. 'Wonderful. He must be six months old by now ... and how is Odile?'

'Very well,' her father said, and dived into his inside pocket. 'Here the latest picture of them.'

Vanessa took it from him. She saw a dark-haired girl, her stepmother Odile, only ten years older than herself, her short black hair shining, her cheek against her new baby son's. He looked to be the image of his mother, his dark eyes looking straight into the camera.

'Oh, he's sweet!' Vanessa cried, looking at Granny Amber then at the photo again and passing it back. 'You must be awfully pleased, Daddy.' And saw the back of her father's neck almost glow with pride.

Granny Amber took her hand. 'It's lovely to have you back, darling,' she said, and Vanessa bit her lip. Then she smiled at Granny Amber and gave her a swift kiss, feeling the soft papery skin against her warm lips.

Granny Amber was the best mother she had ever had.

Chapter Three

April came in with showers and sleet, sudden flurries of snow, and then sunshine warm enough for June. There was a feeling that spring had at least arrived with the birdsong in the mornings, the earth growing warmer, and daffodils in great swathes at the entrance to the park.

Alice Amber's house stood at the entrance to Chantry Park, the original lodge with its gates leading to the long drive at the end of which had stood Chantry Court, an Elizabethan manor house which had burned down at the end of the first world war.

Derelict for some years, it had been developed in the thirties by a builder of taste and discernment. Reputable architects were asked to design homes of quality and distinction, mainly to specification for people who could afford them, with the result that there were examples of reproduction Tudor, Georgian, Victorian and Edwardian residences within the Park. There was a house built like a Chinese pagoda for a retired tea merchant, where a Japanese family lived now, and another as a style setter for its time — a flat-roofed house built on cubist lines with stark white walls and tiny windows. Like a prison, some said, but with its extended white walls, double green trellis gates and white pillars over which tumbled clematis and roses, it had quite the loveliest garden in the Park.

There were no shops in Chantry Park, although Harrods' green vans and Fortnum's distinctive delivery vehicles were welcome sights and the thriving little town of Aysleigh saw to the residents' other needs.

When the lodge had become available, Alice Amber had moved out of her old house. Her new home had a large-sized living room and dining room, and two good-sized bedrooms.

On this lovely morning, she threw a cardigan round her shoulders and went to look in the garden at the azaleas, huge established bushes growing either side of the front door. The deep red one was covered with blooms, striking an exotic note, looking almost out of place beside the white and yellow daffodils and narcissus and the blue and pink of the hyacinths whose perfume filled the air. Scillas, forget-me-nots and grape hyacinths abounded. Everything was allowed to grow in Alice Amber's garden, which was a true cottage garden.

There was nowhere, she decided, more beautiful than England in the spring. She stood beneath the cherry trees — old now for they had been there long before she had arrived, but still their pink blossom stood out against the blue sky. The malus trees were a froth of white and pink lace, the gnarled old apple tree just coming into blossom.

From her pocket she took seeds collected from last year's annuals. There was alyssum — no garden was complete without the scent of sweet rocket — candytuft, love-in-a-mist which she had carried in her wedding bouquet with pink roses. Although it was a little early, they would be safe against a south-facing wall.

She dusted a little earth over the seeds then stood up, adjusting her cardigan as she heard the telephone ring. It was probably Vanessa, telling her whether or not she would be down this weekend. It took Alice a little longer these days to get to the telephone.

'Hallo, darling.'

Vanessa's youthful voice sounded sweet to Alice's ears. That the girl bothered to telephone her delighted her more than somewhat, for today so many young ones forgot about old people. She liked to think that she and her granddaughter had a special relationship.

'Gran, I won't be down this weekend — I have an invitation to a party on Saturday evening.'

'Then you must go, darling.' Alice's voice was firm. 'How are you getting on?'

'The plumber came and saw to the loo, and I know you don't approve of microwave ovens, Gran, but it will be so useful for quick meals.'

'Darling, of course it will! You mustn't take any notice of me – I'm old fashioned. So you're quite settled in?'

'Yes. Daddy's been a brick – and Odile called in when she came up to town.'

'How was she?'

Vanessa sighed. 'A bit – oh, a bit ragged, I suppose you'd say. Not as thrilled with life as I thought she'd be ... They are happy, aren't they, Gran?'

'Yes, yes, of course they are. Remember she has a young baby to see to and motherhood is very new to her. She probably misses her family in France.'

'Yes.' But Vanessa sounded doubtful. 'Anyway, Gran, you're all right?'

'Darling, I'm fine. Going to Sissinghurst on Sunday – Sheila is coming with me.'

'Oh, that's nice. Well, I must fly – due back at the shop.'

'Bye, my dear.'

Alice put down the telephone.

Vanessa had settled down very well in the basement flat in South Kensington which James had procured for her. It wasn't the brightest of flats but it was her own, small and comfortable, with a sitting room, bedroom, bathroom and minute kitchen. He had bought it on a ten-year lease and assured her if at any time she wished to leave it, he would be only too happy to take it over. That, together with her job as an assistant in a rather nice dress shop in Beauchamp Place run by an old school friend, had set Vanessa on to a new lifestyle. It was difficult, Alice reflected, to know just what was right for her, she was such an unusual girl. She wasn't particularly brainy, had not excelled at school, but she was intelligent and bright, good-natured and trusting – a weakness rather than a blessing, Alice sometimes thought. Romantic to a degree – and vulnerable. Anyway, she decided, twenty-two was a nice age at which to marry and settle down ...

Vanessa looked around her tiny domain, well pleased with what she saw. It was her very own and she knew how fortunate she was. Sometimes she thought she might have liked someone to share it with her, but on balance decided she was better off alone and free.

If she thought about India at all these days, it was with fond memories. Strange how you only remembered the good things. The warmth of the sun on your back, garlands of marigolds, women working in the fields — so graceful to watch with colourful saris, exquisite faces, and the bearing of princesses to the manner born. Then the pedlars and the spice stands, riots of colour in oranges and browns, the scents, the elephants, the monkeys, the hot steamy nights she had spent with Karim — it was as if it had happened to someone else, and a very long time ago. If she thought of him at all it was with pleasure and fond remembrance — and a little heartache for something which couldn't be as well as the fervent wish that he was safe somewhere in the vast subcontinent.

It was as if by going to India she had got something out of her system. She had no desire to go again.

Tomorrow was Jane Sparrow's party at her flat above the shop. It would be the usual thing, crowded with lots of very boring people; sometimes Vanessa had the feeling that she still had to discover where exactly she belonged. She found herself growing impatient with empty-headed girls and young men with whom she had nothing in common.

She dressed for the party casually as everyone did these days. Navy blue opaque tights and flattie court shoes, a silk tunic in bright colours that she had had made up from material bought in India, her long fair hair tied back off her face, and the exotic heavy earrings from Nepal which she loved to wear.

She sat in front of the mirror contemplating herself. Fair-skinned, with eyes that were blue and clear as the water in a Scottish burn and a provocative mouth. Her heavy hair was her best feature. She touched up her eyelashes a little to dark them then, satisfied, prepared to leave.

In the flat above the shop she could hear the chatter as she walked up the stairs. She was greeted with shouts of: 'Here's Vanessa! Darling – come and get a drink.'

Jane had called in a couple of girls to lay on a buffet supper, and the guests were helping themselves and finding wherever they could to sit. There were soft drinks and red and white wines, bowls of Oriental nuts and bits placed here and there. Vanessa joined in the crush and found herself a seat at the top of the short flight of stairs which led to the tiny attic rooms. She was joined by Sue and Virgie and Romayne and Sarah – all girls she had met before. They chattered like magpies. Young men brought them drinks and soon the flight of four steps was full of young people. After her second glass of wine, Vanessa relaxed and began to enjoy herself. Later they danced in the tiny space available, and Jane opened the windows to let in the warm evening air.

Vanessa eyed her from her vantage point at the top of the stairs. It was incredible really when she remembered how Jane had been at school. A big girl, she was also tough, a born leader. She played hockey like a demon, was better at tennis than anyone else, a champion swimmer, and had been a bully to say the least of it. She bossed all the other girls, became Form Captain, and ruled them all mercilessly. She had always liked Vanessa, perhaps because she had never been intimidated. Vanessa had always been laid back at school and never got into arguments, but neither cringed nor showed fear.

The one thing no body had expected was that Jane would slim down, become tall and graceful, and turn out to have the most wonderful green eyes – which no one had ever noticed or else had been scared to face because they usually blazed with fury.

But now here she was: an elegant, beautiful fashion plate. When if you had asked her school friends, they would have predicted she would end up being a games mistress.

Chin in her hand, a smile on her face, Vanessa watched

Jane, black hair like heavy satin falling either side of her face, those wonderful eyes, the slim figure — she was surrounded by young men, and no wonder.

There were fewer people now. Coffee was being served from a side table when Vanessa strolled over to pour herself a cup. Beside her stood a tall young man, a stranger she had not met before with black eyebrows and dark eyes and an unruly mass of dark hair. He stood motionless, coffee cup in hand, as though he was lost. Smiling, Vanessa turned to him, holding the cream jug.

'White or black?'

He turned to her, startled. 'Oh, sorry — I was miles away. Er, black — no thanks.'

Vanessa put the jug down and walked away to her favourite seat on the stairs. To her surprise she found he was immediately behind her. 'May I?'

'Of course.'

She smiled at him 'Vanessa Amber.'

'Oliver Maitland,' he said, without the trace of a smile, and sipped his coffee in silence. Presently Vanessa put down her cup and looked at him.

'Are you a friend of Jane's?' she asked politely.

'Jane? Oh — Jane — yes, she's an old friend of mine.'

'Mine too — we were at school together.'

'Really?' He finished his coffee. His tone suggested that this was the last category he would have placed her in.

Rude devil, Vanessa thought, and picking up her bag, made as if to stand up and get past him. 'Excuse me.'

He put out a restraining hand. 'Oh, please don't go!'

She turned astonished eyes towards him, the words were so unexpected.

'I'm sorry to be such a bore, but the truth is — '

Vanessa waited. He really did look rather upset, those dark eyes almost tragic.

'Is something wrong?'

'You could say that,' he said bitterly. 'I've just been ditched, jilted, call it what you like — my girl friend has run out on me.'

'Oh, dear,' Vanessa began. 'I am sorry.' There seemed nothing else to say.

'I only came here to cheer myself up,' he said morosely, and Vanessa bit her lip to stifle a smile.

'Well, it's better than sitting on your own and brooding,' she said.

'I could cheerfully kill her,' he said as a cold statement of fact.

'Surely it's not as bad as that?'

'A Jezebel,' he said. 'Two-faced. She'd been carrying on with this other guy for God knows how long.'

'And you just found out?'

'Exactly,' he said. 'Thank God I found out in time. We might have married.'

'So there's a good side to everything,' Vanessa said brightly. Just her luck, she thought to get stuck with a man who was mooning over someone he couldn't have. 'Would you like some more coffee?'

He handed her the cup and saucer. 'Please, black.'

Walking back to the stairs, she studied him. He was handsome all right – with those strong dark eyebrows that arched attractively, and the burning dark eyes which almost smouldered. If it hadn't been for the scowl, he would have been extremely handsome.

'Here,' she said, and Oliver took the cup just as Jane came up.

'Vanessa – oh, Oliver, you came after all.' Her lovely green eyes were full of sympathy. 'You poor darling, how brave of you to turn up.' He looked up at her soulfully. Like a small boy, Vanessa thought, who has been unjustly punished for something he didn't do.

'Well, you're lucky to have found Vanessa,' Jane said, and Oliver looked at Vanessa as though seeing her for the first time.

'She's rather special so it's your lucky night,' Jane encouraged, but it would have taken an earthquake to shake him out of his apathy. 'Have a little dance, you two,' Jane urged, like an old mother hen.

'Oh, God!' he muttered, burying his head in his hands, and Jane winked at Vanessa. She bent down and kissed the top of his head. 'Be a brave lad,' she murmured. 'Vanessa will look after you.' She moved away to join her other guests.

Thanks, Jane, thought Vanessa. 'Look — ' she began when he still said nothing.

'Would you like to take a walk? It's a lovely evening?'

'Yes,' said Oliver gratefully, jumping up. 'That's a good idea.' And relieved that she wouldn't have to sit on the stairs all night, Vanessa stood up too. Together they walked over to Jane.

'Oliver and I are just going for a little walk.'

'Of course, darling, good idea,' she said, giving him a swift kiss. 'Now, no more tears — she wasn't worth it.' Oliver threw her a reproachful look.

Jane grabbed Vanessa's hand. 'Oh, you forgot your scarf.' She dragged Vanessa back into the room. 'She was an absolute bitch,' she hissed. 'Oliver's had a miraculous escape.'

Then with a sweet smile, Jane propelled her to the door again. 'There, off you go.'

'Thanks for the party,' Vanessa called up from the bottom of the stairs, then together she and Oliver walked up Beauchamp Place and down the Brompton Road.

'Would you like to talk about it?' she suggested, noticing the way his jaw was clenching.

Suddenly he stopped, as if the fresh air had cleared a few things from his mind. 'Look,' he said, 'it's awfully good of you ...'

'Not at all,' Vanessa said. 'What are friends for?'

'I'm sorry to have been such a bore. It was the shock, you see.'

'Of course it was,' she murmured.

'I mean, it's almost a year since I first met her — she quite bowled me over then. Absolutely beautiful. There was no one else to hold a candle to her. Never will be.'

Charming, thought Vanessa. Some girls have all the luck.

'What happened?' she asked him. I might as well get stuck in to this sorry tale, she thought.

'I went round to her flat and he was there — came to the door in his shirt sleeves, the swine! "Who are you?" I asked him. "What's it to you?" he said, or words to that effect. Then there she was, Rosemary, standing right behind him. And I tell you, if ever guilt was written on a Jezebel's face, it was then. "Who's this?" I asked her. I was quite cool.'

'Timothy,' she said, and then this guy turned and put his arm around her shoulders and drew her to him — like — like — ' Oliver couldn't go on.

Vanessa bit her lip. She could see the scene so well. 'Look, you don't have to tell me all this.'

'I felt such a fool — such an idiot.'

'What did *she* say — Rosemary?'

He turned to her with some surprise, eyebrows raised.

'She looked straight at me, as cool as a cucumber. "I'm sorry, Oliver," she said. Just like that.'

'Oh dear,' Vanessa murmured again. There really seemed nothing else she could say.

They had reached the corner of her street. 'Look, I have to go now, but if you want to talk again — '

'Jolly nice of you,' he said. 'Er — Vanessa.' And he held out his hand.

'Goodnight, Oliver.'

'Good night, Vanessa. And thanks.'

Thoughtfully she walked back to the flat. Some party, she thought. Still, Oliver was rather sweet — and somehow the misery she saw in his face brought back the memory of Karim and the awful time when she had lost him.

Three nights later she answered the doorbell of her flat and to her amazement saw Oliver standing there, a bunch of flowers in his hand. This time the frown had gone and he was actually smiling. Weakly, but smiling nevertheless.

'I hope you don't mind? I got your address from Jane.'

'Not at all. Do come in.'

'I say — are you sure?'

'Of course.'

He handed her the flowers and she bent her head to smell them. 'You shouldn't have.' White carnations.

'You were so nice the other evening, I must have made an awful fool of myself — a pretty girl like you.'

She smiled, revealing her one dimple which sat deliciously in her left cheek and only showed when she was happy.

'Come in and sit down — have some coffee. I was just going to make some.'

He sat down on the chintzy sofa, a gift from Granny Amber, and stretched out his long legs, looking around.

'This is cosy. Is it all yours?'

'Yes. I haven't been here long — just a month. Excuse me, I'm just going to put these in water.'

When she returned with the carnations arranged in a slim and pretty jug, he watched as she set it on a side table.

'I really am sorry, you know, about the other night. Was I madly boring? After all, you didn't even know me.'

'No. I felt sorry for you and what you were going through. I'll just go and get the coffee.'

When she returned Oliver was thumbing through a magazine but jumped up to take the tray from her.

'On the table,' she smiled, and sat opposite him to pour the coffee.

'Is Jane a friend of yours?' he asked. He had obviously forgotten their previous conversation.

'Yes, I was at school with her.'

'She's a good sort, Jane — no nonsense about her. Different as chalk from cheese from Rosemary ...' And his eyes clouded over.

Vanessa sighed inwardly.

'What do you do?' she asked brightly. 'What sort of work, I mean?'

'I'm in the city,' he said. 'Merchant banking.'

'I see,' she said, somewhat impressed. She couldn't remember having met a young banker before.

'And what do you do?' he asked, stirring his coffee.

'I work in a dress shop — Jane's.'

'Of course,' he said apologetically. 'She told me.'

'I haven't been there long,' Vanessa said. 'Just six weeks. I used to come up from Surrey, but now that I have this little place — '

'It's delightful. I still live at home with my parents in Sussex. I commute each day.'

'Quite a journey.'

'Of course, I do sometimes stay in town.' He looked into his coffee cup, then put it down.

To stay with Rosemary, Vanessa concluded. Well, young Oliver, you're not going to find another pied-à-terre here.

'More coffee?' she asked sweetly.

'Please,' he said, eyeing her, seeing the graceful arms, the swanlike neck and fair skin. She was unlike the girls he was usually attracted to: dark, small, just like Rosemary ... This girl was like a tall, fair gazelle. Quiet and soothing, somehow. He leaned back against the cushions.

'You can talk about her if you like,' Vanessa said. 'If you want to get it off your chest.'

'You are a very sweet girl, Vanessa,' he said. 'But, thanks. I spent all of Saturday night thinking and remembering, going over in my mind, until I felt I could put it all behind me. Of course she *was* beautiful, and so warm ... I might have guessed it was too good to last.'

'Mmm,' said Vanessa.

'Have you ever had a big disappointment in a love affair?'

'Yes, I have.'

Oliver looked at her sympathetically. 'I say, I'm really sorry. It's the very devil, isn't it? Are you over it now?'

'Yes, quite over it.' She smiled.

'So am I,' he said, looking across at her and smiling too. He really was rather dishy when he smiled, Vanessa thought. Not a good idea, though, to catch a man on the rebound.

'We were going to marry,' he said suddenly. 'That's what makes it so awful, that she should have — '

'Mmm,' Vanessa said again. There was really no need to say anything more. Oliver was quite capable of talking about this Rosemary for hours on end.

'We had so much in common,' he was saying. 'Old films, concerts — although she didn't like jazz and I do. And she liked modern sculpture which I find hideous ...'

'I agree with you there.'

'Who's that?' he asked suddenly, looking at the photograph in its silver frame sitting on a side table.

Vanessa smiled. 'Granny Amber — my grandmother. She brought me up.'

'Your grandmother?'

'Yes, my mother ran off when I was ten and my grandmother came to the rescue.'

'I say,' he said, 'that was jolly rotten, wasn't it?'

After that they talked some more mostly of Rosemary — and when he left, it was with a promise that they would dine together on the following Saturday.

'After all,' Oliver said, 'there's no reason why we shouldn't enjoy a bit of life, two bits of flotsam flung up on life's shore — we have something in common. A broken romance.'

Vanessa bit her lip.

'That would be lovely,' she said. 'I shall look forward to that.'

It was strange, she thought, soaking in the bath later, but all men were small boys at heart. But Oliver *was* rather sweet. And Rosemary for remembrance, she thought wryly ... *she* must have been quite a girl, stringing him along, and others too, quite probably.

She lifted her toes out of the water and studied them. She had elegant feet — Karim had said so. What, she wondered, would Oliver say if her knew about her romance in India?

Her eyes filled with tears suddenly as she saw again Karim's great dark eyes with their incredible curling black lashes. Whenever he looked at her like that, she simply melted. Would she ever feel like that again? Could any other man reduce her to quivering passion as Karim had? She didn't believe so. She would have to live on the memory.

When the telephone rang, Alice Amber was in the garden, taking up the white tulips which she had decided to put in the huge urns next year.

'Hallo, Gran dear — it's Vanessa.'

'Darling, how are you?'

'I'm fine. Are you all right?'

'Yes. Isn't it a super day?'

'Wonderful! Gran, may I come down to Sunday lunch?'

It was a long time since Alice had heard Vanessa so animated and so chirpy.

'Of course you may — your father is coming over with Odile and the baby.'

'Oh, super, I shall see you then. Tell you all about my date — I'm going out to dinner on Saturday.'

'Very nice too. Anyone I know?'

'No — I met him at a party, and I'm doing my good Samaritan act. He's just lost his girl friend and is feeling rather lonely, poor lamb.'

As good a way as any to start a romance, Alice thought.

'Look forward to seeing you then,' she said, and went back to the job of pulling up the tulip bulbs before going back into the house, eventually bringing out the Red Cross box of sewing things and the newly started patchwork quilt. She held it out — just a small section as yet, but when they were all joined together it was going to look very pretty.

She patted her hair into place as she heard the cars coming up the drive, looking through the hall window then opening the front door with a greeting.

'Good morning, ladies.'

Chapter Four

'I had a card from Maggie,' Alice said as they sat round the dining table. 'From Vancouver.'

'She does get around,' Sheila said. 'I'm not sure I should like to do as much of it as Maggie does.'

'I certainly shouldn't,' Ann said. 'I had enough of that when Gerald had to do it.'

'She doesn't always go with him, though,' Joanna said. 'This is a special year I think, because he's been made president of the company.'

'Good thing she has the stamina,' said Ann, squinting to get the thread through the needle and finally succeeding. 'Right, now what do you want me to do?'

'Cut out these blue and white templates,' Alice said. 'Don't you think this is going to be pretty?' She held up the section containing about sixty small octagons. 'This is part of the centrepiece.'

They were all very approving. 'The patches get darker as they get near the edge of the centre.'

'I must say,' Joanna said proudly, 'we're rather clever to tackle this, aren't we? It looks quite professional.'

'Perhaps we shall become known as the English equivalent of the American quilting ladies.'

'Nothing wrong with ambition,' Alice said. *Fame is the Spur*. Did you ever read it?'

'Oh, yes!' they all assented — except Ann, who never read anything except magazines. 'Howard Spring. Why don't they write novels like that today?'

It was just before Gina brought in the coffee that Alice

realised Sheila was rather quiet, and guessed that the coming weekend was the one she had been dreading, when her eldest daughter came home with the friend from Dubai.

'When does Gillian get home?' she asked.

'Friday. I shall go to meet her at the airport.'

'Still bringing what's his name?'

Sheila flushed. 'Oh, don't talk about it, Alice.'

'Very well,' she said amiably. 'What about Alison? Any news?'

'Well ... ' Sheila looked up and faced them. 'She's been impregnated. Did I tell you two of the frozen eggs were no good, so they used the third one.'

'Good gracious!' Anne murmured, making a face.

'So who knows? When and if I get any news, I'll let you know.' And Alice knew that, casually as Sheila appeared to be taking it, really she was going through an agony of doubt and worry.

Fortunately, Gina chose this moment to bring in the coffee.

'Madama – goo' morning, ladies.'

They looked up at her, a bright kerchief round her black hair, her dark eyes darting from one to the other.

'Good morning, Gina.'

She put down the tray and disappeared back to the kitchen.

'Which reminds me, I've forgotten to bring some more shoes for her – Sally's. She buys more shoes than anyone I know;' Joanna said.

'I suppose things are warming up at the hotel?'

'Yes, we're booked solid until mid-way through June, which pleases Donald as you may imagine.'

'Well, you certainly work hard to make them comfortable. Are there many overseas bookings this year?'

'Yes quite a few Americans – that's for the golf, of course.'

'I had a good round yesterday,' Sheila put in. 'Nine holes – it was as much as I could manage. I must be feeling my age.'

'I really should try to keep it up,' Alice said, 'but you know there's always so much else to do.'

'Good exercise, Alice.'

'I think I get that walking and gardening. Still, I will give you a game next week, Sheila.'

'Better not next week, dear — I shall be busy with my visitors.'

'Oh, of course.'

Joanna smoothed her sewing, and glanced at her watch.

'You go, dear, if you want to,' Alice suggested.

'No — I'm all right for a little while.'

'How's Sally settling at the Hon. Lucy's?'

'Very well, as far as I can tell. But you know how she is, Alice. First it was Cordon Bleu, then floristry — we wish she'd stuck to the hotel and catering course, but sometimes I think she doesn't know what she wants ...'

'Still, it was a good opportunity for her to try interior decorating.'

'She seemed to think so — I just hope she sticks to it.'

'How old is she now, Joanna?' Ann asked.

'Almost twenty-one — a year younger than Vanessa.'

'Most of us were married at that age, or going to be. It's a very different story today.'

'And those who do marry break up after a short time — isn't it odd? It seems as if they stand more chance by living together.'

'My niece,' said Ann, 'lived with a boy for five years, then married him, and split up after six months.' And they all laughed, grateful that it was not a child of theirs.

'Pressures are so enormous today,' Alice said as they continued sewing.

'Why is it any different from when we were young?' demanded Sheila.

'Life is lived at such a pace, everyone travels everywhere, young wives want to continue their careers —'

'Then in that case I don't think they should marry.'

'It's an argument that could go on and on. Do you realise, when Joanna finishes that section, the centre will be almost complete.'

She spread it over the centre of the table, and they sat there, eyes full of admiration. 'I say, it is rather nice.'

'Well!' Joanna stuck her needle into the needle case

and pushed in her chair. 'I have to go — hope to see you next week.'

She got into her car, gloved hands on the wheel, gold bracelets jangling. She was a pretty woman of forty-two, with a delicate heart-shaped face, deep blue eyes, and beautiful teeth when she smiled. Sometimes, she thought, the ladies of the sewing circle imagined no one but themselves had any troubles — they probably thought that she and Donald were without a care in the world, with their super hotel to run. But in fact it was really hard work. One of her few breaks came from this couple of hours on a Thursday morning. Staffing problems in hotel keeping could be horrendous. She was glad to escape for a short time.

She turned the car into the drive leading up to the hotel, seeing the sweeping lawns leading up to the entrance, the façade with its great urns of flowers, the heavy gold lettering above the entrance: The Bear Hotel. That's what it had been called in Donald's father's and grandfather's time, and it still was today. There was a great sense of satisfaction running an establishment like The Bear, and she felt it every time she drove in. Now, after taking the car round to the back of the hotel and parking it in the private car park, she hurried inside by the back entrance, removing her gloves as she did so. Her practised eye noted automatically that some of the roses placed by the lift were a little sad. Immediately she went to the housekeepers room to tell her, then made her way to Donald's office.

His face lit up when he saw her coming — he hated her to be away from him for any length of time. A handsome man with greying hair, he was tall, with a fine carriage, the sort of man women dream about. Just the sight of him walking across the foyer was enough to set many a female heart beating faster.

Joanna bent and kissed him, and sat down in the chair opposite him.

'Well, darling, everything all right?'

'Yes, thanks — how did you get on?'

'I did my bit for the Red Cross — any news of the Emir?'

'Yes he wants to come for a week in August complete with entourage — so that makes ten rooms.'

'Good,' said Joanna. She was every bit the business woman once back in the hotel.

'Did Molly turn up?'

'No, I don't think so.'

'Right. I'll go upstairs and change, then see Mrs Tiverton. We can't have much more of this — the girl is so unreliable. I thought she needed the job.'

Donald relaxed. He always felt better when Joanna was around.

Once in her bedroom, she changed out of her slacks and jacket, and going to the wardrobe, took out a dress. She always wore a dress for lunch in the afternoon. This one was in mauve and green silk, the sort of dress the guests liked to see. She rubbed in some hand cream smoothing her fingers, and replaced her rings. Her glance fell upon the photograph of Sally in its silver frame, and a slight frown crossed her face.

How pretty she was. If only she could be certain that she was happy. That was the trouble when you just had one child. All your hopes and aspirations were centred on that one, and it was very hard on them. Sally had tried so many things, and seemed unable to settle to one of them.

When they had heard that the Hon. Lucy Bannerman, the slightly eccentric owner of an interior decorating business, needed an assistant, it had seemed an excellent idea for Sally to apply. They knew the Hon. Lucy well. She had spent many weekends in the hotel in the past; sometimes on her own, sometimes with a man friend. She was delightful company, through somewhat erratic and likely to do anything at any time, and people wondered how she ran such a successful business, but that was part of her charm. Some of the most famous people had gone to her for help and advice, and usually were pleased with the schemes she came up with, for she was never short of ideas, and knew exactly where to go for everything from a curtain pole to a stuffed lion.

Sally had left her course in hotel management halfway through, thus disappointing Donald who had wanted her to learn to run the hotel. With no son to follow on, he had pinned his hopes on Sally, and perhaps it was the slight pressure that he exerted that made her so determined to go her own way. 'Sorry, Daddy,' was all she said.

At boarding school she had been a rebel, always in trouble of one sort or another; all in all she was a rebellious child, but always in favour of the under dog, fiercely fair and compassionate. Having said that, what was her future to be? At nearly twenty-one there was nothing more they could do for her; she had had every opportunity, plenty of boy friends — indeed some would say led a life of luxury and was even somewhat spoiled. One good thing was that she had never shown any desire to move away from home and live on her own, which had pleased both her parents.

Joanna sighed. She so wanted the girl to be happy, and could only remember that at Sally's age she had had the time of her life. Perhaps it was different for girls of today?

She made her way downstairs, her feet sinking into the carpet. She noticed the freshly polished balustrade with a keen eye, checked the flower arrangements, stood just for the briefest moment on the bottom stair before entering the foyer where the commissionaire, Billy, was receiving new guests. At the reception desk, with its bowls of roses, two girls waited to greet the newcomers. Joanna saw the pleasure in the eyes of the new guests as they found themselves finally at The Bear.

She took a deep breath. All was well.

In the interior decorator's shop in Knightsbridge, it was almost time to go home and Sally began to pack up. Lucy was out checking a property she had recently bought for herself and Sally had not seen much of her in the past few days.

She was about to close the door and put on the burglar alarm when the telephone rang and she hurried over to answer it. It was Lucy.

'Oh, Sally, my dear — are you in a desperate hurry this evening?'

'No — not really.'

'I wonder if you'd be a love and bring over the Dessoude

material swatches? Book Five, it is. It won't take you more than a moment or two — if you would be so kind. Can you do that?'

It might be worth seeing the house, Sally thought.

'Yes, Lucy, I'll be round in five minutes. What number is it?'

'Oh, you are a poppet,' Lucy gushed, and told her. Armed with the swatch book, Sally locked up the shop and began to walk slowly up the street. She had always loved this area of Knightsbridge — someday she might have a flat here herself, one never knew.

She looked up at the small narrow house, perfect in its classical design, and saw that the rooms were empty and there were workmen inside. The door was painted black and she rang the brass bell at its side. It was opened by a young man with a shock of red-gold hair and vivid blue eyes. He wore a white tee shirt and blue jeans, and as she noticed that, she was aware too of his tanned muscled arms and the amusement in his eyes, his impudent grin showing excellent teeth.

'Well, well,' he said, smiling broadly at her, and Sally found herself blushing for no good reason that she could explain. 'Who did you want to see?'

'Miss Bannerman,' she said, very much on her dignity. 'Lucy.'

'Luce — Lucy!' he called up the stairs. 'Someone to see you!'

'Come in, come in,' he said and Sally found herself standing in the empty hall, feeling diminutive against this tall, broad-shouldered hulk of a man whose eyes she found difficult in meeting.

There was the sound of Lucy's footsteps coming down the bare stairs, and she peered closely at Sally from behind enormous spectacles.

'Ah, there you are — goodness, you weren't long,' she said vaguely. 'Er — oh, Sally, this is George, my builder. Why don't you show her around, George?' She was busy going through the swatch book.

Sally swallowed. 'Oh, well, I —'

George was staring at her with unconcealed admiration

and Sally, unused to feeling at a loss, spoke softly.

'It's rude to stare,' she said, and he was immediately apologetic.

'Sorry, Miss.' And she rewarded him with a smile.

'Do look around, sweetie, and tell me what you think,' Lucy said. 'I've really stuck my neck out, and it is cost me an arm and a leg.'

'Come on, Luce, you know when you're on to a good thing!' George laughed. He looked down at Sally. 'So what's your name?'

'Sally — Sally Simpson.'

The Hon. Lucy had disappeared up the stairs.

'Is this the drawing room?' Sally asked, going through an open doorway. George was best kept in his place, she decided. Give him an inch and he'd take a yard.

There were two workmen there, one giving the finishing touches to a newly installed marble fireplace, and another working on the polished floorboards.

'My men,' George said proudly. 'Trevor and Jason — Trev's the plasterer and Jason's the carpenter.'

Sally couldn't help smiling. 'How do you do?' she said, and the men looked up at her and smiled courteously.

'Owjedo, Miss.' They went back to their work.

She bit back a smile, George looked so proud.

'This is the lounge — the drawing room, Luce calls it, I s'pose it is really. Great room anyway.'

It was, Sally had to agree. The proportions were perfect, and the walls had been lacquered in a deep rose colour, the paintwork like ivory silk, so well had it been applied. At the long windows she could imagine jewel-coloured drapes. Already she was getting used to the idea of colours and textures and how to use them.

'It's really beautiful,' she said, her dark eyes looking appreciatively around the empty room. She supposed Lucy would have lovely old Persian rugs scattered about the polished floor.

'Wait till you see the dining room.' he said proudly, and led her though the polished mahogany doors to a smaller room which overlooked a tiny garden. Here again the paintwork was in ivory, while the walls were done in navy hessian

— the contrast was startling. 'Oh,' Sally breathed. 'It's very unusual.'

'Yes, well.' And George looked knowledgeable. 'Lucy collects watercolours — really good ones, know what I mean?' He winked. 'And, of course, they have to be protected against the light — did you know that?'

Sally had to look straight at him, the blue eyes searching hers like a school teacher posing a difficult question.

'No, I didn't'

'Ah, well then.' he said, airing his knowledge, 'that's a fact. And of course, they look best against dark walls.'

'Yes, I can understand that,' she said seriously.

He led her to the small kitchen, totally done out in white, with a black and white floor. Although small it had everything to hand, every inch of space being put to good use.

Sally sighed. It was just the sort of house she would have loved for herself. In such a confined area, she was very conscious of this husky young man beside her, his broad shoulders and chest, those strong brown arms. They could certainly hold a girl tightly . . .

'May I see the garden?' she asked hurriedly.

'Yes, sure,' he said, opening the back door which led on to a tiny patio surrounded by trees. It was dark and cool and shady — just the place to sit on a warm summer's afternoon with a good book.

She turned to find George looking down at her, and swept past him.

'I'll go upstairs and find Lucy,' she said, 'I must have a word before I go.'

She hurried upstairs where she found Lucy in the main bedroom, again a small room but enchanting.

'Hello, darling,' she said. 'What do you think?'

'Well, I haven't seen it all, but I think it's adorable. Is it really yours, Lucy?'

'Yes. Well, leasehold, so it's virtually mine for a few years. I've always wanted a house here so I thought — to hell with it! And made George an offer which I'm happy to say he accepted.'

'You made George an offer? You mean, it belonged to him?'

'Of course. Oh, I see – I forgot you didn't know. George is a developer. He buys old properties and does them up – this is his second.'

Sally was puzzled. 'But it must have cost him quite a bit. Aren't properties in this area very expensive?'

'Darling, of course they are – that's what makes them so desirable. That's why he bought it. He took a chance and got a bank loan – you have to hand it to him.'

'Indeed you do,' Sally said, seeing the young man in a new light. Enterprising as well, she thought.

'Go and look at the bathroom,' Lucy said, 'it's a joy. I tell you, with George's building expertise and my flair as an interior decorator, we make a damn good team. There's nothing he won't tackle in the building line, nothing's too much trouble.'

Lucy may look vague, Sally decided, but she really is all there.

'Dishy too,' her boss continued, looking over the top of her enormous spectacles at Sally.

'Really?' she said with what she hoped was a convincing expression.

'Perhaps not your type but I think he's cute,' Lucy said, and sighed deeply. 'Wish I were younger. Well' – and she held out the swatch book – 'What do you think of this for drapes in here and matching bedspread?'

Sally looked at the heavily embossed silk – one of the most expensive in the book as she knew by now – and wondered if Lucy had a lover.

'It's beautiful – and just right.' She smiled. 'And now I must go.'

'Can you see yourself out?' Lucy said, already involved once more in decision making.

'Yes, see you tomorrow. Good night.'

'Good night, my dear – and thanks for coming.'

George was waiting at the bottom of the stairs.

'Did you like the bathroom? It's the latest thing.'

'I didn't see it,' Sally confessed. 'I have to go now, or I'll miss my train.' She saw his disappointment. 'But I hope to see it when it's all finished.'

'You bet.' he said, following her as she went to the door,

and reaching across her to open it. 'Scuse me.'
'Thanks,' she said briefly. 'Good night.'
'Good night, Sally.' She walked swiftly towards Knightsbridge station thinking to herself that, she hadn't realised how warm it was today.

Chapter Five

Alice Amber finished sewing together the pieces of the little jacket she had knitted for her grandson, Edouard. It was thick, navy blue, and minuscule. How times had changed — navy blue for a baby. Why, he even wore little trousers! And nowadays nothing needed pressing — it wasn't wool, anyway, just man made fibres. All that a young mother demanded was that clothes should be instantly washable in the machine. And how, Alice wondered, did babies keep warm with these man made fibre garments? They couldn't be as soft and cosy as wool ... then she was reminded of the amount of hand washing in the old days, all to be dried between soft towels in the old days.

James at eight months would have worn romper suits, which were really dresses with buttons between the legs to differentiate the boys from the girls, and always white. Well, there might have been the occasional pale blue, but mostly babies clothes were white. How she had longed for a little girl so that she could put her in pretty smocked dresses, but it wasn't to be, and by the time she had Vanessa to look after she was ten years old. Now little girls wore jeans and shirts.

Her small grandson wore all the colours of the rainbow, little trousers over his disposable nappies — the idea was unheard of in her day. It had been Harrington squares, two dozen of them, preferably three, with muslin squares to soften inside so that little bottoms didn't chafe. Sturdy safety-pins and now she smiled to herself as memories came flooding back: the nappies soaking in Milton before being boiled, but there was no nicer sight than a whole line of snowy white nappies blowing in the breeze.

So many things had changed, some for the better. Nanny Phillips always said give her a baby brought up with English fresh air and American feeding methods, and she would rear the perfect child.

Odile wouldn't agree, thought Alice, a worried frown appearing between her eyes. Poor Odile — she disagreed with so much that Nanny Phillips did, but since Nanny was the one with vast experience in rearing babies, and James insisted on her being there, Odile didn't stand a chance.

Well, Alice wouldn't interfere — she never had and she had no intention of starting now. James' first wife, Amanda, had solved any problems she might have had by leaving him, and she hoped whatever it was that was worrying Odile would soon be sorted out. She consoled herself with the thought that Odile was French and was probably having some difficulty in adjusting to life as it was lived in England, and in Chantry Park in particular. She had many interests: played golf and tennis, went up to town to meet her old friends, having shown no desire to return to her old job as translator at the B.B.C.

Alice got up, and found a bag to put the jacket in. She would take it round now to Four Oaks, a walk would do her good. It was a glorious morning and she had a meeting of the Save the Children Fund in Aysleigh at eleven-thirty. She glanced at her watch. Just time for a brisk stroll.

She breathed deeply as she walked down the hill to Four Oaks, seeing the laburnam and lilac, the late cherry trees still in blossom. The park was a joy to behold. Everywhere as far as the eye could see was a mass of blossom, and the scent was almost overpowering as she approached a garden full of wallflowers and yellow azaleas.

Four Oaks stood well back from the road, a dark redbrick house with large mullioned windows. Pre-war, it looked solid and very English. In fact, Odile had said that the house was one of the things that had helped her decide to marry James. She had said so openly, she fell in love with it at first sight, and when James proposed it was the thought of being the new mistress of Four Oaks that had tipped the balance in his favour.

Alice walked down the gravel drive and saw Odile just climbing out of the car.

'Alice, how nice to see you!' She bent and kissed her mother-in-law, and her perfume wafted towards Alice. 'Mmmm,' she said appreciatively. 'Lovely scent.'

'Do you like it? It is an old one — Maman gave it to me for my birthday. Bal à Versailles.'

It's true then, the thought flashed through Alice's mind, that perfume reacts differently on people. I remember being given that and hating it.

'I brought Edouard's new jacket — I finished it last night.' She handed Odile the bag.

'Oh, thank you, you are kind — and you are such a beautiful knitter. Would you like some coffee?'

'No, thank you, my dear, I have to go to a meeting this morning, but I would like a peep at Edouard.'

Odile's face clouded over. 'I expect Nanny has finished with him, he's probably in his pram in the garden.'

Alice followed her through the wide hall with its oak panelling and lovely oriental rugs, noticing fresh flowers in the fireplace. It was the one room Odile had not changed when she married James.

In the kitchen Nanny Phillips was at the sink preparing vegetables for Edouard's lunch. Her tall figure with its white apron over the blue dress, was ample, matronly. A commanding figure of a woman, you would have said. She wore a stiff white headdress, much as she had thirty years before. Nanny Phillips made no concession to the passing years.

'Good morning, Mrs Amber. Lovely day,' she boomed, as Odile unpacked her basket of shopping.

'Yes, isn't it, Nanny? Is the baby in the garden?'

'Yes. You may have a peep if he's not asleep.'

Alice walked over and undid the door to the garden. In the shade of the apple tree, Edouard lay in his pram, a high navy blue one, his eyes watching the moving branches as they swayed gently in the wind, his little legs kicking nineteen to the dozen.

Alice took his hand. 'Edouard?' And his face broke into a lovely smile as he recognized her. She smiled back because the sight of this darling baby was sheer delight. She laid one finger gently on his soft cheek, and he grabbed her hand and kicked even more.

'Oh, you are a little love!' she exclaimed. Really, she could have sat and watched him all day. After some more words of appreciation and nonsense talk, she bent and kissed him lightly then made her way back to the kitchen.

'He is a beautiful baby, Odile,' she said.

'Thank you, Alice,' she said, escorting her to the door. 'And thank you for the little coat. Are you sure you won't — ?'

'Yes, thank you, my dear. I must be off. Give James my love.'

'I will,' Odile said, and waited until Alice had reached the end of the drive, before gently closing the door.

She was fond of her mother-in-law, liked her as a person. Alice never interfered. Perhaps it would be better if she did, for she had an idea that Alice knew that she hated having Phillips around. Ghastly woman ... Odile made her way back to the kitchen.

'I'll be upstairs if you need me, Nanny.'

'Right you are, Madam,' Nanny Phillips said.

Odile sat in her bedroom overlooking the garden, seeing the baby lying there in his pram. It was all so different from how she had imagined it would be when she was pregnant. She had been overjoyed at the idea of a baby, longed for a son, but now that she had him, she had never really been at peace with herself. Sometimes she wondered if it might be post-natal depression that one heard so much about nowadays, but couldn't bring herself to believe it was that. She was healthy, a sportswoman, loved being married to James, had longed for a son — so what was the matter with her?

Several times she had tried to analyze it, and knew that for her, if only Nanny Phillips were not there, things would be different. But James wouldn't hear of it.

'You need help, especially with a first baby. I don't want you to be tied hand and foot in his first year. I want you to be able to come out with me, for us to be together.'

'In fact, you don't want Edouard to come between us?' He had looked shocked.

'What an extraordinary thing to say. That's not it at all.'

'You did want him, didn't you, James?'

'Dearest, you know I did.'

'Then why — ?'

But it was no good, argue she might. What he didn't realize was that she was pretty desperate. Everything had got on top of her, and the more morose she became, the more James saw her as needing extra help.

The worst thing was, she had begun to brood about Amanda, someone who in the early days of marriage she had hardly ever thought of. She knew James had been desperately unhappy when his first wife left him, but that was years ago. She and James had fallen in love, she was quite certain he loved her still, though what she had seen in this older man with whom she had so little in common, was a mystery to most people.

Had she perhaps fallen in love with the idea of marrying an Englishman fifteen years older than herself, who could give her stability, a fine home, a really English life, security? Well it may have had some bearing on her deciding to marry him, but if she was truthful, she had to admit that he had swept her off her feet with his good looks and lovemaking, which had brought her to passionate heights such as she had never found with a younger man.

In those first few months after their marriage, they were so idyllically happy she had never given a thought to Amanda. But now, suddenly, the unknown image of the first wife loomed large.

What was she like?

There were no pictures of her, no photographs, not even a picture of her with her daughter Vanessa. Surely that was a little odd? The girl never mentioned her, Alice never spoke of her, certainly her name had never crossed James's lips.

He was a man who knew his own mind, and once that

was made up, it was difficult to change it. That was what came of marrying a Q.C. she thought. James thought things out logically, and having made up his mind, stuck to it. His strength was one of the things she admired about him, but James had rules and didn't like them broken. Was that the things that had caused Amanda to flee?

Odile herself had always found a way round his strictures — as a Frenchwoman, she prided herself on the fact that she knew how to handle a man — but in the case of Nanny Phillips, she was getting nowhere. It made her think James didn't believe her capable of bringing up their son, when really she thought she was the person to do it.

Could it be that he wanted a son — and decided to remarry in order to obtain one? He loved the boy almost ferociously. Now that he had his wish, perhaps *she* didn't matter ... perhaps he had never got over Amanda, perhaps he still loved her, his first wife ...

She got up suddenly and found she was gripping her hands tightly. She must get outside the house, take a walk round the garden.

Thank God she had changed all the rooms round when she arrived. She couldn't have lived with Amanda's schemes — and James had been only too happy for her to do so. Now there was a cool element everywhere; no more chintzes and flowery chairs and sofas, pale rugs and jugs of flowers. She had replaced them with subdued lighting, darker rooms, lace hung windows. Much more like home, like France. Perhaps, she thought, that is what I am missing — my home, Papa, Maman, Jean-Paul, my little brother. Sometimes she imagined herself married to a Frenchman, living in Paris, pushing her pram around the Tuileries. How different life might have been if she had not come to work in London.

Yes, she decided, she was homesick for France, although it was the first time she had felt like this since she had come to England five years ago. She had wondered what James would say if she suggested that she flew over to Paris for a couple of days.

She was still toying with the idea when the telephone rang two mornings later.

She heard a man's voice, unmistakably French, ask for

Madame Amber, and recognised in an instant the voice of Louis Marraux.

'Louis!'

'Odile? C'est tu? Comment ça va?'

'Oh, Louis, it's good to hear your voice again! Where are you?'

'In London, chèrie.'

'That's wonderful — are you staying long? It would be nice to see you.' She hoped she was not being shamelessly forward.

'That is why I rang — I arrived in London this morning, but I have to go down to Surrey for an overnight conference on Wednesday. I am staying at a hotel called The Bear in Cheyning — is is anywhere near you?'

Odile couldn't keep the excitement out of her voice.

'Yes! Yes, it is, just ten minutes away.'

'And in the morning — Thursday — I am playing golf with an American who is also over for the conference. At Chantry Park — isn't that where you live?'

'Yes.'

'Then what about meeting up for a drink? I have to lunch with him but I can arrange something.'

'Oh, that would be wonderful.' It would be, she thought. To talk over old times — just what she needed — and what better company than Louis Marraux?

'Thursday, you say?'

'Yes, can you manage that?'

'I think so.'

'About twelve then, in the club bar. I may be a little late.'

'Don't worry.'

'I'll hear all your news then. Au revoir, Odile.'

Who would have believed it? She thought as she replaced the receiver, dark eyes shining. The last time she had seen Louis he was in London on a long visit. It had been in the days before she met James. What a coincidence ... but he was just what she needed, someone to talk to, an old friend. They had gone out together a few times in the past, had been drawn to each other, mainly because they were both French and away from home — but it hadn't amounted to anything.

They each saw other people, there had been no spark between them, and when he had returned to Paris, she had forgotten all about him. Well, until now ...

Coming out of her bedroom on Thursday morning, she passed Mrs Jackson, the daily help, on the stairs, her basket of dusters and polishes over her arm. She was a friendly soul from the village, and a very good worker.

'Lovely day, Mrs Amber,' she said.

'Yes isn't it, Mrs Jackson?'

The cleaner paused for breath at the top of the stairs. Some of the women in these houses didn't know they were born. She wouldn't wonder if this one was going out for a game of golf, judging by her flat polished shoes and pleated skirt — but, oh, she was a pretty thing, with that black hair and those lovely dark eyes.

'I'm going up to the golf club.' Odile informed Nanny Phillips at the kitchen door. 'If anyone rings I shall be back sometime after lunch.'

'Right you are, Madam,' Nanny said. 'Everything will be all right with me.'

I'm sure, Odile thought sourly as she checked that her golf bag was in the boot, and got into the driver's seat, starting up the car.

You never knew, there might be time for a quick round after lunch. It was lovely and fresh up on the golf course — you could see for miles from there. It must be almost nine months since she had had a game, before Edouard was born. She was a good golfer, having learned in France. Her father had taught both her brother and herself. Now she parked the car and made her way to the impressive club house.

She looked up and smiled as Louis came towards her in the club bar, his hair damp from the shower. Those good looks, so French in appearance, the familiar walk, the slight arrogance.

His white teeth gleamed in a smile of recognition as they kissed on both cheeks.

'I cannot believe my good fortune.' He looked down at her fondly. 'What can I get you? You used to drink wine — do you still?'

'Please.'

'Dry white?'

'What a memory.' She smiled, looking after him.

When he returned, he put the glasses down and she saw that he was drinking Scotch.

He sat down beside her. 'You are more beautiful than ever,' he said admiringly.

'You haven't changed. You used to say that every time we met.'

'Did I? But it was true. Except now, you have matured, there is a look about you of contentment — of fulfilment.'

'I expect that's because I am married and have a baby son.'

'Ah,' he said. 'Congratulations. Let us drink to his health. What is his name?'

'Edouard.'

'To Edouard.'

They drank and put down their glasses.

'And you, Louis?'

'It is a long story — but I have changed my job and travel back and forth from Paris ... sometimes New York.'

'Are you married?'

'No. I nearly married — twice — but each time, I escaped.'

'The eternal bachelor.' She smiled. 'One day someone will catch you.'

'The only girl I ever wanted to marry was you,' he said, his heavy-lidded eyes showing the warmth and sincerity which she knew he could express at will.

'Then it is a pity you let me go,' she bantered.

'Ah, you know me too well,' he laughed. 'Anyway, tell me — are you happy?'

'Blissfully,' she sighed.

'And your husband? Would I know him?'

'No, his name is James Amber, and I am quite sure you would never have met him. He is a Q.C.'

'Oh, I'm impressed'. He glanced around the bar. 'Are you a member here?'

'Yes, we both are, but I haven't played since before Edouard was born. He is six months old now.'

'I envy you,' he said. 'Like most Frenchwomen you make a good mother, I expect.' And seeing her face cloud over, realised that he had touched a weak spot. Something was bothering her, he could see it in her eyes.

'You must come down and see us one day. James would like to meet you.'

'Thank you, that would be fun,' he answered pleasantly. 'Where exactly are you?'

'In Chantry Park itself — do you know it?'

He shook his head. 'No, I am not familiar with the area. Do you ever come up to town — to London?'

'Sometimes.'

'Would you lunch with me one day — in town?' He saw her hesitation. 'Would your husband object? Is he very English?'

'He is, as a matter of fact. But, yes, I would like that.'

They talked of old times and places they knew, and the time flew by. He ordered sandwiches for her, and after an hour had passed Odile felt better than she had for a long time. She had relaxed. It was surprising how meeting an old friend took her mind off her problems.

Louis glanced at his watch. 'Well, chèrie, I'm afraid I must go.'

'It was good to see you again.'

'May I ring you about the lunch date?' He saw her hesitation, but she answered. 'Yes, please do.'

He stood up. 'I think Odile chèrie, that a day in town, a little shopping and lunch with an old friend, is long overdue — n'est ce pas?'

His dark eyes twinkled roguishly, the way she always remembered them. He was such a charmer.

When he left he took both her hands and kissed them, much to the amusement of Sheila Barrowby who was sitting in a corner with a friend after a game of golf. Most definitely French, she decided, looks a bit like Charles Boyer. At least that's how we liked them to look in my day — which is more than can be said for this Depardieu that all the girls are mad about today.

'Penny for them, Sheila,' her friend said.

'What? Oh, nothing, really. They're not worth it.'

When Odile arrived home she bathed and changed and went downstairs where the vegetables had been prepared by

Mrs Jackson. She could see Nanny Phillips coming down the hill, pushing Edouard in his pram. For some unaccountable reason her eyes filled with tears. Angrily brushing them aside, she went to the fridge and took out the lamb for the evening meal. She was a good cook and liked to serve unusual dishes. She had brought all her cook books with her from France, and now she took out of the cupboard and the old pantry all the things she would need. She was very methodical about her cooking: checking the butter for sealing in the frying pan before making a casserole, chopping the onions finely, taking a sprig of basil from the pot on the window sill, skinning and seeding the tomatoes, and putting everything on a plate ready.

James said he loved her cooking. Perhaps, she had suggested once, that was why he married her? He had laughed, and admitted that she had discovered his guilty secret.

That, she thought now, was probably why — that and wanting a son. What, for instance, had Amanda cooked for them? What sort of housewife had she been? Had James's pigheadedness been the reason for his first wife's swift departure?

The pram was outside and Nanny was carrying Edouard in. At sight of Odile, he held out his arms — and Nanny Phillips handed him to her.

'He has been a very good boy, Mummy,' she said, eyeing him as Odile held him close to her. Oh, how adorable he was — how could she have been away from him for an instant?

'We'll go upstairs to the nursery and play,' she said to him, kissing his cool cheek. She was so glad to have him to herself while Nanny got on with her tea.

'Don't forget to pot him,' Nanny shouted from the kitchen.

Oh, go to ... thought Odile. Just go away — and leave us alone.

'Well, and what did you do today?' James asked indulgently as they sat in the drawing room with a pre-dinner drink. 'It was a beautiful day, I believe.'

He wouldn't have seen much of it in court, Odile thought, feeling sudden sympathy for him. How handsome he was.

So dignified, so English, that dark hair just turning silver, grey honest eyes, the small moustache. And when he smiled, something about the way his eyes crinkled at the corners captured her heart every time. By comparison, Louis seemed almost rakish.

'I played a round of golf. Well, eight holes to be exact — and I played very well.'

'On your own?' James asked, looking at his lovely wife.

'Yes, but I didn't mind — it was lovely up there today, James. The sun, the birds singing, the trees all in bloom.'

He sighed. 'Yes, I'll have to see if I can get a game in this weekend. We are not doing anything special, are we?'

'No.' She toyed with the idea of telling him about Louis, then took the plunge.

'I had lunch with an old friend at the club — someone I knew long before I met you.' She hesitated.

'That was nice,' he said. 'What was she doing in this part of the world?'

'It was a man,' she said, furious with herself for feeling guilty.

'Oh.' His voice was polite but just perceptibly cooler. 'No one I know?'

'No, James, I told you — someone I knew before you. His name is Louis — Louis Marraux.'

'That was nice,' he said politely.

'We had a drink at the bar, and some sandwiches.'

'Well', he said, as though that was the end of the matter, 'That made a nice change.' And opened his paper.

'I said he must come and visit us and meet you,' she said, and saw him frown.

'Is that a good idea, darling? What does he do?'

The eternal English questions: what does he do, where was he at school?

'I am not sure now,' she said. 'He used to be in public relations.'

'Oh, PR,' James said, thus writing Louis off, firmly and forever.

But Odile was in a dangerous mood. 'He asked me to lunch sometime in town.' she said, wishing she could see James's face behind the newspaper.

'Well, my dear, only you can decide whether or not you want to go,' he said. 'How was the boy today?'

Edouard was usually in bed by the time James arrived home.

Her irritation gone, Odile smiled, dark eyes warm as she got up and stood behind him, putting her arms around his neck.

'He is adorable, darling. Every day he does something new.'

'We'll give Nanny the year round,' he said, 'then we'll see ... I've engaged her for twelve months, Odile.' And she saw by the set of his mouth that he was not to be swayed.

'Do I not have any say in the matter?' she asked, her lip trembling.

He could never bear to see her upset, and put the paper down. 'Now, how would you be able to go and play golf and meet old friends and that sort of thing, eh, without a Nanny in charge?'

'Oh!' And Odile almost stamped her foot. 'I wouldn't want to play golf if I had him to myself.'

He came over and lifted her chin. 'And that, my dear would be a mistake,' he said. 'You'd soon get tired of looking after a baby all day if you had him all the time.'

What was the good of arguing? Odile asked herself.

She went into the kitchen to check the oven, thinking all the while it might be an idea to meet Louis for lunch sometime — it would be something to look forward to. She would wait and see if he telephoned her, but she had an idea he would.

In the meantime she had promised herself some shopping in town, and possibly lunch with Vanessa. She might, if she could pluck up enough courage, ask Vanessa about her mother, something she had always vowed she would never do. It would be awfully difficult to do so without appearing to be jealous of her, and of course she wasn't, not at all. Just curious.

Chapter Six

The lilac trees in Alice's garden were drenched with spring rain, and the perfume that filled the air gradually seeped into the house through the lowered sash windows in the dining room.

She put on her Burberry and hat, closed the front door and got the little M.G., which was twenty years old, out of the garage. It was eight months old when she had bought it from someone going abroad, and she had looked after it and loved it ever since. As long as she could still drive, she would keep it, even though the insurance premium was high, and as long as she could climb into it she would keep going. The first sign of back trouble or arthritis and that would be that.

She was on her way to Sheila's, the first time she had seen her since Gillian had visited the week before, and she couldn't wait to hear how Sheila had got on with the friend her daughter was bringing home.

Sheila's house, named Windrush, was mock Tudor, smallish with an oak porch and a black and white upper story, heavily beamed. Inside it was traditional, with oak-lined walls, polished floors, Minton fireplaces, low sofas and chairs, pretty lamps. A delightful interior. Sheila herself was very artistic and full of ideas, which contrasted oddly, Alice always thought, with her love of sport.

There was no reply when she rang the front doorbell and she made her way through the garage, stepping over boxes and baskets of dried flowers to see if Sheila was in the garden, which was likely even on a rainy day. Henry, Sheila's cream Labrador, got up slowly out of his basket and yawned, ambling over to Alice.

She bent down to pat him. 'Where were you when I arrived?' she said to him fondly.

'Oh, it's you, Alice dear,' Sheila said, appearing round the corner. 'I thought I heard a car.' She took off her rain hat and shook her hair.

'He's about as good a watchdog as a tortoise,' Alice laughed.

'I know,' Sheila patted him. 'Good boy,' she said. 'Come on, let's go into the house and I'll make some coffee. I've been dying to see you.' She took off her raincoat and hung it up. 'You know I'm really pleased with that new little heather garden I've planted. If all goes well it will cut down the work on that grassy slope — it's always been such a nuisance and looked nothing.'

Alice sat at the big scrubbed deal table in the large kitchen. The Aga reigned supreme at one end of the room, and there were enormous lofty cupboards all round painted a pale greeny-blue — my French colour, Sheila always said — while the door panels were hand painted with various flowers. Alice sometimes wondered if Sheila realised how talented she was. She felt she could have earned her living painting furniture.

Sheila made the coffee, talking all the while until she remembered the cake. 'Ah,' she said, as the timer went off, and opening the oven door, her thick kitchen gloves on, removed the cake maker from the oven. Taking the lid off the cake maker, she looked inside at the golden brown cake sitting in its tin.

'Do you know, I can't think why I bother to bake cakes when there's no one to eat them.'

'Do you always bake a cake in that thing?' Alice asked.

'Yes,' Sheila said, 'and if there is any other way to make a cake successfully, then I don't know what it is.'

She left it to stand before turning it out, then took out another tin from the pantry. 'Try a piece of this, Alice,' she said. 'It's a new recipe.'

'Cake in the morning!' she wailed. 'And I'm trying to watch my diet.'

'Why? You're thin enough already,' Sheila said, and cut

them a small slice each. 'Do try it, Alice, it's a Fuller's walnut cake. Well, not Fuller's, its mine, but it's as near as dammit. Here's a fork.'

'Well,' Alice said, spearing a piece of cake. 'Come on, I'm waiting to hear how you got on with Gillian and – ' she saw Sheila's eyes cloud over as she put down her fork.

'I was hoping you wouldn't ask – but of course, everyone will know sooner or later. Thank God she didn't go out walking.'

'What do you mean?'

'My dear Alice, she wore a – jelli – something – you know, a full black robe. She looked like one of those Arab women you see in Harrods.'

Alice's hand flew to her mouth. 'Oh, Sheila.'

'And I wouldn't have minded, but he was in ordinary clothes. You know, sports jacket and so on.'

'What's he like?'

'Who, Abdul? Dark-skinned – you could say black, if you like – quite good-looking, speaks decent enough English, thank God.'

She sat still. 'They want to get married.'

Alice took a deep breath. So much depended on her answer, she knew.

'Well, what's wrong with that? Does she love him?'

'She's besotted more like – and not just with him, but the whole of the United Arab Emirates. She's being taught his religion and customs – although she must be well versed in those already.'

Alice could see that Sheila felt quite bitter.

'I mean, Alice – why? She's always had this fascination for Middle Eastern things – you remember, even when she was younger, she said she was going out to Dubai where her Uncle Roger was? I have to admit she's excelled in her studies ...'

'What does Abdul do?'

'Wait for it, Alice. Nothing. He is out of a job.'

'Oh, well then. They can't marry yet.'

'You're putting difficulties in the way, Alice. And not unreasonably. But that doesn't stop them. She earns enough to keep them both, she says, and he has a large and supportive family. There are six sons and three daughters. You should hear her, Alice! To be part of this large Muslim family is apparently all she asks of life. They come from Jordan originally, it seems, misplaced. The father owned land — I really couldn't take it all in. All the time she's telling you, he sits there politely listening, smiling ... I tell you, Alice, I was glad when the visit came to an end. I feel I don't know her any more.'

'But Sheila, I do think you're getting too het up over this. There's nothing wrong with her marrying someone like that. Why not?'

'It's not your problem,' Sheila retorted.

'How do we know? Vanessa may yet end up marrying —'

'Not likely. She's not in the least like Gillian.'

'But it's not beyond the bounds of possibility, dear.'

'Alice, if she marries him I don't know what I shall do.'

She got up and went round to her friend, seeing her shoulders tense, the set line of her mouth.

'Look, it's early days. She'll probably get tired of the idea after a while. After all, I am sure life is very different out there, and while she may be impressed now, there may come a time —'

'Alice.' Sheila sat still and faced her friend. 'When Giliian was at college, her first real boy friend was Turkish, the second Egyptian. I don't know why they broke up, I expect they returned home, but you see what I mean. She's fascinated with this way of life, their religion, the people.'

'Then accept it,' Alice said. 'You can do nothing, it's her life.'

'Then I shall lose her. Once she goes back and marries, that will be that. Do you know what I've been doing these past few days? Yesterday I went up to the Embassy — I've bought books on the subject — and do you know something? If they have children, she will have no right to them, none at all. He can take a second wife or throw her out, and keep the children ... can you imagine, Alice?' And she covered her face. 'Two daughters, one unable to have children, the other about to cut herself off from me entirely.'

'You're feeling upset now,' Alice said, 'but you'll see it differently in a while, once you've got used to the idea.'

'No, Alice, I won't. I'll never get used to it. You're different from me, you're tolerant. I'm not. I feel bitter about it — I feel somehow, there's an element of showing off. Look, I'll show you what I mean.' And she went over to the dresser and from a drawer took a large photograph.

Alice took it, seeing Gillian's lovely face, with those dark eyes so like her father's. You would never have thought she was an English girl, for apart from the eyes she was completely covered in a shapeless black robe.

She handed it back to Sheila wordlessly.

'They had a prayer mat with them in her little bedroom. You remember, Alice, when I decorated it for her in pinks and greys.'

She nodded.

'They both prayed, four or five times a day. They would go up there and kneel and pray or whatever they do . . .' She turned away. 'It's like losing a daughter, Alice.'

Alice's heart was torn for her, knowing Sheila could never accept a situation like this. For Alice, it wouldn't have been the end of the world, but it was for her friend.

'Well,' she said brightly, 'they won't be getting married yet awhile — I expect they'll wait until he gets a job. If he speaks English that well, it shouldn't be difficult.'

What else to say? She thought.

'If Don had been alive — well, I'm just glad he isn't,' Sheila said sadly. 'He would never have agreed to it. Never. I feel so helpless — '

'She is twenty-one — there's not much you can do,' Alice said practically. 'The thing is to take your mind off it, Sheila. We'll go out somewhere — have a game of golf.'

'I did that on Monday,' she said, 'but all the time I'm playing I'm thinking of Gillian out there in Dubai — it's very hard.'

Doubly so, Alice thought, seeing that Sheila was widowed so early, and worried as she must be about Alison.

She picked up her handbag. 'I must go,' she said.

'Look, it's stopped raining and the sun has come out.'

She kissed Sheila and smiled at her. 'Things are never as bad as they seem, dear.'

Sheila brightened. 'No, you're right, I'm growing to be a misery. Shall we go to a garden on Sunday?'

'Yes — unless Vanessa's coming down. I'll let you know.'

'By the way, I saw Odile up at the club.'

'Did you?' Alice looked surprised. 'Oh, I'm glad she's getting some golf in — it's what she needs. Who was she playing with?'

'I don't know. She was in the bar with someone or other,' Sheila said evasively.

But Alice knew her friend well.

'A man?'

'Yes, it was a man — they looked like old friends, I didn't recognise him.'

'Well I'll give you a ring,' Alice said. 'See you on Thursday then.'

'Oh, Alice,' Sheila called, 'don't say anything on Thursday, to the others. You know — about Gillian.'

'Of course not,' she said stoutly, and getting into the M.G., drove thoughtfully home.

Poor Sheila, she had so much to contend with. If you had her temperament, then it would be hard to accept the situation. Alice knew that it would never worry her, she lived by the policy: live and let live. It was a pity Sheila couldn't find something to occupy her more. The odd game of golf, gardening, cooking and flower arranging was not enough. She needed to meet people, to get outside the house more.

As for her daughter-in-law Odile ... well, she didn't take much notice of Sheila's observation of her with a man.

Alice turned the car into her own driveway, still thinking. It might be a good idea to take Sheila along on Friday mornings when she helped out at an antique shop in Aysleigh. Sheila was quite knowledgeable, had inherited some fine small pieces from her family, and Alice was sure she would enjoy the shop. Adele Grainger who owned it was always glad of someone to take over so that she had more time to go out buying. It wasn't the pin money Alice needed so much as the interest of having something enjoyable to do.

The telephone was ringing as she unlocked the front door, and she hurried to answer it.

'Oh Vanessa! Darling, how are you?'

'I'm fine. Just ringing to ask you if I could come down on Saturday to lunch?'

'My dear, of course you may.'

'And bring a boy friend, Gran?'

'Of course.'

'I met him at that party, remember? He's on the rebound from a love affair but he's rather sweet ...'

'Look forward to meeting him,' Alice said. 'Come as early as you like, I shall be here.'

She put down the telephone. That meant she and Sheila could go to a country garden on Sunday.

Vanessa walked home from Harrods with two salmon steaks, tiny Jersey potatoes and small mange touts, strawberries and cream for dessert, and a selection of cheeses. Simple enough. All she had to do now was to buy the wine. Oliver would be pleased with whatever she gave him — he loved coming round to dinner. She had been seeing quite a lot of him recently, and the more she saw of Oliver Maitland, the more she liked him. They would walk through the park or sit listening to tapes on wet evenings, while the rain outside splashed the pavements and the sea of coloured umbrellas gave the streets the look of a French impressionist painting.

It was the first of June and summer had arrived. Knightsbridge was full of girls in thin summer dresses and young men in shirt sleeves, the trees were almost in full leaf, and flower sellers on the corners added a splash of colour.

Oliver was still inclined to talk about Rosemary, treating Vanessa like an old friend he could unburden his heart to. 'It's such a relief to be able to confide in you,' he often said.

'That's what friends are for,' Vanessa had said, more than once.

Sometimes, as she listened, she closed off her ears to the tales of Rosemary and her infidelities, her beauty and her charms, and studied Oliver dispassionately, as a friend. It was strange to be so close to a man without any romantic interest, although she did sometimes wonder what he would be like as a lover. He was handsome enough, tall with rather nice dark eyes — not the burning passionate eyes of Karim, but spaniel-like eyes. His mouth was a nice shape too ...

'I like your grandmother,' he said as they finished their meal and sat drinking coffee by the open window.

'So do I,' she said. 'She's more like a mother to me than a grandmother.'

'That was a pretty rotten thing, your mother going off like that. You must have been devastated.'

'We were,' Vanessa said. 'My father even more than me.'

'What was she like?' he asked, and saw her blue eyes cloud over.

'I remember her being really beautiful. And sort of — not there very much. She went out a lot. There's not much more to tell about her really,' she finished abruptly.

She smiled suddenly, and he saw the blue eyes and that wonderful mane of thick fair hair, and realised that she appeared differently to him now that he had got to know her better. He liked her, had grown fond of her.

'You know, Vanessa, I can't imagine that you had an unhappy affair. The chap must have been mad.'

She blushed furiously at the mention of her past love. She had never talked about it to anyone — never, not in India, nor since she had arrived home.

'That's the difference between us, I go on and on about Rosemary but you never talk about — what was his name?'

'Karim,' she said softly. It sounded so strange how on her lips, foreign. She saw the merest flicker of Oliver's lids.

'Karim? He wasn't English?'

'No,' she said clearly.

'Tell me about him — where did you meet him?'

Slowly her eyes up came to meet his, and as she looked steadily at him, he dropped his gaze.

'In India,' she said. 'I spent a year there when I was twenty-one — my father gave the trip to me as a birthday present.'

'Why India?'

'I'd always wanted to go there, even as a child. It might have been because of the stories Granny Amber told me when I was young — she spent some time there as a young bride.'

He said nothing and she went on, 'I loved it. It was all I'd ever dreamed of — romantic, dirty, exciting. There was squalor — and beauty.'

She hesitated before going on.

'Karim was a gardener — at least, that's what he was doing when I met him. He was quite well born, the son of rich man, but a rebel.'

'And you fell in love with him?' The disbelief in Oliver's voice was plain.

'Yes — hopelessly,' she said, happy to admit to it now that she could talk about it.

'What happened?'

'Disillusionment, I suppose. Many reasons. It was doomed from the start.'

'What would your family have said?'

'It didn't seem to matter at the time,' she replied honestly.

'Do you still love him?' Oliver's voice was cool.

'No.'

There was silence as she waited.

'Are you shocked?' she asked finally.

'No, of course not,' he said instantly. Too quickly, she thought.

'But are you surprised?' she said. 'You didn't think ...'

'Not at all.'

'And what about Rosemary?' she asked curtly, unable to resist the jibe. 'Is she free, white and twenty-one?'

'Vanessa!'

'Oh, well. I hate bigotry — and people who discriminate.'

'Meaning me?' he said shortly.

'Yes, if you like.'

He rose to his feet, very much on his dignity.

'Very well. I think it's time that I left.'

'Vanessa folded her arms. She could have hit him with pleasure, and seeing his discomfiture made her want to add to it even more.

She walked to the door in front of him and opened it,
'Goodnight, Oliver.'
'Goodnight, Vanessa.'
'And you can take your precious Rosemary with you,' she said on a half sob, closing the door with a bang.

Stupid man, she thought, and began to clear away the dishes as though her life depended on it.

She discovered to her annoyance that she missed him, even his eternal talk of Rosemary. How could she have become fond of someone who thought as he did? That people were different — that it mattered what colour they were, where they came from?

Out, Oliver! she said to herself. I've wasted too much precious time on you — I should have told you about Karim when you first went on about Rosemary. Ugh! How she hated the name.

She went to bed early and lay thinking. It was strange how Karim now belonged firmly in her past — she no longer felt anything for him but fond memories. Times past, she thought. As to worrying, she worried more about Oliver Maitland than she did about Karim. He was stupid she decided, not at all her sort of man. Not the type she liked. It was just that she had grown used to him ... but that wasn't love. Not as she had come to understand it when she fell passionately in love with Karim. And how could you like anyone who had no time for India or all things Indian?

She fell asleep eventually and woke crossly to face the day, the previous evening's events crowding back until she remembered suddenly that this was the day Odile was taking her to lunch so she had better put on something rather nice. Odile always looked so elegant — so French.

They met in Harrods and queued with a tray for their lunch.

As they ate Vanessa came to realise that Odile was not really herself. As she had suspected lately, her stepmother had something on her mind. Yes, Odile said, Edouard was well, James was playing golf again after a long spell of hard work, they might take a trip somewhere later in the year ... but her eyes were far away, as though fixed on a distant problem.

'I expect you find your days awfully busy with a baby?' Vanessa suggested after a while.

'Not at all. I have Nanny Phillips and excellent help in the house.'

'What do you do all day?'

'This and that,' she said. 'And you — do you enjoy your new job?'

'Yes, it's not bad — it seems a little timewasting sometimes, but what else could I do? I'm not qualified for anything really clever.'

'Don't underestimate yourself,' Odile said sharply. 'Do you take after your mother, Vanessa?' The question was sudden and unexpected.

She was so surprised, she almost dropped her fork. No one ever mentioned her mother these days. She thought hard.

'Do you know, I don't really know ... I don't think so.'

'What was she like?' The dreaded question was out, and the moment she asked it, Odile wished she hadn't.

It was as if a warning light flashed in Vanessa's brain, and she chose her words carefully.

'To tell you the truth, Odile, I don't honestly remember,' she said at length. 'I was ten when she left — and, well I suppose over the years she's become like a ghost really. A shadowy figure.' She felt a moment's apprehension. Was that what was worrying Odile — was she jealous? Odile decided not to become involved. Her mother was a closed book as far as she was concerned.

Her face brightened and she spoke confidentially. 'Odile, you would have loved the outfit I sold this morning, I thought of you — it was yellow with a white jacket. Lagerfeld.' She hoped that she had taken Odile's mind off her problem. Bad enough worrying about Oliver, she thought gloomily, without having Odile on my mind as well.

Somehow they got through the lunch without any further questions from Odile, and with a promise from Vanessa that she would go down to Four Oaks as soon as she could.

It was two weeks later, on a sunny evening, that she opened the door to Oliver. He was carrying a sheaf of red roses this time. Vanessa flushed as she realised who it was, and at the look on his face, she found her heart beating wildly.

'May I come in?' he asked pleasantly.

She said nothing but opened the door wider. Once inside, he put the roses down on the table and took her in his arms.

'Oh, Vanessa.'

'Oliver — '

'I've come to apologize.'

'It doesn't matter.'

'How could I — '

She took his hand and led him through the little hall.

'I've missed you.'

'Me, too.'

They stood looking into each other's eyes, hearts beating wildly, neither moving, wonder on their faces. She would never forget this moment as long as she lived, Vanessa thought. His dear face, she knew every line of it, why hadn't she realised before how much she loved him?

Slowly their lips came together and Vanessa's heart stood still. His arms went round her and she clung to him, lips parted, her spirit soaring, the need for him rising within her. She didn't think at all of Karim, only of Oliver close to her, the strength in his arms, the way he kissed her lingeringly, caressingly.

What a difference, she thought, none of the urgency that Karim had; the times when often he had had his way, leaving her still and unsatisfied, unhappy beside him.

That was different. Oliver teased her with his caresses, cared about her reaction. He put his arm round her shoulders and they walked into the little sitting room where they sat side by side on the sofa and he kissed her until the desire rose in her to have more of him. How could she ever have let him go? Suppose he hadn't come back? She might never have known this was possible.

She sat up suddenly, and pushed back her hair from her face. 'Oliver — '

'Yes, darling?' he murmured, lifting her hair and kissing her ear.

'How — I mean, when did you — '

'Realize that I loved you? That night when I arrived home.

I sat in the train and thought about you, and I was so jealous!'

'Jealous? You?' she said incredulously. 'Jealous of Karim?'

'Yes,' he said sullenly. 'I felt I wanted to knock him down with a straight punch to the nose.' And she laughed.

'Don't you feel like that about Rosemary?'

'I hate her,' Vanessa said simply.

'Well, then.' And he kissed her again, his hand on her breast rousing her until she put her arms round him and drew him to her, sighing deliciously.

'Oh, Oliver — '

Much, much later, warm and drowsy she awoke from sleeping in his arms. His eyes were on her, the depth of his feeling for her as clear as a bell. She took a deep breath.

'I never thought I could be so happy,' she said softly.

'If this is love on the rebound, then I'm all for it,' said Oliver. 'You know, I've had an idea — I don't know what you'll think of it.'

'Mmmmm?' she murmured drowsily.

'Will you marry me?'

She sat bolt upright. 'Oliver! Marry you — why, I hardly know you.'

He raised his eyebrows. 'What more do you need to know?' he said, eyes twinkling mischievously.

'Actually,' she said at length, 'I quite like the idea. But I suppose we should wait a while — just in case.'

'In case of what?'

'Well you know, just in case this is a flash in the pan.'

'What an extraordinary expression,' he said, bending towards her and kissing her lingeringly. 'Is that what you think it might be?'

'Oh, no,' she sighed.

'Then,' he said, 'will you give the idea your prompt consideration?'

'I certainly will,' she replied, smiling up at him with eyes of brilliant blue.

'For starters,' he suggested, 'I think we should go down to Sussex on Sunday to visit my mama — she's dying to meet you.'

'Does she know about me?'

'Of course she does — she wanted to meet the girl who'd put me in such a bad temper,' he said. 'She'll be delighted.'

'You haven't met my father yet,' Vanessa said.

'No, but I've met Granny Amber, and I suspect if I pass muster with her, then everything will be all right.'

'You're very sure of yourself.'

He gathered her into his arms. 'No, I'm not, not really. Oh, Vanessa darling, please say you'll marry me?' And he hugged her so tightly she could hardly breathe.

'This is a form of blackmail,' she said dreamily.

'I know, but isn't it nice?' Oliver said, kissing her, again.

Chapter Seven

Gina, Alice's Thursday help, was swanning around the kitchen in a very expensive yellow two-piece suit which had belonged to Joanna Simpson. The skirt was tight and rather short, so that Gina's plump Italian calves emerged like upturned Chianti bottles. Her shoes were black Gucci, discarded by Vanessa, their bright brass buckles shining like a beacon, and over the suit she had tied a black apron. She was in a good mood on this July morning, pleased with life and her looks, as well she might be.

She was given to singing Italian arias, particularly by Verdi, and now Alice could hear Aida in full spate coming from Vanessa's bedroom. It made you feel good when Gina was in a good mood, for she was as transparent as a baby. When she was cross, she was very cross indeed. It usually had something to do with some unfairness in working conditions at the hospital where Gina was spokeswoman for the dining-room maids and, so Alice had heard, a fair match for the authorities.

The dining-room table had been prepared for the sewing bee. The precious patchwork quilt had at last taken shape. It was quite a thing of beauty, the centrepiece of blue and white octagons set off by a border of pale yellow and blue in a design thought up by Sheila, and now they were embarking on the next border, each person working separately on her own piece.

The basket of cottons in place, a fresh bowl of roses on the side by the open window, the room was ready when the telephone shrilled and Alice went to answer it.

'Alice! Alice! It was Sheila in a state of great excitement.

'Yes — what is it?' It was a long time since she had heard Sheila so animated.

'Alice — Alison is pregnant! It worked — oh, Alice, I'm so excited I could cry. May I come round right away?'

'My dear, of course you can! What wonderful news!' But Sheila had already put the telephone down and was on her way.

Alice waited by the front door, seeing Sheila's small car come into the gravel drive. She got out of the car, and slammed the door, her face wet with tears, looking happier than Alice had seen her for a long time.

'Sheila, my dear.' Her arms went round her friend and they hugged each other as Sheila shed tears of joy.

'You can't possibly imagine how I feel ...'

'My dear, of course I can. Come in, and tell me all about it. I'll ask Gina to get us some coffee.'

Sniffing and blowing her nose, Sheila went into the dining room and sat herself down at the table.

'Well,' said Alice, coming back, 'what wonderful news, Sheila! How is she?'

'She's fine, bless her. Apparently she's known for some time, but didn't want to say anything. When they gave her the implant, she said they were hopeful that this one would work and — well, it has! She's just gone two months, which is past the danger stage apparently. Ten weeks, in fact.'

Alice felt near to tears herself. 'Sheila, I can't tell you how delighted I am. Alison must be over the moon.'

'She is, and says she feels fine. She and Ben are coming down for the weekend in two weeks' time — I asked her if it was all right to travel as you know they're in Gloucester, but she said no problem. The doctor says now that she's conceived, she's perfectly healthy and everything should be quite normal.'

'Well, I shall keep my fingers crossed,' Alice said. 'This is the most wonderful news you could have had.'

'If you knew how I'd prayed,' Sheila said. 'For her sake — she wanted a baby so desperately. And of course they'll monitor her all along the way, so she's in the best hands.'

Gina came in with coffee and looked surprised to see

Sheila sitting there, her eyes red from weeping, but looking as happy as a sandboy.

She put the coffee down on the table.

'Is all righ', Madama?' she asked.

'Yes, very much so, Gina,' Alice said. 'Mrs Barrowby's daughter Alison is going to have a baby.'

Gina's black eyes shone. 'Oh, Mama mia — tha's very good — very nice.'

The news seemed to have completed her day for presently 'Come Back to Sorrento' drifted in to them from the kitchen.

'Isn't it strange how everything seems to happen at once?' Alice said.

'You mean the baby — and Vanessa's engagement? I was so pleased, Alice. You've met him, haven't you?'

'Yes, a little while ago, but apparently Vanessa took him down to dinner to meet James and Odile and the baby.'

'What did James have to say?'

'You know him, he keeps a wise counsel, but he seemed pleased. Pleased for Vanessa — I think he'd like to see her happily married and settled down. After the trauma she had as a child, I know we both want that for her, and Oliver is a very nice young man. I did wonder at one time, after her return from India, whether she had met someone out there, but she never said. She'd changed, grown up.'

'I can't imagine anyone being the same after a year out there,' Sheila said. 'So now we have a baby on the way and two engagements.'

'Oh, yes, Gillian's — is she actually engaged to this young man?'

'She says so. He's given her a ring. But you know, Alice, I can't take it seriously. It's not like an ordinary wedding, is it?'

'I don't see why not. Where will she get married?'

'Over there — in Dubai.'

'You'll have to go, Sheila.'

'Wild horses wouldn't drag me,' she said grimly.

'Sheila, you must! It would be cruel not to. You are her mother, after all.'

'She can come back home. I shall never accept her as being married unless it's done in our church.'

Her lower lip stuck our belligerently.

'Ah, the bell,' Alice said gratefully, as she heard Gina go to the front door and let in Ann and Joanna.

'Not a word about Gillian,' Sheila hissed.

'Of course not, but we are going to tell them about the baby, aren't we?'

Sheila's face lit up.

'Of course we are!'

Ann and Joanna settled themselves round the table, and took out thimbles, needles and cotton.

'Sheila has some news for you,' Alice said, taking her seat.

They looked up.

'Alison is having a baby,' she announced.

Joanna let out a little yell. 'Sheila! How wonderful! When?'

'Early next year — all being well.'

'My dear, congratulations.'

'You mean, this is the — er — egg? The frozen egg?' Ann's face was a study.

'Yes, isn't it wonderful what they can do?'

Ann looked down at her sewing — it was really more than she could possibly understand.

The ladies continued their sewing diligently.

'What that poor girl has gone through — but now it's all been worthwhile.'

'Yes,' sighed Sheila. 'I really never thought it would come off, but she had such faith.'

'Just shows you,' Ann said, wishing to change the subject, which for some reason made her feel uncomfortable. 'I thought Maggie might be here this morning. I heard she was home.'

'Oh?' Alice said. 'Well, she may turn up later.'

'So tell about the wedding,' Joanna said. 'When is it to be, and where?'

'October, I think, so Vanessa says. It will be from Four Oaks, and from what I can gather, she'd like the reception at The Bear, Joanna.'

'Then she'd better be quick in letting us know, Alice dear. We get so booked up. I don't wish to sound smug but that's the way it goes today — brides book so early.'

Alice's face wore a woebegone expression. 'Oh, I never thought, you must be taking bookings months ahead.'

'Of course, we could arrange catering, I daresay, if you had it at Four Oaks. A marquee in the garden, that sort of thing. We have a team of excellent caterers, as you know.'

'That sounds a good idea,' Alice said, somewhat relieved. 'Shall I ask Vanessa to telephone you regarding the date?'

'Yes, please, Alice. And as it is such short notice, the number of guests expected — there's quite a lot to go into for a wedding these days.'

'Goodness,' Alice said thoughtfully. 'I suppose this will be the first wedding the family has organized. After all, James and Amanda were married at her home in town, and Odile and James were married in Paris. I expect it will be a fairly small affair, although I really don't know.'

'Do you ever hear from your son's first wife?' Ann said. As a newcomer to the Park, she was not au fait with all the family histories.

'No,' Alice said shortly.

Ann sat thoughtfully, staring in front of her. 'It must be a difficult situation today, with all these divorces and second marriages. I mean, would Vanessa's mother expect to be invited to the wedding?'

'She surely forfeited all rights to that when she walked out on her daughter,' Sheila said tartly.

'Oh, these days it's not uncommon to have second and even third wives and husbands at the wedding — including all the children they might have had.'

Joanna's eyes were laughing.

'How very messy,' Ann commented.

Alice sewed on, deep in thought. It was true, there were complications once a marriage broke up, but each case was different. Would anyone think of letting Amanda know about her daughter? Would she be interested? She had never been in touch, never even sent Vanessa a birthday or Christmas card, which was very unusual. She had simply walked out and it was months before they even knew where she was, and then in a letter to James, with a Spanish postmark, she had merely said that a clean cut was preferable to any signed agreements and conditions. That Vanessa would be better off in the long run without her — she had never been much of a mother. Which was true. You would have thought, though, when Vanessa was twenty-one ... but even then Amanda had not been in touch. The letter went on to say she would provide James with grounds to divorce her whenever he wished, which he had done four years later. That had all been done from an address in Spain.

It seemed such a long time ago, which it was, almost twelve years, and a lot of water had passed under the bridge since then. Fortunately it had not seemed to affect Vanessa, at least outwardly. Who knew what she was thinking half the time? That was why Alice and James were so pleased to hear of the engagement, and Oliver seemed such a nice young man ...

She came out of her thoughts to hear them discussing another forthcoming wedding nearby.

'And how is your other daughter — the one in the Middle East?' Ann asked politely.

'Gillian? Oh, very well,' Sheila said.

'She must be a very clever young lady, scholarships and that sort of thing. Good at languages — so useful today.'

You could say that, Sheila thought crossly. She and Don had been so proud of her. Their clever daughter, they had said, a real brainbox. And now look at her. Teaching at a university in the Middle East, supposedly engaged to marry someone without even a job ... she had thrown all her chances away, and the whole world had been open to her. But she wouldn't think about that today, she would just rejoice in thinking about Alison and her baby.

'Did you think any more about going to painting classes?' Alice asked. 'I enquired in the village and there's a Tuesday morning session run by Mrs Maclaren.'

'Isn't she the modern artist?' Sheila enquired.

'Is she?'

'I thought she's had something in the Royal Academy, I could be wrong. Isabel Maclaren?'

'Yes, that's her. Why don't we go along?'
'I'm game if you are.'

So it was that two weeks later saw them at Mrs Maclaren's home in a class of six aspiring artists, all of them novices. Armed with new tubes of oil paints, a prepared board, charcoal, turps and linseed oil, they felt quite important.

Isabel Maclaren greeted them dressed in an ankle-length Grecian-design skirt, over which she wore a mustard coloured man's shirt, paint bespattered, a knotted scarf round her neck, and open sandals. A thick fringe of hair below a peasant scarf, silver ethnic earrings which reached almost to her shoulders – she presented quite the picture of a successful artist.

She was fortunate in having a studio in the attic of her Victorian house, but today, she announced, it was such beautiful weather, and so warm outside, that instead of drawing and explaining the rudimentary art of oil painting, she intended to take them in her transit van to Sparrowfields, a mile away, where stood an old barn which was very popular with local artists. There she would provide them with easels and leave them free to paint the barn as it appeared to them.

There was much giggling and laughter and high spirits as they set off. At the barn they set down their easels and stands. Sheila and Alice, next to each other, kept up such a barrage of jokes and humour that soon the last thing they were ready for was serious painting.

'Now settle down,' Isabel said mildly.

They all looked at the view in front of them: a perfect blue sky, the great oak tree above the old barn, the fencing across the field, the meadow filled with wild flowers. Then after further admonitions to concentrate from Isabel, they got down to it, finding the first brush stroke the hardest.

Alice took it very seriously, measuring the barn roof against the sky, scrupulous in her relative measurements. Her first attempt looked like an unqualified architect's drawing. Sheila, tongue caught between her teeth, sloshed away happily. Her palette was a mess of violent colours. Alice laughed happily to herself, she was sure the expedition was doing Sheila good.

'At the end of half an hour, I shall come round to judge your work and give you my verdict as to the best painting.'

'Oh,' they all laughed. 'Not mine!'

Putting down her brushes, Alice cleaned them and, when she had finished, strolled over to where Sheila was still working. She bit her lip as she looked at Sheila's handiwork to stop herself from laughing, for if ever she'd seen a child's painting, it was this one. It resembled nothing so much as a glorious riot of colour, with nothing like a barn in sight unless you could call the tumbledown thing in the corner a building.

'Oh, Sheila!' she laughed.

The end of the brush in her mouth, Sheila stood back and considered it. 'Well,' she said finally, 'I don't know what it is, but by golly, I enjoyed doing it.'

'Then that's what it's all about,' Alice said, really quite pleased with her own effort.

They stood still as Isabel approached, saw her stand back and survey the others' efforts. As she neared Alice's she felt a surge of pride, which disappeared swiftly as she saw Isabel's frown.

'I wonder,' Isabel said slowly, eyebrows meeting, 'just what you had in mind . . .' Her words trailed away. 'The roof — we're looking for an impression of what you see, not an exact drawing.' She moved on, the work was obviously not worthy of further comment. Hands behind her back, she came to Sheila's painting. Such a daub, Alice thought, poor Sheila . . .

'Now this!' Isabel boomed. 'This is wonderful — excellent!' Sheila blushed to the roots of her hair, and Isabel turned it round for all to see. Sheila looked quite bashful, the comment was so unexpected, while Alice couldn't believe her ears. 'Look at this, a true artist — my dear, it is wonderful! Original, uncluttered, natural — an unfettered spirit . . .'

By now Sheila had got her wits back and winked at Alice.

She grinned back. Isabel's words had made Sheila's day. Though, of course, if that was real painting, then she, Alice, was on the wrong track. But the point of the exercise had been achieved. Sheila would now have something to aim for.

They were a subdued lot in the transit van going back home, each of them with her own thoughts.

'Next week we shall be indoors, drawing and talking of the techniques of painting.'

'You can have mine, if you like,' Sheila said straight-faced to Alice.

'That's very kind of you, dear,' she said. 'But you keep it – it will make someone a nice wedding present.' And they laughed together until they could laugh no more.

It took some time to surface then Sheila said, 'I could give it to Ann.'

'Oh, you wouldn't!' Alice said, horrified, and they stifled their giggles.

'We must sober up,' Alice said eventually, drying her eyes. 'Isabel will think we're mad.'

'Which we are,' Sheila said. 'Still, it was good fun, wasn't it? You will come next week, won't you?'

'Wouldn't miss it for the world,' Alice said, tongue in cheek.

'Alison and Ben are coming this weekend,' Sheila said happily. 'I can't wait to see her, Alice.'

'Give her my love, and ask her what she would like me to knit for the baby. It's all different today, Sheila, if Edouard is anything to go by. When we had our babies we automatically knitted a white layette – now it's dark colours, serviceable and sensible.'

'Baby clothes,' Sheila said dreamily. 'What fun it's going to be.'

'Have you seen those nappy service vans driving round the Park?' Alice asked. 'Isn't it wonderful?'

'We were born at the wrong time,' Sheila said, 'although I think you were worse off than we were. By the time mine came along, things had improved.'

'My best time was in India when James was born. Ayahs for everything, I didn't have to do a stroke of work – but of course it wasn't all as rosy as it sounds. There were lots of drawbacks.'

'Your husband was in the diplomatic service, wasn't he?'

'Yes — and very nice it was too, while it lasted.'

Sheila stole a glance at her friend. She was so fond of her.

'Well, my dear,' she said, as they collected their things and went towards the car for the journey home, 'I'll see you on Thursday.'

'Yes, Thursday.' Alice said.

Chapter Eight

It was pouring with rain outside the Hon. Lucy's pretty shop in Knightsbridge as Sally Simpson prepared to close up for the night. The shop always smelled so pleasant, of lavender and apples and wax candles, and there was usually someone looking in the window at the beautiful decor. It was a joy to work in such a place.

She came out of the shop, locking the doors behind her and wishing she had brought her raincoat this morning or at least an umbrella, but the day had started fine and sunny. A shadowy figure blocked her path, and when the man turned, she was astonished to see George the builder standing there holding up an enormous umbrella. Gratefully she smiled up at him, unexpectedly pleased to see him.

'Hello.'

She joined him under the umbrella. 'Were you waiting for me?'

'I'd be lying if I said I wasn't.' He grinned. 'Are you going my way?'

'Which way is that?' she parried.

'Knightsbridge Station.'

'Then I'll join you if I may,' she said gratefully, picking her way through the puddles. 'Thanks very much.'

'My pleasure,' he said, and she walked alongside him feeling pint-sized to his six feet whatever. He had been waiting for her, and somehow she was not as surprised as she might have been.

'I s'pose,' he ventured, 'that you wouldn't like to come for a coffee at Guido's?'

She thought swiftly. On such a miserable evening — why not?

'Just the thing,' she said, and saw his smile of pleasure. He wore a light raincoat over his jeans, and she could not help noticing the girls who passed them eyeing her with envy. It was true, he was quite someone to be seen with. But she would watch her step — he was not exactly backward in coming forward.

In the Italian restaurant, he hung up his raincoat and her jacket, and she saw that he had on a cream sweater over his blue shirt, that he had newly shaved, and glancing down at his hands noticed they were nicely kept, the nails short and scrubbed. No one would have thought he had come straight from a building site.

He sat across from her, those blue eyes looking into hers, and she smiled back at him.

'Bit of a turn up for the book,' he said.

'You could say that.'

'Where do you live?' he asked her.

'In Surrey.'

'And you travel up every day?'

'Yes, to Victoria,' she said. 'It's not long, you get used to it.'

'I used to come up to town from Sydenham — when I lived at home with ma, but she died last year and now I've got a flat in Ladbroke Grove. It's a bit of a dump. Still, it suits me at the moment. One of these days I'm going to move up West.'

'You have plans, then?' Sally asked seriously.

'Oh, yes. You can count on that.'

'I'm sorry about your mother.'

'Are you an only child?'

'Yes, what about you?'

'Yes, me too.'

'I wish I'd had more of a family.'

The waitress brought the coffee and looked at George with undisguised admiration.

Sally smiled to herself. He really had an extraordinary effect on people.

She stirred her coffee. 'How did you come to be in

the building trade?' she asked, finding herself genuinely interested.

'My dad had a building firm in Sydenham — wanted me to take over but he died when I was fourteen.' He stirred his coffee. 'So I went to grammar school,' he added proudly.

'Good for you,' Sally said, hoping she didn't sound too condescending.

'So you decided you would like to go into the building trade anyway?' she prompted. His background sounded so much more interesting than her own.

'Yes, my mother encouraged me — she apprenticed me to the best builders in South London. I did it all, but I like being the boss best — it comes natural to me, like my dad.'

Sally finished her coffee.

'Would you like another cup?' he asked anxiously.

'No, really, thank you. I should be going.'

'Oh.' he said apologetically, standing up. 'Miss!' he called, and the girl came over instantly.

'My bill, please,' he said, and she dimpled. He gave her an enormous tip and paid at the desk.

Outside he put up the umbrella. 'Thanks for the coffee,' Sally said. 'It was nice.'

He looked pleased, smiling down at her, his eyes very blue on this dull, wet evening.

They had almost reached the station.

Sally stopped. 'How do you get home?'

'I park my car in a garage round the corner.'

'Well, thanks again, George,' she said awkwardly.

'My pleasure,' he said, and watched her disappear into the crowd.

She thought about him all the way home, in the tube and on the train, trying to imagine what life had been like for him, brought up in an atmosphere so very different from the one she had known. She had never met anyone like him before.

Two days later, the shop buzzed with excitement as Lucy announced that work on her house was finally complete.

'Do come round after we close and I'll open a bottle of champagne. You know, if it hadn't been for George it never would have been finished by now, but he knew I wanted to move in by August and really put his skates on.'

Sally could believe it.

When they arrived the front door was open, and the pretty chandelier in the hall shone brightly. Through the door they could see two or three people already inside and Lucy hurried in, her face wreathed in smiles. 'Oh, you lovely people! I've brought Sally with me, my assistant — isn't she a darling?'

Over their heads, Sally could see the tall figure of George, smiling at her and giving her a wink.

'Hallo, Sally.'

'Hallo, George.'

'Good luck, Lucy — all the best.' Their eyes met over the champagne glasses and once more Sally found herself almost swept away.

Two more people arrived and soon the small house reverberated to the sound of laughter and popping champagne corks.

Holding her glass, Sally whispered to George, 'Could you take me round now — before the others start moving? I really would like to see it properly.'

He took her arm and led her upstairs. The main front bedroom was finished now, every light switch in place, the small fireplace filled with a basket of flowers, the windows cleaned and polished, the bookshelves waiting for Lucy's envied collection of old books.

'No fitted furniture?' Sally remarked.

'No, it will be free standing. It's the latest thing,' George said knowledgeably.

The walls had been washed over in dark crimson, and it needed no imagination to see how attractive and cosy it would look when furnished.

'I'd like a place like this, wouldn't you, Sally?' asked George.

She smiled back at him. 'I should say. Anyway, at the rate you're going, you'll soon achieve it.'

'It'll take a few more conversions yet.'

'Let's sit down here.' She nodded towards the floor. 'Tell me what you had to do to get this house right.'

George sat down beside her. 'Well, for starters, the roof had gone for a Burton, and there wasn't a floor in the sitting room. No fireplaces, no banisters ...'

'What do you mean?' she asked in astonishment.

'Pinched,' he said laconically. 'Vandals — oh, didn't you know? P'raps they don't do that kind of thing in Surrey but up here — well, you daren't leave a place empty for a day or so or they're in like sharks.'

'But that's robbery — stealing!' Sally said, shocked to the core.

'That's it,' he said. 'And there's nothing anyone can do. They're in and out in a matter of minutes.'

'Even with locks and bolts on the doors?'

'They don't care about little things like that — they go through the skylights or the windows and yank the stuff out. It's criminal.'

She could see how much it upset him.

'So you had to put new floors in, a new roof. What about the ceilings?'

'They'd mostly fallen down.' He grinned. ''Course, it was in a bit of a two and eight — state, I mean — when I bought it, but I could see that it had potential. And that's what you need, location. When you're buying property, Sally, location.'

'Hmmm.' She was thoughtful. 'So how did you go about it?' she asked.

'Well, it was the second one I'd done — the other one was in Wilton Crescent.'

'Where's that?'

'Victoria — not as nice as this, not by a long chalk, but when it was finished I sold it and got a bank loan to buy this. I think Lucy's pleased with it — she seems to be.'

'Of course she is!' Sally said firmly. 'Listen, I can hear them coming upstairs.' They got up and began to walk towards the next room.

'And this,' George said proudly, 'is the bathroom.'

Like everything else in the house, it was small and beautiful. A sunken white bath, an enormous bowl, bidet and pan edged with blue true lover's knots, and a pale blue carpet.

'I've never seen a bathroom suite like this,' whispered Sally.

'You must remember that Lucy knows where to go for everything,' he said, giving her wink, and led her back down the stairs.

Lucy, her eyes shining with excitement at the joy of it all, was standing beside an elderly man with white hair and a military bearing. He had a silver-topped cane at his side and was looking down at her affectionately.

'And is this the young lady you were telling me about, Lucy?' he asked.

'Yes, this is Sally,' she said. 'Isn't she a poppet, Basil?'

He held out his hand. 'How do you do?' he asked with a smile. 'I've heard a lot about you.'

Sally felt her hand enclosed in a warm grip, then other people came along and presently George took her arm and led her away.

'His Lordship took a great fancy to you,' he whispered in her ear.

'His Lordship?'

'Lord Duncross,' he said. 'Now for the garden.'

'I've seen it,' she began, but he stopped her.

'This way,' he said, leading her through the doors on to the tiny terrace where candles burned in glass shades.

'Phew!' he said. 'The smoke in there — I can't stand cigarette smoke.' He dragged her towards a seat beneath a laburnam tree.

''Course, she's not likely to have kids at her age, is she?' he laughed. 'Otherwise I should get rid of this tree — the seeds are poisonous, and you never know with little kids. I used to try everything like that when I was a nipper.'

'George, you didn't! You might have died!'

'Yeh,' he said looking at her. 'Would you have been sorry, Sally?'

She raised her eyebrows. 'I might,' she said finally, and changed the subject.

'So who is Lord Duncross?' she asked.

'Lucy's boy friend,' George said. 'He's a banker — something in the city. I think it's him that's put up the money.'

'Oh, I see,' Sally said. He seemed a bit old for Lucy. Was she really his mistress? Sally couldn't imagine it.

'So ...' she turned to George. 'What are you going to do next?'

'Good question. I've got my eye on a little place in Montpelier Street — '

'That would be very expensive.' She frowned. 'Would you have enough money?'

'No.' He laughed. 'But I could borrow some more. Otherwise it's a place in Bayswater — not much, but I could do something with it.'

'Is its location as good as this?'

He laughed out loud. 'No, not by a long chalk. You know, you're a very nice girl. Most of the girls I know only want to talk about themselves — '

'I haven't started yet,' she joked.

'You make me feel a right Charlie,' he said. 'Tell me about you.'

'No, you'd only be bored.' She got up and brushed down her skirt where a few seed pods had fallen off the tree. 'I really must be going home — why don't we walk past the house you're interested in in Montpelier Street?'

His face lit up. 'Really? Shall we?' She nodded. 'Let's find Lucy.'

'I have to go now,' said Sally, having found her. 'I think the house is absolutely lovely — can't wait to see it when you have it furnished.'

'I move in two weeks' time,' she said happily. 'Ah, George — must you go?'

'Yes, I'm walking Sally to the station.'

Lucy smiled and whispered to her, 'Lucky girl.'

George took her arm which Sally found very pleasant. It was good to be escorted by such a tall and handsome man. When he stopped before a house with a FOR SALE board in front of it, she knew this was the one.

'Could you really find enough money to buy this?'

'It's up to the bank,' he said. 'They did it before, and they know they're on to a good thing. 'Course, the big boys may beat me to it — '

'The big boys?'

'The big building organizations — there's a lot of opposition out there, Sally.'

'And you never thought you wanted to join them — one of the big organizations, I mean?'

'No, I never did. I'm a one off, like my dad.'

'Then I think you should carry on as you are — get known for being interested in very special properties. Location, George.'

He gripped her arm. 'Now you're talking.'

After they had gone a way, he said. 'You do realize you're encouraging me, don't you?'

'You don't need any encouragement, George.'

When they arrived at the station, he took her hand.

'Bye, George — good night.'

'Night, Sally,' he said, but still held her hand. 'Er — would you come out with me one night next week?'

She thought swiftly. If she accepted his invitation she would be establishing some sort of relationship ... Did she want that? Up to now there friendship had been to do with Lucy and her new house.

She found herself saying, 'Yes, although it depends which evening.'

'Tuesday? Wednesday? Thursday?'

She smiled back at him. 'Wednesday.'

'Fine,' he said. 'Pick you up outside the shop — and this time we talk about you. Do you realize, I know nothing about you?'

'What do you want, George — credentials?'

He grinned back at her. 'See you Wednesday then.'

She sat back in the train and closed her eyes. It was quite extraordinary how much of her waking time was spent thinking about George. The idea of him as a boy friend wouldn't wash — not with her parents at any rate. But why not? Each time she saw him she fell a little more under his spell. He had such joy in life, such purpose, he was the only man she had met up to now who could come any way near to the pedestal on which she placed her father.

That had always been a problem. She adored her father — for her there was no one like him in the whole world. She idolized him. Even friends at school, those strongly made attachments one formed at boarding school, could never hold a candle to him in her affections.

He was everything to her, and she had gone through agonies of jealousy over the way he worshipped her mother. For there was no doubt that, much as he loved his daughter, it was Joanna who had his whole-hearted attention. Sally had lagged behind as an also ran, knowing that he loved her, but that she would never hold the place in his heart that her mother did.

He was handsome and kind and clever, a successful business man, charming — all the qualities she admired in a man. It was no wonder that she used him as her yardstick, and any boy friends she had had up to now were like young colts beside him, brash, too young, silly. Whereas George ...

Yes, George she admired. There was something about him that she could look up to. He had ambition, he worked hard, he was attractive. In a different way, of course, and she smiled to herself as she guessed what her parents' reaction would be if she took him home.

'Nice lad,' she could hear her mother say. 'But not for you, darling.'

While her father would like him, she just knew he would, but would be kind but firm, and say that he hoped Sally was not serious about this young man ...

Oh, yes, she could hear them, but oddly enough it only strengthened her desire to see George again. She was quite old enough to know what she was doing, and he tugged at her heart strings more than anyone she had met up to now.

Her mother was in their private apartment at the hotel when she arrived home, that special time of day before she emerged into the hotel for the evening session.

She looked up with a smile when Sally came in. 'Hello, darling — had a good day?'

Sally shook back her hair and smiled at her.

'Yes, fine thanks. I went for a drink with someone I met at Lucy's'

'Oh, that was nice,' Joanna murmured.

She had really got into her stride at the Hon. Lucy's and

was learning all the time, Sally thought. The business side of things was something she'd never thought she would find interesting, yet it was turning out to be something she really enjoyed, and not just because of George. She had grown fond of Lucy too, despite her quirkiness.

'The man's mad, of course,' Lucy said when she arrived the next morning, referring to her latest client, a famous pop star who had bought a very expensive home in a very famous square.

'I had to inform him that the council would not allow him to paint the outside of his Queen Anne house red – I don't think he realized that with such exalted neighbours he was bound to come unstuck – but anyway, inside it's to be canopied in scarlet silk. Each room, Sally dear, and the rest of it stark black and white. Interesting ... I've done that scheme many times – not my cup of tea, but who's going to argue? Not I! Now, we're going to need acres of scarlet silk – the mind boggles at the cost of this. Well, it's his money.' And she rolled her eyes heavenwards.

Sally laughed. 'What sort of black and white?'

Lucy consulted her notes. 'Well, ground floor white marble – that's quite nice, darling, white walls everywhere except for the dining room, which will be black. Silver everywhere – chrome furniture. No curtains, please, no drapes, no pictures. And I can tell you, darling, he has some very strange pieces of furniture indeed!'

'Oh, Lucy! It sounds awful!'

'Yes, my dear, I agree, but you will be surprised at the wonderful effect it will give. Not for living in – at least not for you or me – but for this remarkable young man who has a great deal of money and is able to buy just what he likes ... who are we to argue? Now, to the warehouse.'

Later that day, Sally was sent to a flat in Park Lane which needed to be done over in an entirely new scheme. She came prepared to take notes.

'You're rather young, aren't you?' the middle-aged secretary said, looking at her askance. 'I thought Lucy was coming herself.'

'She was late back from another appointment, so if you don't mind I've brought some samples over and now I'd like to take measurements.' After she had made several good suggestions, the woman completely relented and they ended up having coffee together.

'Lucy will be along tomorrow,' Sally said. 'In the meantime I'll leave these samples and swatches with you.'

'It will be the board's decision,' the woman said, 'but I know which I'd have.'

'So do I,' Sally said, happy that she had taken another step forward.

On Wednesday she found herself longing for the shop to close so that she could see George again.

Lucy was with a client, and was just seeing her to the door when he arrived.

'Hallo, George,' she said, eyeing him up and down with approval.

He grinned at her. 'Hallo, Lucy. I've come to pick up Sally — I'm taking her out for the evening.'

'Are you now?' she said with a look at him then Sally. 'Hmmm. Well, enjoy yourselves.'

Sally glanced at her watch. 'It's not quite — '

'Oh, be off with you!' Lucy said. 'And don't be late in the morning . . .'

George took Sally's arm and began to walk towards his garage. 'I thought we'd go for a walk in the park, then have something to eat at Londini's — do you like Italian food?'

'Love it,' Sally said, her eyes sparkling.

Later they walked over the cobbled stones in the mews where he had a lock up garage. Inserting a key in the lock, he opened the door to reveal a white Mercedes sports car.

Sally opened wide eyes. 'Is this yours?'

'Sure, why not? I've got to spend my money on something. And I've no family, and no girl friend . . .'

'Ahhhh,' Sally commiserated.

'So I bought this. I've had her for two years — of course she's not new, but who cares?' He swung into the driving seat and drove her out of the garage. 'Always aim for the best,' he said, going back to lock the doors. 'Right, hop in.' And Sally got in beside him.

They drove slowly through Hyde Park, before he

brought the car to a standstill in a narrow street in Kensington.

'I hope you like this place,' he said. 'It's quite small but the food's good.'

Sally wondered if it might be the red wine or the delicious meal but halfway through the evening she knew without any shadow of a doubt that she was falling in love with him. She wanted nothing more than to be with him always, for evenings like this to go on forever. When he took her hands across the table, she let him. When he looked at her in that special way, she looked back into those blue eyes and knew that what she saw there was for her.

Almost wordlessly they made their way out of the restaurant and drove through the park, where he stopped the car. Without any demur she went into his arms. When he kissed her, she was lost. Never had she imagined anything like this. Just the touch of his lips was enough. She quivered like a bird coming to life, feeling sensations she had never felt before. He was everything she had imagined him to be: gentle but passionate, loving, yet strong. She found herself aroused as a woman for the first time, wanting to give all of herself, not just to respond, but to give ...

'Sally, Sally,' he whispered, looking down at her as if unable to believe she was really here, like this, in his arms. She put her arms round his neck and drew him down to her. 'Don't stop,' she said. 'Please keep kissing me.'

Presently they broke away from each other and he looked down at her, smoothing her hair.

'Did you know it would be like this?' he said. 'Did you know we were going to fall in love with each other?'

She shook her head. 'I hadn't the faintest idea,' she said, eyes like stars.

'I never really liked the idea of Roedean girls,' he said thoughtfully.

'Didn't you, George? We're quite a nice bunch, really. And I must admit, I never envisaged falling in love with a builder.'

He kissed her. 'Property developer.'

'That sounds worse,' she said. 'Aren't all property developers suspect?'

'Not the ones like me.'

'George, you're incredible — and adorable,' she said with a sigh.

'You're a bit of all right yourself.' He smiled, holding her tightly.

They sat for some time until she wriggled free.

'George, I really must go.'

'I'll drive you home,' he said, kissing her again.

'What? To Chantry Park? Of course not, I wouldn't hear of it — there are plenty of trains.'

'But I don't like the idea — '

'Sorry, I insist.'

He grinned at her. 'Little madam,' he said, and she reached up and kissed him.

They swung through the park towards Knightsbridge.

'How do you get home from the station?' he frowned.

'I left my car in the station car park,' she said.

He nodded, parking his car as near to the station as he could, and putting on the brakes.

Sally looked at him seriously.

'You must come down and meet my parents,' she said.

'I had a thought,' he said. 'The week after next I'm taking a week off — I've booked a few days with an under thirties group going to Sardinia. Why don't you come with me?'

'With you?' she repeated, startled. 'But — '

'If you're going to say Lucy might not let you have the time off, leave it to me. I'll get round her. I've never been before, and I don't know anyone who's going. What do you think?'

Sally's smile grew wider. 'Oh, it would be wonderful — I can't imagine anything I'd like to do more. Let me think about it.'

He put his arms round her. 'I can't bear to be away from you for too long. Tomorrow?'

'George, dear, I can't. I promised ...'

'Never mind. Friday?'

'Yes, that's fine.'

'Same time, same place.'

She clung to him for a moment then got out and ran into the station.

When she had disappeared he drove the car back to the garage and returned to the station, running down the escalator in time to see her train disappearing round the bend.

The sooner he had her under his wing, the better. She would be safe then.

Chapter Nine

It was the end of July and the last Red Cross sewing bee until the middle of September. This morning only Alice, Sheila and Joanna were in attendance. Even Gina had gone to Italy for a visit home, and Ann was in Portugal.

The windows were wide open to let in the lovely summer air, and the scent of Alice's roses beneath the window permeated the room.

'What is this lovely climber peeking in the windows?' Joanna asked. 'I remember you planting it but it's grown so much.'

'Schoolgirl,' Alice said. 'I planted that for Vanessa.'

'She and Sally are lunching today,' Joanna said. 'It's nice that they're in town together. Did Vanessa mention that Sally is going to Sardinia next week?'

'Yes, she did.'

'I think she'll enjoy it – all young people together. It's ages since she wanted to come away with us! Not since we used to rent that house in the south of France, and we all went. Do you remember, Alice?'

'I'll say. It was great fun then ... I expect it's not as nice today.'

'They were still schoolgirls then,' Joanna said wistfully.

'I know you're not supposed to look back, but it's nice to sometimes.' Sheila looked up. 'Since Ann isn't here – and I don't know why I have such a hang up about her – I can talk more freely about Gillian. She's coming home next week to discuss the wedding. It's all on, you know, Alice.'

'You mean she really is going to marry this Abdul?' Joanna

asked. She and Alice felt so sorry for Sheila, knowing how badly she was taking it. 'I can't help feeling you're being a bit difficult about it,' Joanna continued. 'The world is such a small place today, and if she loves him — '

'She's totally fascinated by the lifestyle, and in my opinion, would marry any one of them, just to become a proper Muslim. Of course she's coming home for the first week in August because August is Ramadan, and most of the wealthy Arabs come to England at that time.'

'What exactly is Ramadan?' Joanna asked. 'I've often wondered since we get lots of visitors from the Middle East in August. We have quite a few this year.'

'It's one of the five Pillars of Islam or basic beliefs,' Sheila said. 'I know because I've been reading it up, and I'm quite horrified that an English girl, especially my daughter, can even consider becoming a Muslim. They fast during Ramadan, which means abstaining totally from food, drink and tobacco from dawn until sunset.'

'Golly,' Joanna said. 'Nice if you want to slim.' But saw at once that Sheila had totally lost her sense of humour on the subject.

'Well,' she sighed, 'I suppose at the end of the day, Sheila, you have to accept it. There really isn't much you can do about it, and if that's what she wants — it's her life.'

'How would you feel?' Sheila said bitterly. 'How would you feel if it was Sally?' Her eyes fell accusingly on Joanna, but all she met there was sympathy and understanding.

She picked up her sewing. 'I'm sorry. I'm being an absolute bore about it all. I just wish Don was here — it wouldn't seem so bad. But then if he had been alive, perhaps she wouldn't ...'

Alice stood up and put an arm around her shoulders. 'I am going to make us some coffee,' she said. 'We could all do with a cup.'

'Anyway, how's Alison getting along?' Joanna asked, and Sheila's face changed in an instant. 'Oh, Joanna, she's positively blooming! She is like a woman transformed. Isn't it amazing what having a baby does for you? And her skin! It's smooth and clear, and she looks so well — '

She smiled apologetically at Joanna. 'I keep telling myself

what a lucky woman I am — it's just that I want Gillian to be happy, too, and I don't think she will be ... She hasn't found herself yet — she only thinks she has. I don't want her to go through with becoming an Arab wife and all the misery it might entail.'

'I know,' Joanna said. 'Still, you don't know that she will be unhappy, do you?'

'No, that's true,' Sheila said. 'I suppose there are mothers who would take it in their stride and not mind too much, but I'm intensely English — to the core — and there's nothing I can do about that now. I don't even like us being in the Common Market.' And Joanna laughed out loud.

'Now that's something else,' she said, as Alice came in.

'What is?' Alice asked, putting down the tray.

'We're talking about the Common Market,' Joanna said.

'Oh, that old thing.' Alice laughed, and began to pour out the coffee. 'Help yourself to biscuits.'

'You haven't told us yet, Alice, about Vanessa's wedding dress. Will she have it made?'

'Yes, I think so. She rang you about the reception, did she?'

'Yes, I think she said about seventy. Is that right?'

'About that.'

'Alice, isn't it rather a lot for you to do — invitations, church service, that sort of thing?'

'I shall be guided by what Vanessa wants, and I can hardly hand the whole thing over to Odile, can I? As a new stepmother, she's hardly concerned at all. No, I brought Vanessa up from the age of ten, it will be my pleasure. Sheila will give me a hand, and you and Donald are looking after the catering side of things. I think it's going to be very exciting.'

'October can be nice,' Joanna said, sipping her coffee. 'We used to go away in October, a break after the summer trade to gear ourselves up for Christmas.'

'Where will they live?'

'She hasn't said. Her flat is too small, I imagine, so I expect they'll probably try to find another one. She can always sell that — that's if she is going to keep on the job she has with Jane.'

Joanna looked down at her expensive cotton dress. 'I bought this at Jane's — she has some awfully nice things.'

'Yes, I like that,' Alice said. 'Vanessa says she's going to wear cream, not white. White really doesn't suit her — she's too fair.'

'That's true,' Sheila said. 'She's such a lovely girl, that wonderful hair — I always think of the pre-Raphaelites when I see Vanessa, especially when she wears long flowing skirts.'

'She's a poppet,' Alice said proudly, putting down her cup as a ring came at the front door. 'Who can that be?' She hurried to answer it.

They heard her shriek of surprise. 'Maggie!' And there were squeals of pleasure from both of the others when Alice came in followed by their friend, a vision in white, slim and sun-tanned, gold chains jangling, gold sandals, gold earrings, her red hair bleached by the sun.

'Just like a bad penny!' she laughed, taking a seat at the table. 'Oh, it is good to see you! Any coffee left?'

Alice hurried into the kitchen.

'Where is everyone?' Maggie demanded. 'Just the three of you?'

'Ann's away — and there are just four of us nowadays,' Joanna said.

'My dears, I do feel so guilty,' Maggie said, her heavily mascaraed lashes sweeping down over vivid blue eyes. 'But needs must.'

'We'd probably do the same, given half the chance,' Joanna laughed. 'Well, tell us all about it. Where have you been?'

'Everywhere,' Maggie said. 'You name it, I've been there, done that.' As Alice came in with fresh coffee. 'Oh, bless you, Alice.'

She sat down and picked up her sewing. 'Now you can keep us amused while we work.'

'What are you making? What happened to the squares?'

'We got bored,' Joanna said, 'and Alice had the idea of making a patchwork quilt. What do you think?'

'My dears, it's absolutely beautiful. Who's it for?'

'We're going to raffle it,' Alice said. 'And we expect you to buy tickets.'

'My dear, of course I will — '

'So, what's your news?'

'Well — Alec has been given the whole of the Far East so you may imagine what a step up that is ...'

'Oh, well done! Do congratulate him for us,' Alice said. 'So what does that mean for you?'

'That we shall be based in Hong Kong for the next two years.'

'Oh.' Joanna made a face. 'Will you like that?'

'Not much choice,' Maggie said. 'Still, it could be worse — Hong Kong is a very exciting place.'

'And interesting,' Sheila said, 'now that it's coming to the end of its British run.'

Maggie glanced at her watch. 'So tell me all the news — I'm dying to hear what's been going on.'

'What will you do with the house?' Joanna asked.

'Let it,' said Maggie. 'Both the children are living away from home — they're not interested, and there's no point in letting it sit there. Alec doesn't want to sell it — we do intend to come back to the Park, after all. Actually, we shall probably be home for a few days at Christmas. If the house is let, we'll stay at The Bear.'

With just half an hour left, time sped by. After Maggie had gone, Joanna and Sheila stayed on for a while.

'I don't envy her,' Sheila said afterwards. 'Imagine having to live in Hong Kong for two years.'

'Oh, I don't know,' Alice said. 'I wouldn't mind the chance.'

'Not me,' Sheila said. 'Give me England every time.'

'You know, Sheila, you're very insular, considering you're so imaginative and creative,' Joanna remarked.

'What's that got to do with anything?' she asked.

Closing the door on them, Alice pondered how much Sheila had changed since Don died. Some widows made a new life for themselves, but Sheila had never been able to accept Don's death. Something, a spark, had died within her, and somehow she had never got it back. That new grandchild, she thought, was going to be a miracle for someone else beside its parents.

She took the coffee cups and saucers into the kitchen. This afternoon she was going to tea at Four Oaks with Odile and Edouard. She couldn't wait to see him again.

They sat on the lawn, on this perfect summer's day, beneath the enormous oak tree which provided shade. On a rug lay young Edouard, kicking his bare fat legs and trying hard to sit up. When he finally achieved this he looked surprised until he rolled over again and made the effort once more, grinning at them with the joy of success.

Alice lay back in the chair, watching him. He really was perfect: his strong little limbs, six baby teeth, his fat little feet. He was all a grandmother could ask.

'You must be very proud of him, Odile,' she said. 'He's beautiful.'

'Thank you, Alice.'

It was difficult to see her expression behind those enormous dark sunglasses but Alice thought Odile looked pale and tense. These days she was never relaxed as she was before she'd had the baby, and Alice was at a loss to think what the reason could be.

'I often think,' she began, 'how different your life must be since you married James. I know every wife starts off a new era when she marries, but yours couldn't be more different. You have adapted yourself so well, from a young Parisienne with an exciting career in front of her. Now here you are, married to an Englishman with a baby son — are you enjoying life with us in Chantry Park?'

'Yes, of course,' Odile answered. Too quickly, Alice thought. 'Why shouldn't I? I have the best of everything — a beautiful house, a wonderful husband, and an adorable baby.'

So she must have told herself, over and over again, Alice thought.

'I hope James isn't being too — strict.' Alice smiled. 'He can be. It's the result of his legal training, I suppose?'

But Odile was not to be drawn.

'I am waiting for one thing, Alice,' she said. 'For Phillips to leave at the end of the year.'

So that was it. 'But surely, if you don't want her ...?'

'James thinks we need her, so that is that.'

'Well, it is true to say that it's nice to have help with a first baby — '

Odile smiled, as thought to say, 'You see, you will be on his side.'

'But if you really don't want her, my dear — '

'I would rather have had an au pair,' Odile said. 'A young French girl I could have trained. There are some excellent ones, with good references.'

'I am sure there are,' Alice murmured, wondering if she had stirred up a hornet's nest. She knew now what the trouble was — James could be immovable if he thought something was right. And Odile was so young and so vulnerable. James was years older, a divorced man with a grown up daughter. Perhaps the price she was paying for security and a lovely home was too high.

'By the way,' said Alice, changing the subject, 'are you happy — you and James — with what we are doing about Vanessa's wedding?'

'Oh, Alice, of course we are! I wouldn't have an idea in this world how to go about it, and James is much too busy, and happy to leave it all to you.' She turned anxious eyes to her mother-in-law. 'If you are sure it is not too much trouble? I know we were quite surprised at home as to how much there was to arrange for my wedding. It may be different here, of course.'

'I expect it is the same,' Alice said. 'It is exciting though, isn't it? Oliver is driving Vanessa and myself down to his home for lunch on Sunday.'

'How nice,' Odile said politely. How can I ask her? she thought. How can I mention Amanda's name? Will she, as Vanessa's mother, be asked to the wedding? Should I discuss it with James? Vanessa? Alice?

It was on the tip of her tongue, and still she held back. Surely when the wedding invitation list came round she and James would discuss it? How strange it would seem, talking about his first wife. They never had, up till now. Where was she, anyway? Had no one any idea what had happened to her? Was James secretly in touch with her? Would he have told her if he was?

She jumped up. 'I will make some tea,' she said. 'Stay there, Alice dear, and look after Edouard for me.'

And she ran across the lawn, a young, lithe figure in a navy and white cotton dress, her dark hair dancing on her shoulders.

Alice sat up and put out a hand to Edouard who grabbed it and levered himself up into a sitting position.

'There's a clever boy,' she said, thinking hard. How she hoped that James had not treated the girl harshly. It was one thing to be in court, prosecuting a villain, but surely in dealing with his own wife he was more flexible? Had that been the trouble with Amanda? She'd never known — they had never discussed it.

When Odile came back with the tea things, Alice remembered the Save the Children Fund. They were holding a fête in August to raise money, and she herself had the bric-a-brac stall. Sheila was doing cakes.

'Odile, if you come across anything that would do for my stall, anything at all ... Old clothes you may be tired of, some of James's perhaps. They always sell so quickly.'

'I'm sure there are lots of things,' Odile assured her, 'I'll have a good turn out and see what I can find.'

Presently, as they finished tea, the formidable figure of Nanny Phillips appeared on the lawn, and Alice saw the frown that crossed Odile's pretty face.

'Now then, young man,' the nurse boomed, 'time for tea. He is looking well, isn't he, Mrs Amber?' Thanks to me, were her unspoken words.

'Yes, he's a fine little chap,' Alice said as Nanny's starched, immaculate figure bent down and picked him up as though he was a feather.

She could think of many women who would give their eye teeth to have their babies so expertly cared for. But there it was, Nanny Phillips didn't suit Odile.

'I must go, too,' she said, getting to her feet. 'Lovely cake, my dear, and of course you made it.'

'Thank you, Alice — yes,' Odile said, accompanying her

across the lawn and into the house. 'Do you think Sheila would like some cakes for her stall?'

'My dear, she would be delighted!'

When she had gone, Odile carried the tea things back into the house and went upstairs in search of oddments for Alice's charity fête. There were so many things that needed to be turfed out, many of them she had put into the attic when she first arrived at the house.

In her bedroom she sorted out a few clothes which she laid on the bed, then went into James's dressing room. It always gave her a slightly awed feeling to be in here. It was such a masculine abode with its massive inlaid wardrobe; the Georgian chest containing his underclothes. When she had married James, she had lined the drawers and cupboards with pot pourri paper as she had done at home, and now the contents as she riffled through them gave off a musky, scented odour that reminded her of Paris.

The long wide drawers held vests and pants, and one was set aside for his official trappings as Queen's Counsel, all wrapped carefully against moth and dust. In the top drawers were socks and handkerchiefs — not a lot to throw out here. She was careful to see that his old clothes were replaced as soon as she saw any sign of wear. James was immaculate with his clothes, fussy to a degree. She would be more likely to find things upstairs in the attic. Still, there was a perfectly good sweater which he had never liked, and socks which he never wore.

Closing the drawers, she smoothed the contents down. It was in the top left hand drawer that she felt something beneath the lining paper. She drew it out. It was a photograph, still in its parchment folder, and she knew before she opened it what she would find.

It was of Amanda and Vanessa, taken when Vanessa was about ten years old with her mother's arm across her shoulders. And it was obvious then that Vanessa was going to be taller. Odile looked out at them both, laughing into the camera — and sank down heavily into the nearest chair, her hands shaking, heart beating wildly.

So this was Amanda! But she was beautiful, much more beautiful than Odile had imagined. Dark cascading curly hair, one arm lifted to take it off her face, lovely smile, beautiful eyes, the other arm on Vanessa's shoulders. Oh! Odile could hardly bear it. How had it come to be there, unless James had put it there — and not all that long ago because she herself had lined the drawers and it hadn't been there then. It was hidden, hidden — and she could hardly bear the thought. No wonder he had been devastated when his wife left. She peered hard at it. How happy Amanda looked! Why had she gone, left her husband and her child? There must have been a good reason. Vanessa looked to be about ten, and her mother had left then — so what had happened to change her from this lovely, happy young woman to one who had deserted her family?

Almost with a sob, Odile took one last look and thrust the folder back under the lining paper, closing the drawer slowly.

She felt weak, all the life gone from her limbs .... Did he, James, take it out from under the paper every night before he came to bed? Tonight, for instance, she would lie and wonder. When he was a few moments too long, was he staring hard at the picture of Amanda? She buried her face in her hands.

This way madness lies, she told herself, but making her way up to the attic, could not throw off a feeling of fear and despondency.

She looked around as she unlocked the door, at the crates and boxes facing her, and lost all heart to sort through then. A lot of things belonged to Amanda and James, had been wedding presents which he had banished to the attic when she left. 'Keep what you like and throw the rest out,' he had told Odile when they married, and she had thought, poor James, only too anxious to make a fresh start and throw things away that reminded him of Amanda.

But he been unable to get rid of everything that reminded him of her. She wished now that they had talked about Amanda in the beginning, easily, naturally. Now, if she had anything to say, it would be stilted, forced. How could she say to him: 'James, I found a picture of Amanda in your dressing chest?' He had every right to say, 'What were you doing, probing in there?' He had every right, after all, to keep a picture of his first wife if he so wished.

She had never felt so miserable in her life.

Chapter Ten

'Sardinia,' Sally read aloud from the guide book, 'is one hundred and sixty-eight miles long and forty-five miles across. It had five hundred years of Spanish rule before becoming Italian in 1861.'

'Very interesting,' George said, taking the book from her hand and holding it instead.

Sally smiled, eyes closed behind dark glasses. Beside her, stretched out on the sand, lay George, his navy and white striped swimsuit showing off to perfection his golden-tanned skin.

'You know, you're lucky, George,' she said. 'I mean, being so fair, to go that lovely gold colour. I just get darker and darker.'

'And more mysterious,' he said, lifting himself up on his elbow, removing her glasses and bending down to kiss her soft mouth.

Her lips parted under his as his tongue sought hers. Wave after wave of desire swept through her, and she clung to him. They were on a deserted cove to the north of the island, with nothing in sight apart from the crystal clear sea and the lofty mountains seen through a gap in the rocks, their hired motor boat tied to a post.

'George . . .' But his lips were on her breasts until the nipples rose taut, and he moved his mouth down the slim flat line of her stomach as she arched her back in desire.

His arms went round her, lifting her to him as he entered her, his thrusting movements arousing her to a frenzy where they came together as one in those ecstatic moments that seemed almost too wonderful to bear.

He lifted his head and looked down, seeing the flower-like mouth, damp and soft and warm beneath his, almost bruised, so intense had been their passion. He put out his tongue and licked her lips, feeling the salty taste in his mouth, feeling the desire rising in him again, and this time he entered her slowly, taking his time, until she almost cried out in passion. She held him to her, forcing him in even higher, ever closer inside her, and this time it was as if the ground rocked beneath them when they climaxed together.

Presently he rolled off her, perspiration curling his hair into tight little gold ringlets, his blue eyes looking down into hers with that special look just for her which by now she knew so well.

She looked like a satisfied kitten lying beneath him there on the sand, her amber-flecked eyes with their long fringed lashes smiling up into his.

'Did I ever tell you that I think you're the most beautiful girl I've ever seen?' he asked her.

'No, George, you didn't.' She looked interested. 'But tell me now.'

'I think — ' But she closed his mouth with a kiss that caused him once more to stroke her breasts deliciously, until the sound of a passing motor boat brought them back to earth.

'There can't be,' she said slowly, 'a more idyllic spot in all the world.'

He got to his feet, naked as a baby, and pulled at her hand. 'Come on.'

She took his hand and ran with him over the sand to the sea where they plunged in, gasping for breath at the shock of the water. They held on to each other kissing below the water, George holding her tightly until she laughed, pressed against him. 'Oh, not again, George, you are insatiable.'

'Be interesting, though, so see what's it's like — ' he began.

'Come on,' Sally laughed. 'Race you to the rock.'

They had spent four days so far like this, lazing on

deserted beaches in the sun or making love, never seeming to get enough of each other.

'Three more days,' he said that night as they sat in a small restaurant in a village high up in the mountains.

They looked into each other's eyes across the table, and George took her hand in his.

'You know what I think?' he asked. 'I think we should get married.'

'George!'

'What's so odd about that?' he demanded.

She laughed. 'Nothing. Nothing at all. Simply that I wasn't expecting it. Are you really asking me to marry you?'

Sally wished they didn't have to go home, that this short break would last forever. England seemed so far away. Another world.

'Yes, I am.' He looked at he seriously. 'I mean it – why not?'

'Darling George, I do love you.'

'But?' he said. 'There's a but, isn't there?'

'Not really – I'm wondering what my parents would think. After all, they've never met you.'

'Well, that's easily remedied, isn't it?' he asked her with his engaging grin.

'Of course it is – when we get home, that's the first thing we'll do. I shall invite you to lunch.'

'Then that's settled,' he said happily. 'Are we engaged?'

'Not yet, George,' she said.

'I see. First hurdle coming up. Well, I'm ready when you are. I love you, Sally Simpson.'

'And I love you,' she said, as the waiter appeared at their table for their order.

'I have some news for you,' George continued when they were alone again. 'I waited until now, because – well, because I thought business could wait ... I thought you'd like to know that before we came away, I got the promise of a loan from my bank manager.'

'George! That's wonderful!'

'So I've put an offer in on the place in Montpelier Street – and as far as I know I shall get it. I shall know when we get back.'

'That's great!' she said. 'So what's next?'

'Same as I did on Lucy's place. We'll go to see it when we get back — when I've got the key. Oh, I don't let the grass grow under my feet, Sally.'

'No, I've noticed.'

He put down his fork. 'You know, it seems to me we'd make a good team.'

'I think the same thing.'

'No — I mean, business wise. If I'm to stay in the property business, then I need a business partner — and that's where you come in.'

Sally held her breath.

'Well, I do the places up and you could do the decor — after all, you've learned quite a lot about that side of things working for Lucy, which is more than I have. We could be on to a good thing. Adams and Simpson — how about that?'

She was thinking how much fun he was to be with.

'My dad's firm was Adams and Son — he meant me, of course, though he died before I could do anything about it.'

Sally Adams, she thought, Mrs Sally Adams. Mrs George Adams.

'It was a very good firm, Sally. Prestigious, old established, you know. None of your fly by night cowboys.'

'I'm sure it was.'

'So what do you think?'

'You've taken me by surprise,' she countered. 'It would be a big thing — going into business with someone, especially in the West End.'

'Not if we were married.'

'That's true,' she said.

It was amazing, she thought, that they had so much to talk about. They had very little in common, and yet conversation was never stilted; she never found herself at a loss for words. What a comfort George was. He was so sure of everything, so confident.

What, she wondered, would her parents think of him?

The day before they were due to return home, he took her sailing. It never ceased to surprise her how well George did most things — and sailing apparently was one of his hobbies.

They made for the north of the island and the headlands with their dramatic rocks shaped by the wind where there was good underwater swimming and skin diving and water-skiing.

While George did a spot of skin diving, Sally lay stretched out on the sand, her eyes closed against the sun, listening to the sounds of bathers and sea birds and the lap of the water nearby. Presently she sat up and looked around her. There were not many people about — a few couples here and there, and lone swimmers. Her eye was taken by a man and woman sitting by an upturned boat. The man was handsome and sunburned, he looked like a native Sardinian, and was busy with what looked like a fishing net.

The woman lay flat on the sand, face down, her long slim brown legs stretched out, her hair a dark mass round her shoulders. Presently she sat up and put on her sun glasses. The man smiled at her and, leaning forward, kissed her gently.

Sally smiled. Lovers, she thought, though they weren't young. The man looked to be around fifty. He had broad shoulders and a slim waist, and his luxuriant hair was greying — it shone silver in the sun — while the woman must have been in her forties ...

She turned over and propped herself up on her elbows. There was something vaguely familiar about this woman, yet Sally couldn't think what it was. She had the most beautiful profile, and large dark sunglasses, and her thick riotous hair was tied back carelessly. Even as Sally watched her, the woman sat up and took off her sunglasses, massaging her face with cream or oil, and Sally could see that the bone structure was classically beautiful. She frowned, jogging her memory. Was she an actress, a model, possibly someone famous whose face appeared in magazine or periodicals?

At that moment the woman stood up. She was very slim, thin almost, her figure honed down, the skin as brown as berry. Then she stretched before running down to the sea and plunging in.

Well, Sally thought, Sardinia was the playground of many

celebrities, but just who this one was, she wasn't sure. She looked for George and saw him just emerging from the sea and taking off his flippers. The woman didn't stay in long, and Sally noticed that the man with her watched her every movement, never taking his eyes off her. Then she emerged, like a dryad from the water, shaking her long hair and making her way slowly back to the boat. I know her, Sally thought, I really know her — who can she be? The man threw her a yellow towel which she wrapped around her shoulders, standing up and shaking her hair, and for a brief moment she looked across at Sally, looked away then back again before finally putting the towel down and lying on it.

Sally's heart gave a sudden leap as enlightenment dawned. Unless she was mistaken the woman was Amanda Amber, her godmother! But she couldn't be. After all this time ... But why not? Sally had adored her, the most glamourous godmother any girl could have had. She was almost ten years old when she'd seen her last but she had a long memory — and unless she was very much mistaken, this woman was her Aunt Amanda.

After the first year or so of Amanda's flight, Sally had stopped asking about her. It was better, they told her, kinder to Vanessa, not to keep mentioning her name. She was, after all, Vanessa's mummy; think how heartbroken she must be. But Vanessa had never seemed to mind very much. She had her adored Granny Amber, and then she went away to boarding school, a different one from Sally, so they didn't see each other very often except in the school holidays. Sally still had the gold bracelet which had been her christening present as well as all the trinkets she had been given by Aunt Amanda on her birthdays — that is, until she was almost ten. After that, all the presents had stopped, and a year later, no one even mentioned her name. Sometimes, wearing the bracelet, she thought about Amanda, but by then she was a shadowy figure and apart from the picture of her holding Sally at the christening, you might have thought she had never been.

Now, remembering the photograph and the way Amanda looked in it, in a dark dress and a large hat, Sally knew, despite the years, that this was the same woman. She would stake her life on it.

'Hello, poppet!' It was George bending down to kiss her, and her face broke into a smile of greeting.

'I shall have to teach you how to snorkel, my darling,' he began – but Sally interrupted him. 'I think you've taught me quite enough on this trip for the time being,' she said primly. He lay down beside her on the sand.

'Did you miss me?'

'Well, George, I might have done, if I hadn't discovered someone whom I really do believe is my godmother. I haven't seen her for eleven years.'

He sat up. 'What? Your godmother – here?'

She took off her glasses. 'See that couple over there? That gorgeous hunk of man and that beautiful woman?'

'You've probably got a touch of sunstroke watching the fella,' he said.

'Well, a bit,' she admitted. 'But really, George, don't you think that's the most fantastic coincidence?'

'Yes – if it's true. What makes you so sure?'

'Oh, I don't know, just something about her – the way she looks, the way she moves her head, just something.'

'A bit vague,' he said. 'Has she seen you?'

'She wouldn't know me,' Sally began – and told him all that she remembered about Amanda.

'Well, I don't like to disappoint you, but I think the odds are that it's not her. Still, if you're sure, why not go over and introduce yourself?'

'Mmm, I've been debating that,' she admitted. 'It's difficult while he's there – after all, if it is Amanda, she might not want him to know who she is – or that I'm someone from her past, as it were.'

'See what you mean,' George said, putting an arm round her and drawing her down to him. 'Think about me instead.' He looked at her imploringly.

'That's easy,' she said, pullling him close and kissing him.

But as he closed his eyes and drifted off to sleep, Sally sat up again and saw that the man had gone to the edge of the sea, perhaps to swim or snorkel, leaving the woman alone. She made up her mind in an instant.

Treading over the sand, she drew nearer to the woman,

and as she did, knew without a shadow of a doubt that she was right. It was Amanda Amber.

'Hello,' she whispered softly, and the woman stirred. She had not been sleeping. She opened huge dark eyes, heavily mascaraed, and seeing her closely, Sally realized she was not as young as she had first appeared.

'I'm awfully sorry to disturb you,' she began.

'Oh, you're English,' the woman said as if that explained everything. She had a low, melodic voice. 'Do I know you?' she asked, frowning.

'No — well, yes, you might.'

The woman patted the towel beside her. 'Sit down,' she said. 'Is that your young man?' She looked across to where George lay.

'Yes.' Sally smiled.

'He's very good-looking,' the woman said. 'Now?'

Sally took the plunge. 'I'm Sally Simpson,' she said, and saw the realization in Amanda's lovely eyes.

'Sally?' she whispered slowly. 'My god-daughter. You can't be — '

'You haven't seen me for a long time.' Sally smiled. 'But I remember you.'

Amanda's eyes were wide with shock.

'Oh — I shouldn't have told you like this,' Sally said, contrite. 'I'm sorry.'

The woman blinked and a tear ran down her face which she brushed away hurriedly.

'My dear, don't mind me — what a suprise!' she said, pulling herself together. 'And what a terrible godmother I turned out to be!' Then she was glowing, smiling, a lovely smile which lit up her face. 'How nice of you to come over and speak to me. I'm so glad you did, even though I thought I was dead to everyone in England and no one would want to know me.'

'I'm sure that's not true,' Sally said, remembering that she had never really known what lay behind Amanda's flight.

She was saved from saying anything else by the reappearance of the man. Amanda seemed relieved to see him. 'Oh, Pepi, look who's here — someone from my past. My god-daughter, Sally.'

Sally found herself looking into the handsome face of Pepi, who was every bit as good-looking close to as he had appeared, and saw concern in his eyes for Amanda.

His voice was deep with a French accent.

'Mademoiselle.' And he held out his hand.

'Pepi is half French and half Hungarian — what a mixture,' Amanda laughed.

He smiled at Sally, a warm and friendly smile.

'Darling,' Amanda spoke to him in French, 'do we have something nice to eat this evening?' She leaned over and took his hand.

'He does all the shopping,' she explained to Sally.

'Mais certainement,' he said.

'Then why don't you and your young man come and have dinner with us this evening?' Then as she saw some doubt in Sally's eyes: 'Please — I cannot possibly let you go now that we have met again. And I want to hear all the news.'

Of course she did, Sally thought, it was only natural. 'We're going home tomorrow,' she explained doubtfully, 'and I don't know if George has anything planned.'

'Then run over and ask him,' Amanda said. 'We live just over there — the whitewashed villa on top of the cliff.'

What a perfect place, Sally thought, excited at the prospect.

'I'll go and ask him,' she said. 'Excuse me.'

'Well, I'll be damned,' George said. 'So you were right. Well, if you want to ...'

'You don't?' Sally's face fell.

'Darling, I want you all to myself — but I'm being selfish. If you'd like to — well, we'll go. It's not every day you meet your godmother on a beach in Sardinia.' And he grinned.

'Oh, George, you are a poppet!' And she raced back to tell them.

'Around eight-thirty?' Amanda said.

'That would be lovely.'

'Take that path — you can see where it starts — it's quite a climb from the sands.'

That evening they climbed slowly up the rocky path: Sally in a brief green silk shift, gold sandals on her bare feet, long jade earrings which somehow brought out the amber flecks in her eyes; George in white cotton slacks and tee shirt, carrying a bottle of wine.

The sun was just disappearing behind the mountains, the sky all shades of mauve and translucent green, as they stopped for a moment to embrace.

'It's been the most wonderful holiday I have ever had,' Sally whispered.

'For me, too,' George said.

Amanda and Pepi were sitting outside when they reached the patio which was a riot of colour with geraniums and petunias, bougainvillaea and a scarlet trumpet-like flower which climbed and cascaded over the walls.

Pepi stood and held out his hand.

'This is George,' Sally said, and Amanda smiled.

'Hello, George,' she said in her low seductive voice, and Sally saw his face break into a warm grin while his blue eyes blazed in greeting.

'I think drinks are called for and Pepi has put some champagne on ice – nothing else will do,' Amanda said imperiously. 'After all, this is a celebration.'

They talked until it was time to eat and the night grew darker. There was the sound of cicadas all around them, and the wonderful scent of flowers which exuded their perfume at night.

It was easy to see where Amanda's fascination lay for she was like a butterfly, skimming from one to the other in her conversation yet never staying long enough to talk really deeply and for Sally to find out the things she was curious to know. They talked of their life in Sardinia, and Pepi's being a fisherman. They had been there six years. Whether or not Amanda had been with him all along, Sally was not to find out.

Amanda asked questions about Sally and about her job in London, never touching on life in Chantry Park. Sally found that she could not take her eyes off her; there was a mesmeric quality about her, even though when he did speak, Pepi was every bit as interesting and amusing. She touches everything, Sally decided, like a ballet dancer on a stage but never really comes down to earth.

Pepi had prepared the meal, which was delicious, of sea

foods and salads, followed by excellent cheeses, fruit and dessert wine. It was only when he disappeared into the kitchen with George to make the coffee that Amanda dropped her butterfly act and spoke seriously.

'Tell me,' she said softly, 'about Vanessa.'

Sally took a deep breath. Now that the moment had come, she was totally unprepared.

'Vanessa? Oh – she's working and living in London, and getting married – in October, I think.'

'Married!' Amanda's eyes glowed. 'Oh, how lovely! Who is she marrying – anyone I would know?'

'I wouldn't think so. His name is Oliver, and he comes from Sussex. A banker, I believe.'

'I see. And is she still as lovely as ever?'

'She's gorgeous,' Sally said honestly. 'Tall, fair ...' But Amanda was miles away, her eyes on the distant past.

'Yes, she was never anything like me,' she said. 'Thank God,' she added with a little laugh.

There were no further questions, about James or his new wife or baby son or even Granny Amber. There was a long silence instead, and Sally realized that this was all she was going to be asked.

'Vanessa spent a year in India,' she said at length.

Amanda opened her eyes wide. 'Did she now?' she asked. 'I wonder why she did that?'

There were sounds from the kitchen of the two men returning. Sally could hear the clink of coffee cups and saucers on a tray.

'How I would love,' Amanda said as the men returned, 'to see Vanessa's wedding.'

Pepi put down the tray. 'What news is this? Is Vanessa getting married?'

'Yes, darling, isn't it exciting? In October, Sally thinks.'

'How very nice,' he said, and began to pour out the coffee.

When the time came to leave, Amanda got up and wrapped a scarf around her shoulders, then held out her hands to Sally.

'You will soon be twenty-one,' she said. 'I haven't forgotten, you see.' And she disappeared into the bedroom, returning with a small black box.

Opening it, she showed Sally what was inside. 'I would like you to have this,' she said. 'In case we don't meet again. It will match your earrings.'

Sally saw a magnificent carved jade brooch set in gold, and took a deep breath, looking up at her.

'Oh — I can't accept this. It's beautiful!'

'My dear, you must. It is my privilege as your godmother. Take it with my love.' And she bent forward and kissed Sally lightly on both cheeks.

She felt her eyes fill with unshed tears.

Amanda shook hands with George. 'Goodbye,' she said. 'And thank you for coming and spending your last night with us. I shall go to bed, Pepi darling. Will you see our guests safely down the path.' And with a little wave, she had gone.

Pepi led the way down the precipitous slope until they reached the sands, then took Sally's hands in his.

'Thank you for coming. It will have pleased Amanda very much, and I know you will want to tell them at home, particularly Vanessa, that you have seen her. But I must take you into my confidence, sadly, to tell you something I think you should know.'

He gripped her hands tightly. 'Amanda has cancer.' He heard the gasp that came from Sally's white lips. The doctors say she has only three months or so to live so that is why I am telling you, but please, I beg of you, do not say anything about this to anyone. Amanda herself doesn't know how long she has, although she knows she has cancer.'

Sally bit her lip to hold back the tears.

'It was the mention of the wedding that made me realize she might just think she could go — but it would not be a good idea, even if she could. Amanda is a creature of impulse, but such a visit would be disastrous. Naturally I will do everything I can to dissuade her. There is also the likelihood that after all this time her family would not wish her to reappear.'

He took a deep breath. 'I will leave it all to your discretion. I know I can rely on you, Sally.'

She reached up and kissed him briefly.

'Thank you for telling me. I don't suppose I shall see you again — but thank you, and for looking after Amanda so well.'

They walked back in silence, George tight-lipped, Sally saying nothing. Presently he stopped and took her in his arms.

'I'm sorry that we went — and that you had to hear such bad news. It's sad for Amanda — sad for anyone to be so ill — but you mustn't fret, Sally. It will do no good to anyone.'

'You're right,' she sniffed.

'Are you going to mention it to your parents?' he asked.

'Yes, I think so, I feel I must — I'm not sure about Vanessa or Granny Amber.'

'I shouldn't,' he said tersely. 'If I could give you a bit of advice, Sally: "A still tongue in a wise head," my old dad used to say.'

Sally gave a weak smile. 'Your old dad sounds like a very nice man.'

'He was,' George said shortly. 'I take after him.'

Chapter Eleven

Joanna Simpson walked down the wide staircase and through the foyer of The Bear Hotel.

As usual she received many admiring glances, not only for her looks but for her elegant appearance. Always up to the minute in fashion, she wore a natural linen long skirt and thigh length jacket, a cream tussore silk blouse, and gold chains around her neck from which dangled her magnifying spectacles. Her hair was cut short, close to her head, her make up perfect. If you had complimented her, she would have said it was all part of the job.

At the reception desk, she glanced through the visitors arrival book, then walked through the reception area towards the entrance. Standing beneath the eighteenth-century portico, she looked out at the panorama before her. The long sweeping drive, lined with age old oaks and beech trees, the huge urns filled with now pink and white geraniums, the lawns close cut, having been done that morning by the gardener whose father before him had worked in the gardens of The Bear.

Joanna never looked out at this view without feeling a surge of pride. Now she awaited Sally's return with excitement. Her plane had landed, the car had gone to meet her.

When Sally came eventually through the entrance doors, Joanna couldn't help feeling a thrill of pride at the sight of her daughter. She looked wonderful. Her eyes shone, she was darkly tanned, and her step was light despite her heavy holdall. Surely, Joanna thought, surely a man had to be responsible for a girl looking like that!

She put both arms round her and hugged her. 'Darling, you look fantastic — no need to ask if you had a good time!'

'Mummy, it was wonderful!' Sally turned starry eyes to her.

'Did you have a good flight?'

'Super,' she said. 'And the weather was glorious.'

'We got your card,' Joanna said.

'Already? That was good.'

'You must tell us all about it — Daddy's upstairs having a nap. I expect you'll want to bathe? We'll see you at dinner. I have to go and sort out some arrivals.'

'See you later then.'

Soaking in a hot bath, Sally closed her eyes. How strange it seemed to be home again. That wonderful week in Sardinia seemed like a dream. And George? Dreamily, she soaped her legs ... Dear George. She couldn't wait to see him again, and she had taken leave of him less than two hours ago. He had wanted to come back with her to meet her parents, but she had forestalled him. The timing wasn't right. She knew she was going to have to play her cards very carefully, realizing in her bones that once she told them about him, they would have a fight on their hands.

She stepped out of the bath and wrapped herself in a warm towel. It didn't matter in the long run what they thought because she intended to marry George. She didn't want to upset them unnecessarily but she would have to make them realize that her mind was made up.

She unpacked her things then telephoned George around seven, putting the receiver down dreamy-eyed after talking to him. She made her way along the softly carpeted quiet corridors of her parents' private apartment. The large salon held a dining table and chairs which the family often used when they wished to dine privately, as they would want to do this evening, Sally knew.

Joanna and Donald were sitting on the sofa, both with a drink in their hand. When she came in, her father put down his drink and hurried over to her.

He kissed her warmly. 'Sally, you look wonderful!'

She sat down opposite them, curled in a big armchair, and helped herself to a dish of tiny biscuits on the side table.

'Well,' Joanna urged. 'Tell us all about it.'

Sally began with the island and the hotel, the other young people who had been on the trip and the sort of things that filled their days, deftly leaving out George's name for the time being.

When the waiter came in with the meal, she was still chatting nineteen to the dozen. They let her talk on, and if Joanna thought she was being unusually garrulous, she kept the thought to herself.

It was when her parents were eating cheese and biscuits and she herself was indulging in strawberries and cream, that Sally appeared suddenly to remember something.

'Nothing like English strawberries!' she said. 'Oh, I almost forgot — you'll never guess who I met on the beach near the hotel.'

They smiled up at her expectantly.

'Aunt Amanda — my godmother. Amanda Amber.' She saw the shocked look on both faces. Afterwards she recalled that her father had a biscuit halfway to his lips, his mouth open in dismay. Her mother looked quite, well, horrified.

There was a silence. 'Yes, it was a bit of a shock,' she said firmly, as still they did not speak.

'Did she recognize you?' her mother asked in a small voice.

'Well, I knew her at once so I went over to her —'

'Oh, Sally, you didn't!' Joanna cried.

'I did,' she said. 'Why not? She is my godmother.'

'Yes, but —'

'Donald put out a restraining hand. 'Let her tell us, darling.'

'Anyway, she was jolly pleased to see us.'

'Us?' interrupted her father.

'Yes, I was with a friend. And she asked us over to dinner.'

'You didn't go!' her mother said accusingly.

'Yes, I did,' Sally said belligerently.

'Was she — alone?' Joanna said.

'No, she lives with her friend. A really nice man called Pepi — he's half-Hungarian.' She saw her mother's lips tighten.

'She said she knew that it was my twenty-first this year,

and she gave me a simply lovely jade and gold brooch to match my earrings. I had on these jade earrings you and Daddy gave me, do you remember?' She stopped when she saw the expression on their faces.

'What's wrong?' she asked.

'Nothing,' Joanna said hastily. I'm just — surprised that you met her. I mean, there — in Sardinia.'

'Where did you think she was?' Sally asked.

'Darling, I thought she was in Spain ...' Joanna laughed, but it was a tremulous little sound.

'Did she ask about anyone?' she said eventually.

'Only Vanessa,' Sally said. 'I told her she was getting married.' She saw her mother look briefly at her father, who was gazing at the floor.

'She didn't ask anything else,' Sally said miserably, knowing that somehow she had upset them. 'I'm sorry,' she said. 'But honestly, I just couldn't not talk to her.'

'Of course you couldn't, darling,' Joanna assured her, and seemed to make up her mind.

She dabbed at her lips with her napkin and got to her feet. 'Well, I'm sure you must be tired after the journey — an early night would do you good. I'll walk along with you to come to your room then you can show me the brooch — it sounds lovely,' she added brightly.

Sally took the box out of her jewel case and opened it. Joanna gasped.

'Darling, it's beautiful. Must be worth a small fortune.'

'Yes, that's what I thought.' Sally put it back in its box and snapped the lid shut.

'Well.' Joanna bent and kissed her. 'Goodnight, darling, sleep well — see you in the morning. Thank goodness tomorrow's Sunday.'

'Good night, Mummy. I — er won't be in to lunch tomorrow. I'm going up to town.'

'Oh, all right, darling,' Joanna said, and closed the door softly behind her.

This had definitely not been the right time to tell them about George, Sally decided. But what about Amanda? She'd certainly put the cat among the pigeons.

Well, she wasn't sorry for what she had done. For

goodness' sake! Anyway, whatever had happened with Amanda it was past history and none of her business.

Joanna joined Donald in his den where he sat behind his desk, fingertips joined, gazing out into space. She closed the door behind her.

'What an extraordinary thing, Donald? After all this time.'

'Yes,' he said shortly, then got up and came round the other side of the desk to take her in his arms. 'I suppose she was bound to pop up again sooner or later.'

'Sardinia ... well, let's hope she stays there. Do you suppose she's been there all along?'

'Who knows?' he said drily. 'Your guess is as good as mine.'

'I've just seen the brooch she gave Sally, Donald — it's simply beautiful and must be worth a great deal.'

'Probably trying to make up for the missing years as her godmother.'

'Yes, I expect so. Still, it's strange how things happen isn't it — it must be eleven years.'

She was silent for a few moments, then sighed deeply. 'Well, I'm off to bed — don't work too late, darling.'

'I've one or two things to do,' he said as she closed the door after her.

When she had gone, he sat down again in the leather chair, his head in his hands. Please God this would be the last time anyone would talk of Amanda. He could see the unhappiness on Joanna's face at the very mention of her name. Amanda — who had set her cap at most of the men around, but particularly him. She had made no secret of the fact that she wanted him. Everyone knew — except perhaps James, her husband, and he was so busy in the Law Courts he was hardly ever home. Which was probably half the trouble, he thought wryly.

Eleven years ago ... In those days they had been a circle of six, he and Joanna, James and Amanda, Sheila and her husband, the other Donald ... Don had been alive then. They had all belonged to the prestigious golf club, all played a good round, went to all the club dances, the Midsummer Ball, the New Year's Eve

Dance, sometimes lunched up at the clubhouse on a Sunday.

Amanda had a roving eye for the men, and what was more she was damned attractive to them, with her looks and figure, and made no effort to hide the fact that she liked to flirt. Any good-looking new member of the club got her immediate attention. Which was all very fine and large, in fact they all laughed about it — until that last year, when she be came serious about him, Donald. Gone was her banter, her flirtatiousness, her lighthearted approach to the game. She changed, and set her wonderful eyes firmly on him.

She grew quieter and more serious. He wondered sometimes if they all noticed it as much as he did. Certainly Joanna saw it clearly. 'Darling, she really fancies you,' she would laugh, in a off handed sort of way, but he knew that sometimes she was really annoyed.

It came to a head that last summer when they took the usual villa in Juan-les-Pins, a glorious house sleeping twelve with a private swimming pool. There were the six of them and Alice, Vanessa and Sally, and Sheila, and Sheila's two girls, Alison and young Gillian.

They booked it for a month, and all went well until that last week when James shot back to London two days early. It was a Thursday — it was etched on Donald's mind forever. Alice had gone to town shopping for last minute gifts, with Sheila and Joanna, Amanda and the children, while Don went off for a game of golf.

Donald had gone to the bank, and on his return went up to their room to change for swim. He was in his swimming trunks, picking up a towel and his sunglasses when the door opened, and in came Amanda, wrapped in a yellow bath robe. She stood just inside the closed door, back against it, looking at him.

He wouldn't have said why he felt a moment's unease but he smiled at her nevertheless. He had learned in business that to smile is to disarm.

'I thought you'd gone with the others,' he said.

'No, it was too hot. I decided I'd have a swim.'

'Oh,' he said, wondering why she had come unasked into his and Joanna's bedroom.

'Right,' he said prosaically, throwing the towel over his shoulders, 'let's go.' He heard the key turn in the lock, and in an instant she had thrown herself at him, burying her head against his chest, her perfume falling his senses.

'Oh, Donald, I'm so unhappy.'

'What on earth's the matter?' he asked solicitously, his mind searching for the best way to deal with this.

She raised those lovely eyes to his, deep violet with strange gold flecks, holding his gaze until she came closer and kissed him full on the mouth — at the same moment as she let the towelling robe drop from her shoulders and stood before him stark naked.

It was instinctive reaction to close his arms around her and return her kiss, to protect her nakedness — yet even then he knew without a doubt what the outcome was going to be. Short of being pushed away with brute force, she was not going to let go. As she began fondling him the desire to have her rose in him, a physical thing, a basic instinct to take what was being offered, without warmth or even affection on his part, just the desire of a man for a very desirable woman.

There was just one moment when the thought of Joanna, his beloved Joanna, flooded his mind to the exclusion of what was going on, but he stilled it and they subsided to the floor on her towelling robe, even the cold tiles unable to quench her ardour or bring him to his senses.

There was no doubting her experience; a man would have had to be very strong-willed indeed to have thrown off this wanton woman determined to have her own way. His senses reeled at the touch of her delicious body, as she used all her wiles to ensnare him. It had not been difficult to co-operate, to indulge to the full, to respond to every movement, so unexpected was the seduction, so skilfully did she employ every trick in the book on the art of seducing a man.

When it was over and she lay back triumphant, he could not disguise a fleeting pang of admiration for the sheer nerve she had shown, even thought it was quickly followed by a feeling of self-reproach.

'You've always wanted me, Donald, you know you have.' Amanda smiled softly like a cat finishing a bowl of cream.

'You must be mad to come here like this,' he said, shaking his head, 'You've got it all wrong — '

'I wouldn't think so.' She held out a hand for him to take.

Grasping his hand, she swung to her feet, and would have gone into his arms, except that he backed away.

'It had to happen, Donald.'

'No. I'm sorry, Amanda. I should have been man enough to stop you.'

He went to the door and unlocked it, his breath coming fast, some of the disgust he felt for himself showing in his face. For the first time she looked a little wary.

'You and I belong to each other though you may not realise it now — women are always quicker at sensing these things than men.'

'You'd better go, Amanda. Joanna is due back at any moment.'

She put out a hand to take his, but he backed away.

'Keep away from me, Amanda, I warn you.' He closed the door after her, panic rising in him at what he had done.

Under the shower, he wondered what her next move would be, for there was no doubt she must be a very determined woman to have done what she had. It took some pluck to come to his room like that. That she was a slut he was in no doubt — how many other men had she used? Poor James. But his big fear was Joanna's reaction. If ever Joanna found out, he had the feeling that she would never forgive him — because the woman had been Amanda, a friend of the family. In all his married life, he had been true to Joanna — he had never wanted any other woman. Would she understand that it had meant nothing?

Sick to his stomach, he went off for a swim, trying to convince himself that it had never happened.

Surprsingly, the roof hadn't fallen in when Joanna arrived back home. Amanda emerged from her room as she always did for drinks at six o'clock without the slightest sign that anything untoward had happened.

They had a barbecue by the pool, and spent the next day packing.

It was all very much as it had always been, and once home Donald had given a great sigh of relief thinking the whole thing might be forgotten, but a telephone call for him on Sunday was from Amanda, saying she had to see him. When he refused, she became hysterical.

'I must see you, Donald — now, as soon as possible. Can't you get away?'

'For God's sake, Amanda — no! No! Do you hear me? This must stop. Where's James?'

'How do I know?' she asked furiously. 'As if I care ... Please, Donald.'

He put down the phone, his heart beating wildly. God, what a situation to be in — and all because this ridiculous woman ... how could he ever have ... she must be going round the bend.

He would do anything, anything to save his marriage. What a price to pay for a moment's indulgence. And all because a stupid, spoiled ...

But then Joanna came in and Sunday continued on its own inexorable course until Monday dawned, and with it the news that Amanda Amber had run away. Left her husband and her child with a simple note of a few words. Not to try and find her, it was better this way.

Chantry Park had been thrown into a state of confusion, almost disbelief. By midday everyone knew, and the rumours were rife. Was there another man? Had James sent her packing? Everyone knew what Amanda was like. Was she simply tired of married life? Had she a secret lover? How could she do that? Leave a little girl — such a dear little girl ...

It was the worst time of Donald's life. The guilt was almost unbearable. When everyone seemed so puzzled as to the reason for her disappearance, he felt he had the answer. That it was up to him to say, to explain — but he couldn't. Couldn't admit it, not to anyone. Unless the time came when he had to, he was going to keep his mouth shut.

Until now.

All those years, and it had to be his own daughter who

had found her. Truth was stranger than fiction. God, what a mess.

He couldn't blame Sally, it was a natural thing to do. Seeing her godmother, of course she spoke to her — why shouldn't she? But supposing, knowing that Vanessa was to be married, Amanda wished to come to England and see her daughter's wedding? Surely not! And face everyone — even James — after all that time? No, he assured himself, it was extremely unlikely. He had nothing to fear on that score, he would stake his life on it. What incredibly bad luck. The last time anyone heard of her she had been in Spain ...

Now, here he was, on another Sunday eleven years later. He was in the bedroom when the call came — and Joanna answered. She called him from the salon where the switchboard had run through.

'It's for you, darling. It's Alice, I think.' And thank God, he thought afterwards, she had gone from the room.

'Connecting you, to Mrs Amber,' the switchboard operator said.

'Hallo, Alice.'

'It's not Alice, Donald — it's Amanda.'

The deep husky voice, so familiar, turned his blood to water. Even his knees felt unsteady.

He didn't repeat her name. 'Hallo — Donald Simpson here.'

'Donald, it's me — Amanda.' Again that low husky voice, just the same after all these years.

'Hello, Amanda.'

'Is Sally home yet?'

'Yes, she arrived yesterday.'

'Did she tell you she'd seen me?'

'Yes, of course,' he said, keeping conversation to a minimum.

'It was quite a surprise — for both of us,' she said.

'I can imagine,' he replied. 'Is there something I can do for you, Amanda?' His voice was cool.

'Yes, as a matter of fact there is. I would very much like to see Vanessa married — yes, I know what you're going to say. After all these years. But do you think something could be arranged?'

'I'm not the one to answer that,' he said. 'Surely it's up to Vanessa herself — have you contacted her? Or Alice?'

'Of course not. I was hoping you would give me the lie of the land — what the reaction would be, for instance. I know James has remarried — I saw the announcement in *The Times*, and also news of the birth of his son.'

'Well, then ...' Donald began.

'Surely, after all this time, no one is going to object if the bride's mother appears at the wedding!'

Amanda, he thought, had always done what she wanted to do — without reference to anyone else. She hadn't changed.

'That's not for me to say,' he began. 'If you want my opinion, I would say it's not a good idea, more especially since they've never heard from you in all this time ...'

'A lot of water has passed under the bridge since then, Donald. And I have to say, you sound as stuffy as you ever were! Thank goodness your daughter seems to have taken after Joanna.' And she gave a low laugh. 'I was delighted to see her, she's a lovely girl — and it looks as if you might be getting a son-in-law too, a delightful young man.'

Now she had his full attention. A young man?

He heard her sigh deeply. 'Well, Donald, I shall expect you to put in a good word for me. I will ring you again in a week or two.' And she hung up.

The bride's mother after all this time — what a joke! And the young man — Sally's young man? Again, that was not something he could ask her about. He would have to wait until she mentioned it. He decided that he would think over Amanda's words, and contact Alice. She would be the one to know, and if Alice wondered why Amanda had chosen to ring him, well, that was too bad. He hated intrigue.

It was Monday evening, over dinner, when Sally broached the subject of George.

'I'd like to ask a friend down on Saturday or Sunday,' she suggested. 'Whatever suits you.'

Joanna smiled. 'Someone special?'

'Mmmm, sort of,' she said.

'Was he the young man you took to dinner at Amanda's?' Donald asked pleasantly.

'Yes, how did you know?'

'You said you were with a friend.'

'Oh, so I did. His name is George – George Adams.'

'Well, darling, that's easy enough to remember.' And Joanna laughed. 'Did you meet him out there? Was he in the party?'

'No, I met him in London – he was working for Lucy.'

Donald put down his knife and fork and looked up. 'Doing what?'

'Doing up her new house – he's a builder.'

'A builder? What sort of builder?' Joanna seemed genuinely puzzled.

'A sort of property developer,' Sally said. 'He does up houses and sells them.'

Sally saw Donald's fingers tapping on the table.

'Who does he work for?' he asked.

'Himself of course,' Sally said. 'You'll like him, Daddy. Which day shall we say then?'

They looked across at each other then Joanna said, 'Sunday lunch?'

'That's fine,' Sally said. 'Now I must fly. I promised –' But they didn't hear the rest of her words as she hurried away from the table.

'Donald,' Joanna said, a worried frown between her brows, 'you don't think this is serious, do you? She was over the moon when she got back – she looked positively radiant.'

'I shouldn't think so, darling,' he said.

He had something else on his mind.

Chapter Twelve

Alice was sorting out clothes for the forthcoming sale in aid of the Save the Children fund when she came across the blue and white cotton dress she had worn all those years ago in India. Wrapped in blue tissue it had faded only slightly, and she held it up to herself in the mirror seeing the small waist, the puff sleeves and low neckline. Had she ever been that small? She had saved it all these years — pure sentiment, she chided herself. Yet the material was so pretty and now she knew what she was going to do with it. She pulled it gently to test its strength and found it was perfectly usable — it was going to make the next ring border of the patchwork quilt.

She could remember so well the times she had worn it — mainly garden parties and charity events — with a large leghorn hat and long blue ribbons. She had old photographs somewhere but she wouldn't ferret them out now. She had more important things to do. If after washing it was still usable, she would iron it and get out the template for the patchwork quilt.

There were several garments she could donate — it was a good thing from time to time to have a turnout. The trouble was, most women liked to hoard just a little, only grudgingly throwing out something that had worn so well, something they knew that had suited them or bore memories of a happy occasion.

Those pretty sprigged cambric pillowcases of yellow and white striped cotton bought when Vanessa was a schoolgirl and her bedroom had been done out in yellow ... they would make excellent scraps for the patchwork quilt too. It was coming on so well, the others donating pieces of material from time to time – it was beginning to take on a real meaning, with small relics of dresses and linen and discarded curtains.

She hurried downstairs and soaked the blue dress in soft suds, squeezing gently so as not to pull, then rinsed it and shook it out, pleased to see that the colours had not run and that the material was still durable. Presently it hung on a hanger on the clothes line, and she stood smiling, looking at it from the kitchen window in approval.

Bundling the other things together, she made small parcels and put them in the back of the car. This morning she usually visited the local hospital to help with the book round in the wards – there was always so much to do, her days were full, but that was how she liked them to be.

She was almost ready to leave when she saw Donald Simpson walking up the narrow path to the lodge, his beautiful cream Labrador on a lead. Donald was an old friend – she had known him since he was a young man and his father had been in charge of The Bear. Sometimes he called in when he was taking the dog for a walk across the common, and she was always so pleased to see him, particularly as his free time was so precious.

She opened the front door. 'Donald! How nice to see you.'

He bent and kissed her. 'Were you just going out, Alice?'

'Nothing that can't wait. Will you have some coffee?' She bent down to Archie. 'Good boy.'

Once inside they sat at the kitchen table, a pot of coffee between them. Alice guessed this was no idle call – she knew by his expression that he had something to tell her.

He forestalled her question. 'Well, Alice.' And she smiled at him, her strong weatherbeaten face wrinkling into a hundred creases, the bright blue eyes those of a friend.

'I have some surprising news to give you,' he said apologetically.

'I hope it's good,' she laughed.

He put down his coffee cup. 'You knew that Sally had been on holiday to Sardinia?' he began.

'Yes, is she back?'

'She came home on Saturday — and guess who she met there?' He didn't wait for an answer. 'Amanda.'

Alice almost dropped her coffee cup as she put it down in the saucer. 'Amanda? Our Amanda?'

He nodded. 'I'm afraid so.' There was a silence you could have cut with a knife for a few moments as they stared at each other, lost in their own thoughts.

Alice was quite pale. 'Well!' she said at length. And again: 'Well! Did Sally recognize her — after all this time, did she speak to her?'

'Yes, she recognized her — on the beach, it seems — then went over to her and they chatted. From what I can make out, Amanda invited them — Sally and her companion — to dinner at the villa where she lives with her friend, Pepi.'

Alice looked grim. 'Naturally,' she said. 'Did she ask after — anyone? James? Vanessa?'

'Only Vanessa, I believe — and Sally told her she was getting married.'

'What did she say?'

'She mentioned, briefly, that she would like to see her daughter married — that's the sum total of it, Alice.'

'Good God!' she said. It was a long time since Donald had seen her so cross.

'What a nerve! Poor little Sally — what did she say to all this?'

'Just that it was up to Vanessa and her father.'

Alice sighed deeply. 'Well, the least said, soonest mended, I should think. What did Joanna say?'

'Not a lot — what could she say? Amanda gave Sally a beautiful brooch for her twenty-first birthday.'

'Goodness!'

'Alice, there's something else.'

She looked up sharply. 'If that wasn't enough, I had a telephone call from Amanda on Sunday morning.'

'What?' she cried in disbelief. 'You did? She telehoned you?'

'Mmm. To ask me privately what I thought everyone

145

would think of the idea of her coming to the wedding.'

'Why on earth — ?' Alice began and was suddenly silent. Thoughts were racing though her head one after the other, suspicions, conclusions, and a terrible feeling of pity for Donald if he had become ensnared in the wiles of her beautiful ex-daughter-in-law.

She looked up and saw him watching her, his face clear of any deceit, his honest eyes searching hers for help.

She put a hand over his.

'I would rather Joanna didn't know about the call,' he said, 'and I don't know the best way to handle the situation.'

'Poor Donald,' she said softly. 'How did you leave the conversation in the end?'

'That she would ring again in a week or so — I suppose to find out if James and Vanessa were agreeable.'

'I think it a shocking idea,' Alice said firmly. 'Still, I have no right to an opinion, though if I was asked, I would say no. It's up to Vanessa — and of course, James. And I can be fairly certain as to what he would say — not to mention Odile!' They both smiled wanly.

'Oh, what a thing to have happened!' She cried. 'To think if Sally hadn't gone to Sardinia ...'

'I suppose it was on the cards, Alice, that a thing like that could happen anytime.'

'I wonder whether Vanessa will want her there? I can't imagine that she would be bothered that much. And James ...' she said thoughtfully. 'Oh, no, it's out of the question.'

If what she imagined was true, Donald wouldn't want her there either.

'Let's just let it ride,' she said. 'Do nothing, say nothing, and perhaps that will be that.'

'But what will I say when she telephones again?'

'Yes, I'd forgotten that. Look, let me sleep on it, I won't do anything hasty.' She wanted to say his secret was safe with her, but that was pre-supposing too much.

After he had gone, she subsided on to a kitchen chair, her thoughts in the past. Was it really possible, all that time ago, that Donald and Amanda had had an affair? It surely was unlikely — where would they have found the time and the secret meeting place? Donald's life was an open book, and although the same couldn't be said for Amanda, nevertheless Alice doubted very much whether Donald would have succumbed to her wiles. still, he was only human — and Amanda had been quite stunning.

She had to conclude that there was something in it, however brief and regretted by Donald, for he adored Joanna, always had. No good asking herself now if that was the reason Amanda had disappeared — it might well have been. She could, of course, mention it to Vanessa to get her reaction before saying anything to James, but that was not such a good idea.

She fell back on her favourite axiom: least said, soonest mended.

James was in his chambers when the phone rang. His clerk, Rattenbury, took the call, and looking across at James, raised his eyebrows in the deprecating way he had.

'Mrs Amber, sir.'

'Thank you.' James lifted the receiver. 'Good morning,' he said pleasantly, and waited to hear if it was his mother or his wife.

'James — it's Amanda. Amanda,' she said again when he said nothing.

It took a good deal to disturb James's equanimity, but the sound of his ex-wife's voice after a lapse of years was enough to shake him more than somewhat.

'Amanda?' He felt a momentary sense of panic. 'How are you?' he asked automatically.

'I'm well, James, as I trust you are?'

He waited until he felt completely in charge of the situation.

'They may not have told you — ' she began ' — perhaps you didn't know that Sally Simpson recently came to Sardinia on holiday, where we met.'

Good God! he thought.

'I'm speaking from there now, James, and I'm going to ask you to do something for me. A favour, if you like. Sally told me of Vanessa's wedding, and I would very much like to come.'

There was a silence as he digested this.

'James? James – what do you think? Is it on? I mean, coming over to the wedding? How do you think Vanessa would feel?'

'I have no idea,' he said coldly in a voice familiar to many defendants.

'Oh, James, relax a little! It's years ago now, water under the bridge – and I really would like to see her married. After all, I am her mother.'

What good did it do, he thought, to enter into a slanging match? There was no limit to what this woman would do to get her own way. She hadn't changed at all.

'I will tell Vanessa that you rang,' he said politely. 'I really must go – I'm due in court.'

'Of course you are!' she cried. 'When did you ever have time to talk to me?'

'Goodbye, Amanda,' he said and replaced the receiver, aware that Rattenbury was hovering in the corner, and had heard every word.

He gave no more thought to the telephone conversation, concentrating solely on the business in hand as he made his way into court. Then, at lunch time, he thought about the shock of the call from Amanda and what she had had to say, coming to a logical conclusion, the only one of which he was capable. He really hadn't any say in the matter.

It was Vanessa's wedding and Amanda was her mother. Therefore the decision must be hers.

When he returned to the office, he asked Rattenbury to put a call through to Vanessa.

'Daddy!' she cried. 'How nice – it's ages since I saw you.'

'Vanessa, my dear, how are you fixed for lunch – say the end of this week, Friday? Would that suit you?'

She didn't say that she had a hair appointment – she could change that.

'That would be lovely, Daddy. Where shall we meet?'

'The Hyde Park? Near enough for you?'

'Super. I shall look forward to that.'

'Around twelve-thirty, then.'

Vanessa put down the phone. What a nice surprise ... it

was ages since she had seen her father on his own, certainly not since he had married Odile.

He was waiting for her when she arrived, a tall, distinguished man with silver hair, while he saw a delightful fair-haired girl, so like him to look at in many ways, and his heart leapt with pleasure at the sight of her.

'Well, my dear,' he said, when they sat down. 'It was good that you were free to lunch — I'm sure time must be precious to you now that your wedding day approaches. Shopping that sort of thing.'

'I'm fairly well organized,' she said. 'My dress should be ready next week, and Gran is more or less up to date with everything. I don't know what we would do without her.'

'The thing that I want to discuss with you has some bearing on that,' James said, 'but let's eat first.'

It was over coffee that he broached the subject, and he didn't beat about the bush.

'Have you seen Sally since she came back from Sardinia?'

'Sally Simpson?' She was surprised at the question. 'No, we don't see so much of each other nowadays. She has a new boy friend, and I see a lot of Oliver.'

He put down his coffee cup and looked across at her, his grey eyes meeting hers steadily.

'She apparently saw your mother while she was there.'

'My mother?'

To hear those words on his lips was almost unbelievable.

Vanessa was quite pale. 'Really? In Sardinia? Is that where she has been all this time?'

'I have no idea,' he said, dismissing the question, 'but the point is that Sally told her you were getting married, and she expressed a wish to come to the wedding.'

He dabbed at his lips with a napkin and put it down on his plate, then looked up at her.

'Your mother has since telephoned me and requested an invitation to the wedding.'

Used to reading the slightest change in a person's expression, he saw a glimmer of interest in Vanessa's eyes and knew before anything more was said that she was intrigued. He sighed inwardly. He already knew her answer.

'Well!' She sat thinking. 'What a shock!' she said at length. 'After all this time. How do you feel about it, Daddy? After all, it's for you – '

He shook his head. 'No, my dear, the choice is yours. It is your wedding, and she is your mother. Those are the facts.'

'Yes, but I wouldn't want to upset anyone – you or Odile,' Vanessa began. 'Would her coming be frightfully embarrassing for everyone?'

'Perhaps,' he said drily. 'The request is a little unusual after such a lapse of time. Still, if you would like her to come, I will tell your grandmother to send her an invitation.'

Vanessa was absorbed in her own thoughts.

'Fancy her wanting to come,' she said. 'I've never heard from her in all this time.' She wanted to ask him: 'Have you?' but knew that was unwise.

Looking across at her now, he was suddenly assailed by guilt. He had left Alice to get on with it, organizing Vanessa's boarding school while he had opted out for a time to pick up the threads of a broken life. Never, even now, could he listen to the story of the breakup of a marriage without feeling sick inside.

Vanessa looked across at him, blue eyes frank.

'You never wanted to talk about it, did you, Daddy? Why did she leave? Did you know the reason?'

He was silent for a few moments.

'Your mother was unhappy,' he said. 'She tried to make a go of it, but it was not to be.'

He looked down. 'She was beautiful, and she did love you – very much – but she wasn't a strong person and the temptations were too great.'

'What temptations?' Vanessa asked.

'The temptations of the world outside. She felt trapped – marriage wasn't enough for her. She felt that real life was going on outside Chantry Park. There are many people like that, Vanessa, who feel that the grass is always greener on the other side. Are you going to be happy with your Oliver? Is he the one you want? I would like to think you will. It is a father's greatest wish for his daughter.'

She put a hand over his. 'Oh, Daddy, of course I will. Don't worry about me. I'm quite tough.'

He smiled at her.

He would say no more about her mother, she knew.

'You are sure you won't mind? And Odile?'

'Quite sure. I am not certain of your grandmother's reactions. I haven't spoken to her yet, but in any case she will go along with whatever you wish. Would you like me to ask her to send the invitation or will you do it?'

'It might be best for you to do it,' she said, 'although I'm going down to see her tomorrow, so we'll talk about it then.'

'Well, my dear,' and he glanced at his watch, 'I must get back. Don't hurry.'

'Thank you for a super lunch – I did enjoy it,' Vanessa said.

She watched him go out of the restaurant, proud of him, the glimmer of a smile playing around her mouth. Then she picked up her handbag and went out.

She would ring Sally straight away and suggest lunch. Fancy her not saying anything! She couldn't wait to hear what had happened, what Sally had to say about her mother.

She positively skipped along Knightsbridge. Life was so full of surprises.

Chapter Thirteen

September, Odile thought, was a lovely month. A time when the trees in Chantry Park began to change colour and there seemed to be a hush over everything, as if the brightness and vivacity of the summer had gone and nature was taking a deep breath. The garden was a mass of colour still: fiery geraniums and fuchsias, the tall chrysanthemums behind in bud, the fat dahlias hiding their occupants the earwigs who seemed to prefer them to any other flower.

There was a mist outside in the garden as she went about her work of preparing the evening meal. The kitchen, once large and very thirties in style, had led into a breakfast room — called the morning room by James, much to Odile's amusement. When she married him and he gave her carte blanche to do as she liked, her first task had been to tackle the kitchen. Builders had knocked down the dividing wall and fitted out a working area at one end and a dining area the other. With so many woods and finishes available she had settled on dark oak, mainly because she thought it suited the house, and because it was very English to her Gallic mind.

There was a quarry-tiled floor, a beamed ceiling, and Jacobean blinds which lent a rich colour to the dark oak. Then blue and white china and, to make it homely, French Impressionist prints on the white plastered walls at the dining end of the room. She had insisted on a large work table in the centre despite the protests of the kitchen planners, and now she stood at it, a cooking apron over her skirt, hands immersed in pastry making.

She was rolling it out when Nanny Phillips came in before going upstairs to pick up little Edouard from his afternoon sleep.

'May I have a word, Madam?'

Odile looked up, hoping that her hostility and dislike for this woman did not show too much on her face. Every time Nanny said those words, it boded trouble.

'Yes, Nanny. What is it?'

She closed the kitchen door and came into the room.

'I was going to speak to Mr Amber, seeing that he engaged me if you know what I mean, Madam, but I thought perhaps I should tell you first.' She coughed gently and put a hand up to her face while Odile waited.

'I am afraid, Madam, that I have to give in my notice.' And at these words Odile felt a wave of exultation run through her.

She put down the rolling pin carefully and dusted her hands at the sink. Now she could afford to be polite.

'I am sorry to hear that, Nanny. Is there something wrong?'

'Well, Madam, Mr and Mrs Roding — they live at Grey Steeples, you may not know them. She is very young, poor dear. Her first baby is due earlier than expected and I had always said I would be on hand when she came out of the nursing home ...'

'And of course you must!' Odile cried, without waiting for her to finish.

'I know I should be leaving at Christmas but — '

'Nanny, you must not feel guilty,' Odile said honestly. 'We shall be sorry to see you go — but there it is. Edouard is a big boy now, and I am sure I can manage.'

'If you are certain ...'

Odile had never thought to see Nanny Phillips so placatory.

'I never like to leave my mothers in the lurch,' she said. 'But there you are — we can never be sure with first babies, can we, Madam?'

Behind the thick spectacles, her small eyes glinted.

'Indeed we can't,' Odile agreed pleasantly. 'When did you wish to leave, Nanny?'

153

'Well, Madam, if it's all the same to you, I should like to leave at the end of the month — that will give me time to settle in at Grey Steeples.'

'I am sure that can be arranged,' Odile said, trying not to look too pleased at the news. 'I will tell my husband, if you would like?'

'Thank you, Madam,' Nanny Phillips said. 'Well, I'll be up now and see to Master Edouard — I can hear sounds from upstairs, and I expect he's throwing things out of his cot — the naughty young rascal!' And clucking like a mother hen, she went out and closed the door behind her.

Odile almost hugged herself. She had got what she wanted — the horror was leaving — she would have the baby to herself at last! It was a pity though that James hadn't given in to her — it was quite different, Nanny leaving of her own accord. The least he might have done was aquiesce to her wishes, but that was James — he liked his own way. Still, she was delighted. Nanny was going! Things couldn't be better.

She waited until they were having their pre-dinner drink together in the drawing room — Edouard already having been put to bed. She could hardly hide her air of triumph has she settled herself among the cushions and took up her glass.

James glanced across at her. What a joy she was to look at. Her dark beauty, those brown eyes alight with pleasure. He wondered what had caused that. He was pleased, though, for he knew he would have to tell her of the decision to ask Amanda to the wedding and with Odile's mood of the last week or so, he was not too sure how she would take it. She was likely to be up in arms at anything he suggested.

'Nanny has given in her notice today,' she said lightly, knowing he would be shocked and somewhat displeased.

He frowned. It was the last thing he had expected to hear. 'What? What on earth do you mean? She's not due to leave until the end of the year. Is anything wrong?'

'No, not at all,' Odile said, taking a sip and putting down her glass. 'It seems she wishes to go somewhere else in the Park to help a young couple with their first baby. She apologized, of course, but said that is what she wanted to do.'

'I am afraid she can't,' James said firmly. 'She's under agreement to stay for twelve months.'

'Oh, James, don't be so stuffy!' Odile cried. 'What on earth does it matter? If she wants to go, then let her go — I for one am delighted.'

'Yes, I know you are,' he said drily. 'However, a contract is a contract.'

'You mean, she signed a contract to stay for twelve months?' she asked in disbelief.

'No, but it was a verbal agreement, and she has been paid until the end of the year.'

'Goodness!' Odile said, her French upbringing shocked at such an arrangement.

'That's neither here or there, however,' he said. 'I must say, I'm suprised — I thought she was the kind of woman who would honour an agreement.'

'I told her I would inform you and I have,' she said.

He eyed her silently, wondering if she had said anything to upset the woman, then decided to make the best of it.

'Well, there it is then,' he said. 'What will you do?'

'What any mother would do,' Odile said reasonably. 'Look after Edouard myself.'

'You must get help,' he said. 'I can't have you left here with only a daily woman.'

'You seem to imagine I am helpless,' she said with repressed fury. 'I assure you, I am quite capable.'

'My dear, I know you are,' he said. 'Of course you are,' soothing her, 'but I want you to be free whenever we go out — to be able to meet your friends and play golf. All the things other women do.'

'I am not other women,' Odile said. 'I am me — and I am not like them. I am French, for a start, and we like to bring up our own children. I might get an au pair — one of my cousins.'

His face was like a thunder cloud. 'We shall see,' he said. 'I am not in favour of — '

'But I am!' Odile said loudly, almost shouting, as she got up and went into the kitchen.

They sat through dinner in silence until James, having enjoyed what was an excellently cooked meal, dabbed his mouth with his napkin and smiled across at her, filling her glass.

'A simply wonderful meal, my dear,' he said. 'What an excellent cook you are.'

Odile blushed with pleasure. 'Thank you.'

'I never remember tasting pastry like that,' he said. 'What was it called?'

'Normandy plum tart,' Odile said. 'It is a recipe of my mother's.'

'Delicious,' he said. 'Were they our own plums?'

'Yes — from the little tree down at the bottom of the dell. It has been simply laden with fruit — it seems to have been a good year.'

'Yes, judging by the wasps,' he said agreeably. 'I shall have to ask Parkins to see to that nest above the eaves there.'

And so peace was restored — temporarily — for unwisely James, sitting opposite Odile and drinking coffee, decided that perhaps now was the time to mention Amanda.

'By the way,' he began, 'quite out of the blue I received a telephone call from Amanda — from Sardinia.'

Odile went pale — she felt suddenly weak as a kitten when she heard him say the name, it seemed to her for the first time.

'Your wife?'

'My ex-wife,' he corrected her.

'What did she want?'

Her voice sounded quite harsh — not like her at all.

'Apparently, she met Sally — '

'Sally? Sally who?'

He looked at her patiently. 'Sally Simpson — from The Bear.'

'Oh.' She slumped back against the cushions.

'Have you seen her since she returned from Sardinia?'

'No, of course not. I have only met her on a few occasions.'

'Ah. Well, it seems she went to Sardinia, and there she came across Amanda — I am not aware of the actual circumstances.'

'Yes, yes, so why did she ring you? Amanda, I mean.'

How she loathed that name. Amanda — such a stupid name.

'Apparently, Sally told her that Vanessa is getting married, and she — '

'You are not going to tell me she wants to come to the wedding!'

She was almost shouting. James raised his eyebrows and looked straight at her.

'Yes, that seems to be the general idea.'

'Good God! How ridiculous. I hope you told her what you thought of the idea?'

'My dear, it was not for me to say. I have my own opinion, but the answer must lie with Vanessa — after all, Amanda is her mother.'

'It's a bit late for her to remember that now,' sneered Odile, surprising herself with the vehemence of her feelings.

She sat quietly, breathing heavily, her lovely dark eyes smouldering, not looking at him.

'Odile — ' he ventured, and she looked up, hostility in her gaze.

'I can quite understand your reactions — at first, mine were the same.'

'Really?' Her voice was cold.

'We have never talked about Amanda — '

'There should have been no need,' Odile said. 'She was part of your life a long time ago — years ago, long before you met me.'

'Exactly,' he said, pleased at her words.

'Or rather, she should have been.' She emphasized the word 'should'.

'What does that mean?'

'She should form no part of our lives now.'

'Nor will she,' James said, not understanding. He had never thought of Odile as a jealous woman.

'Then why are you even considering her coming to the wedding?'

'My dear, because it's not up to me. The decision rests with Vanessa.'

'Have you spoken to her? Told her about her mother's wish to attend the wedding?'

'Yes, I have,' he said, realizing now that he should have tactfully told Odile first.

'I see, Charming! What I think is of no account.' She bit her lip.

He had never seen Odile like this before. True, she had been off colour lately, and likely to fly into a temper at anything he said, but now her feelings were very real and transparent. She was jealous of Amanda. What reason could she have after all this time? They had been married for two years. The subject of his first marriage had never cropped up. There was surely more to this than met the eye.

'And what does Vanessa say?' she asked.

'She seemed to be quite – ' he searched for a word ' – intrigued by the idea.'

Her lip curled. 'Intrigued? How curious. After what happened to her, I should quite understand if she never wished to see her mother again.'

'Perhaps,' he agreed. 'But, human nature being what it is, and Vanessa about to embark on an important step in her life, she can afford to think generously of her mother.' He coughed. 'At least, that's the way I see it.'

'And is that what you think she should do? Allow her mother to come – just like that?'

'We were speaking of Vanessa's reactions.'

More like your own, Odile thought darkly. All this being planned behind my back, as if I were a child, with no opinions of my own. It is more than any woman should be asked to do. Face a beautiful, erring wife, confront her at the wedding ... Well, if she comes ...

'Odile,' he said gently. 'Shall we talk about this, once and for all? Would that clear the air? Perhaps it would have been better if we had in the beginning, but I never saw the need.'

What was he up to? Odile wondered. Not only did he keep his ex-wife's photograph in his private drawer, but now she was being asked to face her and being made to feel ungracious just because she didn't want her to come to the wedding. What woman would? she argued.

'Was she on holiday in Sardinia too?' she asked suddenly. 'Or has she been there all this time?'

'I have no idea,' James answered quietly, getting up and going over to the drinks cabinet where he poured himself a brandy. I wonder, Odile thought. She watched him and he turned to her.

'Can I get you anything?'

'No, thank you,' she said shortly. So he needed a drink, she thought grimly. She was not surprised. After all, what did she really know about him? Why had Amanda left him? Was it because he was a womaniser? Had there been others in his life? And where would this ex-wife stay? Before you knew it they would suggest she stayed here. It wasn't difficult to imagine a menage à trois ... Her thoughts were so jumpy and incoherent that she decided she had said enough. Best to go to bed early before she said something she might really be sorry for.

'I have a slight headache,' she said. 'It's been quite a traumatic day.' She got up and plumped the cushion behind her. 'I shall have an early night.'

'Please, Odile don't go. Let's — '

'Goodnight, James.'

She almost sobbed as she went up the stairs. Oh, why was she being so horrible to him! She had never realized there was this distinctly nasty side to her nature! If she hadn't found that photograph in his drawer, would she have felt like this about Amanda coming? Was it that her marriage was already doomed? Over? This last three months she had become more and more dissatisfied with her life in Chantry Park. In fact, it was since little Edouard had been born. But why? She simply adored him. He was what she had always wanted — a baby of her own, a son.

When James came in she feigned sleep but was aware that he bent over her and kissed her gently on her brow. Was this, she wondered, how Amanda had felt before she left him. Was that why she had fled?

She was going to take her life in her own hands and do just what she wanted. Everyone else seemed to please themselves. Carrying on as though she didn't exist. Well, they would see about that.

She would write to her cousin Nicole who lived in Nice, one of a family of four daughters. Each of them in turn had been to England to perfect their English, now it surely must be the turn of Nicole, the youngest. Aunt Sophie had had a large family, two boys and four girls, so that they were all very much used to family and children. If she was free, Nicole would be an excellent choice to come and stay to help look after Edouard. It might not be James's idea of a nanny, but it was hers, and it was time she asserted her rights. After all, she had excellent daily help.

Long after she knew James was asleep in the next bed, she lay awake, brooding and planning. Another thing — it might be a good idea to lunch with Louis Marraux again. It was not so much that she was mad about Louis, but that she needed a bit of glamour, excitement ... that was what she was missing. And the time to do it was before Nanny Phillips left. She had almost a month.

Relations between Odile and James were strained for the next few days, not helped by the fact that he was busy at the Law Courts on an important case.

He picked up his briefcase one fine September morning and kissed her as she sat at the breakfast table with Edouard.

'I expect I shall be late again this evening,' he said. 'I'm sorry about this, my dear, but when it's over we'll go away for a few days — would you like that?'

She looked up, a small smile playing around her mouth.

'Yes, James. That would be very nice.'

How cold she had become, he thought. So different from the warm, passionate girl he had married. If he could just put his finger on the trouble ...

At twelve-thirty he took his client to lunch, a Mr Rudemeyer. He was immensely rich, a Dutchman who liked to eat well. James had the chauffeur drive them to Rules.

Divested of hats and umbrellas, they studied the menu seriously, with the approach of men who know exactly what they are looking at.

Having chosen, they went into a deep discussion of the merits and de-merits of the case, and it was not until the oysters had been disposed of and they were waiting for the main course that James's eye was attracted by the delicious profile of a young woman seated some way to the side of him. The man opposite her, dark and handsome in what James would call a slightly effeminate way, was obviously enamoured of his companion, judging by the way he looked at her. Every now and again as she turned or bent her head, James caught a glimpse of a straight small nose, and smiled to himself as he realized that what attracted him was that the young woman bore some resemblance to Odile from the back. Her hair was thick and dark, she wore an elegant, simple black dress, in the understated way that Odile would wear it ...

He returned to his client's affairs with difficulty.

With only half his attention on the business in hand, he found it extremely difficult to keep his eyes away from the girl. The couple were talking so animatedly, engrossed in each other. He watched with envy until she turned her head a little and he caught a glimpse of the pearl earring set in gold which looked suspiciously like one of a pair he had given Odile after Edouard was born. He began to feel a little hot under the collar. That he was over-working he knew, and now told himself he was letting his imagination run riot ...

He concentrated hard for the next few minutes on what his client was saying, and over cheese, decided to have one more glance.

They were still there, smiling at each other, and he decided that he had to be mistaken. Even if it were Odile, which was well nigh impossible, he was too much of a gentleman to intervene, and anyway, it couldn't be her. How could it be? He had left Odile in Chantry Park with his son — it was not likely she would be lunching in Rules with a man, having said nothing to him about it ...

He walked out, followed by Herr Rudemeyeer, knowing that if Odile said nothing, he would never be sure.

It was after eight-thirty when he arrived home and found her sitting in the drawing room with some embroidery.

She looked up with a smile when he came in, and he went over to her and kissed her cheek, feeling it cool and firm against his lips, her perfume lingering. Her eyes were warm and brown and — was it his imagination, or did they seem to glow at some hidden secret? She had the most wonderful eyes — it was these which had attracted him when they first met. Were they the eyes that had looked across the table at the young man today?

'What sort of day did you have?' he asked.

'Oh, so-so,' Odile replied. 'Much as usual.'

'Did you go out?' he asked casually, picking up a paper.

'To the shops,' she replied, which could have meant anything. 'By the way, Edouard has another tooth,' she said with maternal pride.

'Oh, well done,' James said, for the attempt to cross question her seemed suddenly ridiculous and ill timed.

'And how was your day?' Odile asked, bending over her sewing. 'Very busy?'

'Very,' he said laconically. 'By the way, I've eaten — I had an excellent lunch.' He wanted to add: 'At Rules,' but if it had been her, how he would hate to see her embarrassment.

'I guessed you would have eaten,' she said. 'By the way, Alice telephoned — she wants you to ring her back. It's not important, no hurry.'

'Still, I'll do it now,' he said, getting up. If there was one thing he hated it was awkward situations, especially those of his own making.

Why did the feeling persist that Odile was hiding something from him?

Chapter Fourteen

'James, dear,' Alice said, 'I wanted a word with you about the invitation to be sent to Amanda. I had a chat with Vanessa about it, and she seems to be in favour of the idea — what do you think?'

'Well, Mother, the whole thing took me by surprise, as you may imagine. I was not best pleased when I heard. But ...' He sighed deeply. 'I felt it only right to tell Vanessa, and when I had lunch with her the other day, she seemed all in favour of the idea.'

'Oh, James, it's not a good one, is it?' Alice sounded troubled.

'I agree,' he said. 'I am a little surprised that Sally didn't mention it to her, but be that as it may, the deed is done now, and I'm afraid there's no going back.'

'But what will Odile say? Will she mind?'

'Oh, I shouldn't think so,' he said airily. 'She's not the sort of person to object,' but Alice knew her son, and recognized the inflection in his voice. So Odile had minded, she was sure of it. Oh, what a mess! Just because a selfish woman had a whim to come to her daughter's wedding — the daughter whom she hadn't seen for over eleven years! What nonsense. And everyone who had known her fraught at the very idea, not least Donald. She would protect his good name up to the hilt if need be, although she knew nothing for certain.

'Well,' she sighed, 'if everyone is agreeable, then I will send off the invitation.'

'Do you have her address?'

'No, but Sally will have it. I'll ask her.'

'Thank you, Mother, for all you are doing — it's not easy, I know, and jolly good of you.'

'My dear, I am enjoying it hugely — or I was, until —'

'I know, I know,' he said. 'Now you are not to fret over this. I won't have you worried. She caused enough suffering in the past.'

'Oh, I've the hide of a rhinoceros!' Alice laughed. 'Don't you worry about me!' But when she put the receiver down, she was frowning with ill-concealed impatience.

Drat the woman! Why couldn't she stay in Sardinia, or wherever it was she lived?

When the invitation arrived, Amanda was overjoyed. It came when the French doctor was visiting her. Pepi was so pleased for she had been unusually well for the past couple of weeks. Her eyes were brighter, she had lost no more weight and seemed stronger, more like her old self.

Now her eyes shone as she showed the doctor the gold printed wedding invitation.

'My daughter!' she said proudly. She's getting married in October.'

'And I suppose you want to go?' the doctor said, his dark eyes on her animated face.

'Of course I'm going — no doubt about that!' Amanda cried. 'Why, you can see how much better I am.'

He smiled. 'Yes, you are improved, I'm glad to say. But don't overdo things. Take life very easily and build up your strength.'

He went outside to the cliff top path with Pepi, then turned and faced him before walking back down to the beach.

Pepi looked at him questioningly.

The doctor shook his head. 'She is in remission.'

'What does that mean?'

'This happens — sometimes more than once. The patient appears to start to get better, and then —'

He saw Pepi's agonized face.

'You mean, it is not so? She is not getting better?'

The doctor shook his head. 'No.'

Pepi covered his eyes. 'It is cruel, cruel!'

'Yes, my friend, it is.'

'But is it not true — while there is life there is hope?'

'Yes, but I am speaking from experience. She may last a lot longer than I think — she may even get well again — she could surprise us all.'

He saw Pepi's look of anguish.

'But it is better to be prepared, my friend, then the shock is not so great.'

'Do you think she could make the journey to England?'

The doctor smiled. 'Determination is a wonderful thing. I have known people win against great odds if they want something enough.'

'In that case, she will go,' Pepi said. 'There is nothing I can do to stop her.'

'And neither should you,' the doctor said. 'It will be the thought of taking such a journey that will keep her going.'

They shook hands.

When Pepi returned to the villa, Amanda was sitting gazing at the invitation on the stone mantelpiece, her eyes starry, a smile on her face.

He went over and took both her hands.

'Four weeks,' she said softly. 'I shall be quite better by then.'

'Of course you will,' Pepi said. 'And now we must think about buying you some beautiful clothes — clothes for an English wedding in October.'

'Oh, Pepi,' Amanda said, leaning against him, unable to see the tears which had sprung to his eyes.

When the acceptance of the wedding invitation arrived, Alice's heart turned over as she recognized the mauve spidery writing she knew to be Amanda's. It was a formal note, no more, and she went into her small study and put it with the others on her desk.

She stood looking out into the garden beyond, her thoughts going back many years, memories flooding in at the sight of Amanda's handwriting. Amanda as a bride — beautiful, radiant — and James who just had to be the most delighted groom Alice had ever seen. To think that after a short span of years and one child, the butterfly had flown — to settle where and with whom? How could she bear to, how could she dare, face them? It was incredible — but then Amanda had always done exactly as she wanted, taken all that life had offered, hurting people as she went on her way.

Alice sighed. Oh, well, it was done now. She had sent off the invitation as requested, and had the acceptance, and there was nothing anyone could do about it. They had to make the best of it. She certainly wouldn't let it mar Vanessa's wedding if she could help it.

She went upstairs and from the spare room wardrobe took out the folded patchwork quilt, laying it carefully on the bed. Tomorrow was quilt day. After the summer break they would all come back and carry on where they had left off.

It really was a beautiful quilt — better even than she remembered. It would be finished sometime in November, and that would leave just the backing and finishing off in time to be raffled for Christmas — such a good idea. Well, she certainly would not mind holding the winning ticket. It was lovely enough to grace anyone's bed. Mainly light blues with touches of yellow, white, a tiny bit of pink, some heathery mauves and browns — it was the prettiest thing. Single size, of course, for a single bed. They had not been too ambitious and carried away enough to tackle a double-sized quilt.

They arrived early, greeting Alice effusively and waxing enthusiastic over the quilt. Taking their seats and diving into the sewing basket, they talked as though they had not seen each other for years.

The pieces grew under their nimble fingers as they heard each other's news.

'So how's Alison?' Joanna asked.

'My dear, she's marvellous,' Sheila said. 'She looks so well, and really I hand it to her. She's been working in the office — just mornings only, although I think she's giving that up this week. Her point is that it was only starting a baby that was the trouble. Once that was achieved, she's like any other mother — although they monitor her closely, of course. You'll see her at Vanessa's wedding, all being well.'

'That's nice,' Joanna said. 'And what about Gillian?'

Sheila hesitated only for a moment, then decided to tell them. After all, they had to know sometime or other, but she was not going to look straight at Ann. Alice, bless her heart, knew anyway.

'Gillian is engaged.'

'Oh, wonderful! When was this?' Needles were poised in the air. 'Anyone we know?'

'Hardly,' Sheila said, unable to resist a hint of sarcasm. 'No, she's engaged to Abdul, a young man she met at the university in *Dubai*. And as I understand it, she had her engagement party last weekend.'

'Well I never!' Joanna seemed genuinely pleased to hear the news, but Sheila noticed that Ann didn't look up from her sewing and wore a look of disapproval.

'She will live out there, I suppose?' Joanna went on. 'You have to admit, Sheila, she's always been fascinated by the Middle East.'

'Oh, yes,' Sheila agreed, wanting to throw something at Ann whose head was still bent low over her sewing. You'd have thought she'd have said something.

'When are they getting married?' Alice asked.

'In the New Year sometime,' Sheila said. 'This seems to be the season for weddings.'

'Yes, things usually go in threes.' Joanna said. 'I wouldn't be at all surprised if Sally isn't leading us in that direction.' And she peered through the eye of her needle.

'Sally? Really? I didn't know.'

'Yes, she met him at Lucy's — you know, where she works. An awfully nice young man, but of course her father and I wouldn't agree to marriage yet. She's hardly known him long enough —'

Ann looked up. 'What does that matter? Many successful marriages come from brief courtships.'

'What a lovely word!' Alice cried. 'They don't seem like courtships today, although I suppose that's what they are — in one way or another.'

'Of course they are,' Ann said briskly. 'I had only known Gerald for six weeks when I married him.'

And it didn't take you long to discover what a good thing you were on to, Sheila decided, hating herself for feeling so bitchy towards Ann, but deciding that she deserved it.

'How romantic!' Joanna said.

I wish I could be more like Joanna, Sheila mused.

'Anyway, you were saying about Gillian — it looks as if you are in for a trip to Dubai, Sheila.'

She looked embarrassed. 'Oh, I don't know —'

Alice looked at her. 'Of course she is,' she said. 'It will be a wonderful experience. Unless, of course, Alison wants to be married here, at home.'

Sheila grasped at this straw hopefully.

'Mmm, yes, I suppose there is that.'

'And this young man of Sally's — have you met him?'

'George? Oh, yes, he's a poppet, awfully good-looking.'

'What does he do?'

'He's a property developer, I believe,' Joanna said. 'Something like that.'

Ann looked up approvingly.

'Why would you discourage her? It's nice when a girl wants to settle down.'

'Oh, yes, I agree,' Joanna said hastily. 'But she hasn't known him long, and Donald and I feel —'

'At least he's English,' said Sheila.

'Yes, I know what you mean,' Ann said, commiserating with her, making Sheila wish she had said nothing.

'Anyway, how is Vanessa's wedding coming along?'

Alice smiled. 'Well, I believe her dress is almost finished, I can't wait to see it.' She hesitated before going on, 'You heard about Amanda's wish to come to the wedding?'

They all seemed to speak at once.

'Damn' cheek!' Sheila said. 'When Alice told me I couldn't believe it!'

'Wasn't it a strange thing — that Sally should bump into her like that?' Joanna asked. 'Out of the blue. We couldn't have been more surprised.'

'Well, I suppose it was bound to happen sooner or later — somewhere,' Alice said soothingly.

'You're not going to send her an invitation, surely?' Ann asked.

'Yes,' Alice said. 'We told Vanessa and she said, why not?'

'Well, I've never met your ex-daughter-in-law, but I certainly wouldn't have asked her,' Ann said firmly. 'I think it goes beyond the bounds of good taste.'

She resumed her sewing and Sheila made a face at Alice, then Gina appeared with coffee which halted all conversation temporarily.

When she had gone, Alice said, 'Gina is coming to the wedding. She's already bought her outfit — it's quite something, I can tell you.'

Ann looked up, her shocked eyes staring at Alice over the table. 'Gina? This Gina?'

'Yes, dear,' Alice said smoothly. 'She's like one of the family — she's been with me more than ten years, remembers Vanessa when she was a schoolgirl.'

'Oh, it wouldn't be a wedding without Gina,' Sheila laughed. 'What's she going to wear, Alice? Do tell.'

'Well, she went up to town and bought a suit — and, my dear, it really is nice, and quite circumspect for Gina. A sort of navy silk — she says no one in Italy would wear anything but silk to a wedding! It has white lapels and a white collar, and with it she will wear a large navy and white hat, really super — and you know how well she wears anything on her head. I tell you, we shall have to look to our laurels. Not only that but, bless her, it's all new, so you can imagine how she enjoyed buying it. The money seemed to be no object. "What else do I spend it on?" she said.'

'I have bought,' Joanna said, 'the prettiest pink outfit — at Jane's, as a matter of fact — did Vanessa tell you?'

'No.' Alice smiled. 'She never says anything about clients at the shop.'

'That's good,' Sheila said. 'I do like Vanessa — she takes a bit of knowing, but she's an awfully nice girl. I'm dying to meet him, Oliver.'

Alice put down her sewing.

'I don't suppose you will now until the wedding,' she said.

Joanna glanced at her watch. 'I'm sorry, have to fly. We have some friends coming in to lunch today — friends of Donald's from Scotland.'

'My dear, you hurry along,' Alice said. 'I'll pack up your pieces.'

'Thanks, Alice, you are a dear. Shall we be seeing you on Friday afternoon for bridge?'

'Of course,' she said. 'We shall be there, won't we, Sheila? Margery's at two, isn't it?'

'That's right,' Joanna said. ''Bye then, I'll see myself out.'

Driving home through the park, her beautifully kept hands on the wheel, her diamond rings sparkling, the expensive handbag at her side, her thoughts were mainly on Sally — and on George who was coming down for the weekend, unless she was mistaken with a view to sounding out Donald and herself about marrying Sally.

Weddings were infectious, she thought, it had always been the same. When friends got married, you wanted to follow suit. Of course, it didn't apply so much in these days when couples lived together. Still, there was an air about Sally these days. She had changed since she met George. Joanna had decided straight away that Sally was in love with him. Understandably, she realized, but marriage was another matter. She hoped Sally would fall in and out of love several times before the right man came along. But somehow you knew when he did. Was George the man for Sally?

'Darling,' Donald said, when she greeted him. He looked pleased to see her, as he always did.

She had been so lucky, she thought. To have found the right man almost at her first real grown up dance. It was a charity affair, held at The Bear, where she had gone with her parents. She and Donald had looked into each other's eyes, and from that moment their future was decided. They were blissfully happy, the parents approved — not everyone was so fortunate.

'Have the Macphersons arrived yet?'

He glanced at his watch. 'No, plenty of time.'

'Right, I'll go up and change,' she said. 'See you presently.'

George and Sally sat on the floor of the first-floor drawing room in Montpelier Street. George's arm was around Sally's shoulders as they looked at what he had achieved in the last four weeks. The windows were pushed up to let in fresh air to combat the smell of paint, plaster and new woodwork.

'I love this house, George,' she said. 'Wouldn't it be wonderful if we could live in it after we were married?'

He nodded. 'It would — but that's not going to be, Sally, my girl. We'll end up here eventually — but in the meantime we're going to have to make it the hard way.'

'Are you going to ask for my hand in marriage?' she asked, her dimple showing.

'Ask who?' he said.

She pushed him. 'My father, idiot!'

'If you want me to — I will certainly mention it to him.' And his blue eyes crinkled in that special way that made her want to kiss him.

'It would have been nice to have got engaged before Vanessa's wedding,' she mused. 'Then I could have flashed my ring around.'

'I see, that's the main reason for wanting to marry me, is it?' he teased.

'Of course — if I get you thrown in as a bonus.'

He put his arms around her and kissed her, then leaned back and looked at her.

'Your father isn't going to like this, is he? By that, I mean he won't think I'm good enough for you.'

Sally flushed. 'Oh, George, it isn't that. But I suppose they hoped I'd marry someone they know.'

'One of your own sort,' he said laconically.

'You are my sort — and I don't want to hear anything more about it. I'm going to marry you, and that's that.'

'I'd rather have his approval though,' George said.

'So would I, to be honest,' Sally confessed. 'But you never know. They may say, great, go ahead.'

'Born little optimist,' George said, hugging her. 'Still, the point is, we want to get married — blessing or not — is that right?'

'Absolutely,' she said. 'Are you proposing, George?'

'I already did.'

171

'Ask me again,' Sally said, closing her eyes and lifting her face for his kiss.

'Will you marry me, Sally Simpson?' George bent his head and kissed her eyes and her mouth. She pulled him down to her.

'Oh, George,' she murmured. 'Of course I will, of course I will ...'

Later they walked over the house, checking every room, locking the windows and doors, finally making their way down the stairs.

'It will look absolutely beautiful when it's finished.'

'As soon as it is, it goes on the market.'

'Isn't it a bad time, George — the housing market isn't having too good a patch, I understand.'

'You're right,' he said. 'Still, places in this particular spot are usually snapped up — people who have this kind of money aren't usually affected by recessions or slumps — and let's face it, they're more often than not foreigners.'

She sighed. 'Oh, well, the main thing is for you to repay the bank loan, isn't it?'

'Now you're talking.' He grinned. 'I shall put you in charge of the accounts. I bet your dad never imagined his daughter was going to end up keeping the books for a jobbing builder.' And they both laughed, arms entwined, as they made their way through the rain now falling in Knightsbridge to the station.

He took her in his arms and kissed her. 'Goodnight, my lovely.'

'I'll see you on Saturday, come to lunch, then we can go for a spin in that super car of yours.'

'Now you take care,' he said firmly. 'Don't sit in an empty carriage.'

'And don't speak to any strange men.' She smiled. 'I know, darling, I won't.' And he watched her go until she was out of sight.

He didn't think he ever would be able to tell her how much he loved her.

When Sally arrived home, she went straight to her room, before going in to see her parents for a pre-dinner drink, a ritual which they observed every evening, her mother and herself with a glass of wine, her father with his usual malt whisky.

As she lay in the bath, she went over in her mind just how and when she would tell them that she intended to marry George. She felt in her bones that she would not have much trouble with her mother, but her father — well, that was a different matter. And she was not choosing the best time, it seemed, for lately he had been very preoccupied. Even her mother had noticed it.

He had smiled apologetically when Joanna mentioned it. 'I think I'm ready for a holiday, a few days in Scotland — we haven't done awfully well on the holiday stakes this year, have we? Still, we mustn't complain. Business is good, and that's all that matters at the moment.'

Poor darling, Joanna thought. The hotel was always booked up, but that didn't mean that it was going to continue. They were affected like everyone else in a recession, and if it were not for the wonderful chef they were lucky enough to have, things might be very different. She had learned very early on in the trade how important that was.

Anyway, she was getting excited now about Vanessa's wedding, having had the organizing of the marquee and the caterers to do, and the flowers — something she did so well. Getting in touch with the best people for the job and those who gave the best service was second nature to her after all this time.

Sally came into the drawing room, freshly bathed, wearing a long black skirt and crisp white blouse, her hair still wet from shampooing, her lovely dark eyes positively glowing.

How pretty she was, Joanna decided, but mere good looks did not account for that air of suppressed excitement about her.

'Here, darling,' she said, handing her a glass of wine.
'Where's Daddy?'
'Just coming.'
'I'm sorry I missed the Macphersons.'
'Yes, they left soon after lunch — send you their love. Ah, here he is.'
'Hello, Sally.'
She went over and kissed him. He looked strained.

'You're working too hard,' she said severely. 'Long hours.'

'Listen to her.' He smiled at Joanna, pouring his whisky.

'And how is the house coming along?'

'Nicely, thank you,' Sally said, sipping her wine. I don't think, she decided, that I can hold out much longer without telling them.

'Is that a new blouse?' Joanna asked.

'Mmm,' she said. 'I bought it yesterday.' She put down her glass.

'Um — I don't know if this will come as a shock to you, but George has asked me to marry him.' She smiled at them brightly, willing them to react with pleasure.

They both stared back at her, open-mouthed.

'Well?' she laughed after a moment.

Joanna let out a breath. 'Yes, it is a shock in a way. We hadn't realized.' She looked at Donald whose face was expressionless.

'I don't know what the protocol is these days but we — George — thought he would like to talk to you about it at the weekend when he comes down. If you're not too busy?'

'And what do you want?' Donald asked coolly. 'Do you want to marry him?'

'Oh, yes!' Sally said fervently. On her mother's face she saw a look of sympathy and understanding.

'Well,' Donald said, putting down his glass, 'I suppose what you both want is my — our — blessing, but I can't give it to you, Sally. You know nothing about this young man, his parents, who he is — he's just someone you met that you happen to like. And I can understand that. He's a very likeable young man. But I can't see myself handing over our precious daughter into his hands, I'm afraid, and I'm sure your mother can't either.'

'Donald, dear, don't be too hard on her.'

'Marriage is a serious business, Sally, and not to be entered into lightly. Background is very important — more than you think. You went to a good school, you have always had what you wanted — riding, tennis, golf, everything we could give you — that is your background, your status in life. What does this young man have in common with you? Nothing, I suggest, nothing at all.'

'You sound like a Victorian father,' she muttered. 'Things have changed, things are different today.'

'Yes, that's what we are told, but in reality things don't change that much, Values are important.'

'It's just George's bad luck that he hadn't the advantages that I've had. He'll make up for them, you'll see. He's going places — I know he is — and I shall be right beside him. I know he's going to be a success.'

'I don't doubt it,' Donald said, 'but it isn't just that that I mean. Are you happy to take him everywhere — to the sort of places and homes you are used to? To introduce him to your friends? Won't he feel like a fish out of water? It's not fair on him. Let him find a nice girl of his own —'

'Class,' Sally finished bitterly. 'How I hate that word!'

'You'd like to pretend that it doesn't exist, my dear, but it does.'

Joanna stood up, looking distressed. 'Let's not talk about it now, otherwise we shall all be upset, and we have a long evening in front of us ...'

'I'm sorry, Mummy.' Sally went over to her, seeing an ally, someone who might not approve, but who understood. 'Perhaps I shouldn't have broken the news to you like this. I'm sorry — I'm going to bed now. Goodnight.'

Almost in tears, she made her way back to her room.

Chapter Fifteen

Donald and Joanna lay awake for a long time after Sally had gone to bed.

'You were very hard on her, darling,' Joanna said. 'She is in love with George, she adores him — can't you remember what it was like?'

'I'm not that old,' he said, 'and I am thinking of her. After all, he might have got the idea that Sally is a good catch — which she is, from that point of view.'

'You're being cynical.' Joanna said. 'I must say I like him, and I think they make a very nice couple — good for each other.'

'Perhaps, but it would be so much better all round if she married someone who fits in, as it were. Someone in our line, perhaps, who can take over the hotel when we are older. After all, there will be grandchildren, hopefully, and we want to keep it in the family.'

'You're looking so far ahead, darling.'

'We have to. This chap is a builder — not the remotest connection with our trade — or family — or —'

'That's a snobbish point of view, and not like you, Donald. I would have thought you'd be thinking of Sally's happiness before everything else.'

He sat up abruptly and switched on the bedside light. 'That's exactly what I *am* doing, dammit!' he said. 'This could be just a passing phase — after all, she's not known many boys, nor had a special boy friend. I think she's got carried away by this chap — and her new job.'

'I think you're forgetting she's twenty years old, soon to

be twenty-one. After all, Vanessa went off to India when she was that age. We have to let her go sometime. Every father thinks the man his daughter marries isn't good enough, isn't it partly that?'

He sat staring at a picture on the opposite wall.

'After all, some girls would not have consulted you at all, but gone off to live with the man.'

'Sally isn't like that.'

'No, perhaps not, but it's what they do today. And I suggest that if you make it too hard for her, that's just what she might do.'

He turned to her, shock written all over his face.

'She wouldn't!'

'Darling,' she put an arm on his, 'we don't want to lose her, do we? And that might happen if you are too rigid.'

'I can't understand you, Joanna. I would have thought you'd have wanted — expected — more of her. A good marriage . . .'

'Who can say what a good marriage is?' Joanna asked mildly. 'Ours is, but we are the exception rather than the rule — and we have been lucky. Be kind to her, darling, she's all we have.'

'That's just why —' he began, but she reached up and kissed him.

'We'll talk about it again tomorrow. Everything looks different by daylight.

Donald buried himself beneath the bedclothes, but it was Joanna who hardly slept.

Sally seldom saw her parents before she left in the morning. Their day ended so late, and the lifestyle of an hotel was unlike that of a normal family. It was evening before she saw them again, and when Joanna handed her the glass of wine, Donald had not yet appeared.

Joanna's heart was torn as she saw the anxiety in Sally's eyes. She wanted to go over and comfort her, reassure her.

'You really love him, don't you?' she asked gently. Sally nodded.

'Yes, I do. Oh, I know, Mummy, he's not perhaps the

man you might have chosen for me, but honestly he's as straight as a die, and with such a sense of humour. And he loves me, I just know he does. I mean, things he doesn't know — I can teach him, show him. He learns quickly, I can tell you, and he knows what's what. Honestly.'

'Your father was upset, I think, with one thing and another, and he's not been himself lately so all in all your timing wasn't the best.'

Sally laughed. 'Did he say any more?'

'No. I think we'll wait and see what happens when George comes down. Have you told him to expect a battle?'

'Oh, he knows that!' Sally laughed. 'He's not stupid, not by any means — and, Mother, he does know how to use a knife and fork correctly!'

Joanna had the grace to blush. It was not often that she was embarrassed.

'Touché, Sally.'

'I won't have dinner. I'm just off for a swim at Jennie's. Is Daddy around? I must have a word with him before I go.'

'Somewhere,' Joanna said. 'Try the office.'

Donald's private den was empty when she arrived, but as she was leaving the telephone on his desk began to ring. She answered it, to find it was the switchboard downstairs.

'I'm sorry, Michelle, he's not here just at the moment. Can I take a message?'

'No, it will wait, Sally.'

She put the telephone down and saw the mass of papers and brochures and paraphernalia that covered Donald's desk. Her father had such a lot to do always — so much of the business was his sole responsibility. She straightened a few things and, in doing so, her eye was caught by a pad with a number on it which seemed familiar. Where had she seen that before?

She stared out of the window. Sipiato 96 — and then she remembered. Surely that was Amanda Amber's telephone number in Sardinia?

Hurrying back to her bedroom, she took her diary out of her handbag and turned to the back. There it was. Aunt Amanda Cipiato 96 ... What was her father doing with

Amanda's telephone number? She had never given it to him, no need, although she had given Aunt Alice Amanda's address. How had her father known the telephone number? Had he been in contact with her?

She flopped down into an easy chair and began thinking. Was she making something out of nothing? She recalled the night she had returned, and how shocked her parents had been at the news that she had seen Amanda. Both of them ... Was there something behind all this that she didn't know?

When she had told her parents, they had looked at each other. She had thought at the time that their reaction to her news had been pretty odd. The more she thought and wondered, the more she asked herself if perhaps this was the reason for her father's preoccupied manner. Hadn't it stemmed from that date? She was not about to sit in judgement, but she had to know. It was pretty obvious, as she saw it, that they didn't want Amanda to come to the wedding, and they might not be the only ones.

She made up her mind — she would ride over to see Aunt Alice instead of going for a swim. Putting on her shorts and a sweater, she got her bicycle out of the garage and rode down the hill and into the Park. At the entrance, she propped up her bike and knocked on the door of Chantry Lodge.

Alice looked pleased to see her. 'Why, Sally, what a nice surprise! Come in, dear.'

Sally kissed her. 'What were you doing? Have I interrupted anything?'

'No, of course not, my dear — I was just putting together some quilt pieces. I expect your mother told you we are making a quilt?'

'Yes, she did. Oh, how pretty! Aren't you all clever to make something like this? They're worth an awful lot, these days.'

'We hope it will be someone's heirloom,' Alice laughed. 'Now do sit down — can I make you some coffee or — '

'No, I'm fine. I thought I'd pop in to you see you — just for a moment — to ask you how the wedding is coming along?'

Alice sat down at the table. 'Very well, my dear. All underway, as they say. The wedding dress is finished.'

'What's it like — did Vanessa tell you?'

'No, it's a dark secret. By the way, thank you for Amanda's address — you must tell me all about it. Your holiday and meeting her.'

'Yes, wasn't it a strange coincidence? I saw her on the beach, and she looked familiar, somehow, I couldn't tell why. Then, watching her, I was sure. I went over to her.'

'Did you.' It was a statement rather than a question.

'Yes, and course I knew it was her then.'

'Was she with someone?' Alice asked casually, folding the quilt carefully.

'Yes, Pepi. She lives with him in the cutest place on a cliff top. It's more like a cottage than a villa.'

'How did she look? As attractive as ever? I don't suppose you remember.'

'Of course I do! I knew her in an instant — someone like her doesn't change that much. The same lovely eyes, the hair. Of course she's very tanned and slim.'

'She was always slim,' Alice said.

'Yes. Anyway, she asked us to dinner —'

'Who's us?'

'My friend, George.'

'Oh, that's your new boy friend? Your mother was telling me.'

'He's the man I'm going to marry — but that's another story, Aunt Alice!'

'I see.' Behind her glasses Alice wore a quizzical look.

'Tell me about her. She is my godmother, after all.'

Alice frowned. 'Do you know, I'd forgotten that.'

'She's such a fascinating character, and now that she is coming over for the wedding ...'

'Who told you that?'

'I thought you'd invited her?'

'Yes, we have, but I only heard yesterday that she's coming.'

'Oh, I am glad. I liked her enormously.'

'Did you?' There was that look again, the same one her parents wore. It was fairly obvious that Amanda Amber was not going to be a welcome guest.

'Of course,' Sally said hesitantly, 'I suppose no one knew why she left Uncle James and Vanessa.'

'Well, it was no one's business,' Alice said sharply.

'No, of course not,' Sally said quickly. 'I didn't mean to pry.'

'Of course you didn't, child. But it's a prickly subject.'

'I'm sure. I remember her from when I was little, I thought she was so glamorous.'

'Yes, she was that.'

'Do you remember those fantastic holidays we used to have in the south of France?'

Alice was silent.

'And then the parties. So many of us — barbecues, that sort of thing — we had a wonderful childhood, Vanessa and I. Oh, I don't mean that. For Vanessa, I mean, it must have been awful ...'

'Yes, it wasn't quite so wonderful for Vanessa. Still she is surprisingly adult and well balanced for all her early experiences.'

It was strange, Sally thought, but she got the impression that Aunt Alice had clamped down, that she was not going to find out anything in this direction.

'Where will she stay?' Sally asked suddenly.

'Stay? Oh, I've no idea,' said Alice.

'Well, if there's anything I can do to help,' Sally said, getting up. 'I'll be on my way. I hope you'll get to meet George at the wedding,' she said, giving Alice a farewell kiss. 'You'll like him.'

'I'm sure I will,' she said, smiling brightly now that her guest was going.

Sally mounted her bicycle and rode away.

Alice stood looking after her. Now why did she get the impression that the child had come for a purpose — almost to find out something?

Surely she had not stumbled upon Donald's secret — if there was one. Alice went quite cold as she wondered if Amanda herself had hinted at anything. She wouldn't put it past her. Oh, what a hornet's nest had been stirred up!

Sally rode home, more than ever convinced that no one wanted Amanda to come to the wedding. But why?

Apart from the usual reason of good taste. It had to be something more.

As soon as she returned, she telephoned Vanessa.

'Hi, are you too busy to have lunch on Friday?'

'Mmmm, can do. If it's early.'

'Twelve — twelve-thirty?'

'That's fine. Come here, I'll find a snack. Then you can see my dress — it's just arrived. Oh, it's simply gorgeous, Sally. As long as you don't tell anyone ...'

'Of course not, silly, as if I would.'

Mischief alight in her dark eyes, Sally went to bed, telling herself that all was fair in love and war.

Vanessa was as beautiful as ever, even more lovely now with the radiance of a bride around her. Her blue eyes seemed deeper in colour; that wonderful silver ash-coloured shining hair was pulled up carelessly off her neck and face, showing the lovely line of her jaw.

'Oh, it's wonderful to see you. I haven't seen you since you got back from Sardinia ...'

In the tiny dining room, Vanessa had laid the table with wine glasses, cold salmon, a French bread stick and a mixed salad.

'Lovely.' Sally's eyes glowed. 'I'm starving.'

'Good, tuck in — I've to be back at the shop at one.'

Vanessa poured a glass of white wine and pushed the salad towards Sally.

'So you met my mother? I couldn't have been more surprised — well, shocked is the word.'

'Yes, how about that?' And Sally told her, word for word, watching Vanessa's expression change as the tale went on. By the end of the story, her eyes had misted over.

'Isn't that amazing? Fate ...'

'Yes, I suppose it was. So she's coming to the wedding?'

'Yes, of course. I hope no one minds. I certainly don't — it adds a romantic touch. Daddy didn't seem to care — I was quite surprised, but then you know him. He keeps his feelings well hidden. Still, if he had — minded, I mean — I would have known.

'It will be strange, though, Van, won't it?'

'Yes, I suppose, except that it must happen frequently these days. It's the oldies who don't seem able to take it.'

'Well, you can understand, can't you?'

'What's the man like she's living with? Is he coming?'

'I don't know. Remember, she only mentioned that she would like to see you married. I didn't know if everyone was agreeable or that she was coming until your grandmother told me.'

'I can't wait to see her,' Vanessa said.

'It's strange really,' Sally said. 'I thought you might be right off the idea — after all, it would be quite understandable.'

'It's so long ago,' Vanessa said. 'Now I only remember the nice things about her — she was so beautiful, and always wore such lovely clothes. I think all the men were in love with her.'

'Who do you mean?'

'Well, don't you remember the parties and things, and the holidays, Christmas ... I was always sure that Uncle Don — and even your father — were mad about her. I used to see Daddy looking at her sometimes, his lids half-closed.'

'Really? But you were only —'

'Eleven when she left,' Vanessa said. 'I always wanted to be like her as I grew older. You know, have that wonderful way with men, the secret looks, the way she enticed them — but, of course, I wasn't the type. Tall and skinny where she was small and dark, and so — well, you know.'

'Sexy,' Sally said, for that was the word. Amanda was, even now — and suddenly Sally felt a pang. Wishing that she hadn't started all this. She had thought perhaps she could twist her father's arm about George — but what a cruel thing to do. If, and it was a doubtful if, there had been anything between her father and Amanda, how awful it must have been for him. And for her mother, if she had known. She was suddenly sick of the whole subject.

Glancing at her watch, she waited as Vanessa poured the coffee.

'Thanks, then I must fly. Have I time to see the dress?'

The door stood open to Vanessa's small bedroom. There

on the bed lay a froth of cream silk and masses of tissue paper.

'Oh, Vanessa!' It was so lovely Sally felt she wanted to cry.

'It is gorgeous, isn't it? I had it made. I can't wear white but this is the palest ivory. And the back — '

'No, don't tell me' Sally sniffed. 'I'd rather see you in it. Oh, Vanessa, you're going to look absolutely beautiful.'

'Well, I don't know about that — ' she began, and was interrupted by a man's voice.

'Vanessa? Are you there?'

'Oh, it's Oliver!' she said. 'He must have let himself in. I'm just coming — don't come in!'

Sally followed her out. 'Hello, Oliver.'

He kissed Vanessa, and put an arm round her shoulders. 'Sorry, I didn't realize.'

'It's all right, darling, Sally came to lunch — good thing you didn't come in to us, it's unlucky to see the wedding dress!'

'I must fly' Sally said. 'Thanks for the lunch. Goodbye, Oliver. See you on the fateful day.'

His long, handsome face broke into a small smile.

'Jolly good. 'Bye, Sally.'

She walked back to the shop in a thoughtful mood.

That Friday evening she was especially nice to her father, seeing him in a new light, trying to imagine what his feelings must be, having to face someone from his past — perhaps not a pleasant memory. Having met Amanda she could quite understand how a man might be swept away, and you couldn't tell her that her father had made the running. He adored her mother too much for that. The indications were that perhaps her mother had had no idea about it, and that was even worse. She would put the whole thing at the back of her mind and concentrate on what was the most important thing in her life: marrying George.

She was waiting in the foyer when he arrived, having parked his Mercedes at the back of the hotel. She greeted him with a kiss, much to the interest of the receptionist who then discreetly looked the other way. Some girls had all the luck, she thought.

'You're in room twenty-three,' Sally said. 'Come upstairs and I'll show you. I have the key.'

The room was large and beautifully furnished in an old English style. Its windows looked out over parkland beyond. Beneath the window flower beds blazed with autumn colour, and the chestnut trees flanking the drive had already begun to change colour. The Wellingtonia stood like a sentinel, the faint breeze lifting its heavy branches and causing shadows to dance on the green lawn.

George looked out silently. 'And you were born here — grew up here?' he said finally.

'Yes,' she said.

'I expect you realize what a fortunate girl you are?'

'Yes.'

'I can't give you anything like this,' he admitted as she came up behind him and put her arms around him. 'Are you still game?'

She hugged him tightly, and he turned round and took her in his arms.

'Then let's start from here,' he said.

They drove down into Sussex for a pub lunch, exploring the countryside and the villages until it was time to return for dinner.

Holding his hand, Sally took him into the small drawing room where her mother sat reading.

Joanna looked up with a friendly smile and held out her hand.

'Hello, George.'

'Hello, Mrs Simpson.' She found her hand held in a strong grip.

'Where did you go this afternoon?'

'Down as far as Nymans — we saw the garden.'

'It must look lovely this time of the year. It's ages since your father and I went.'

She beckoned a chair. 'Do sit down, George. My husband will be here presently.'

When Donald came in, George was on his feet in an instant.

'We're having dinner in the main dining room this evening,' Joanna said. Sally raised her eyebrows, then realized that of course it was not so private and there would be less chance of any discussion about their engagement.

The evening passed pleasantly enough, until Joanna decided that she would retire, followed by Sally, who gave a meaningful glance in George's direction to bolster his courage until she saw that he seemed to be very much in charge of the situation.

'Will you join me in a brandy, George?' she heard her father say.

Her heart beating fast, she looked at Joanna.

'Oh, I do hope Daddy will be nice to him!'

'I think George is quite capable of standing up for himself,' she laughed. 'Come on, let's have a nightcap in my room. You can tell me all you've been doing.'

It was not until early the following morning that Sally crept along to George's room, only to find it empty. He was already up. Her heart missed a beat. What had her father said? Had George gone back to London?

She dressed hurriedly, putting on slacks and a shirt, and flew down stairs where she found George in the foyer with his Sunday newspaper. He looked up casually as she came in.

She bent down and kissed him. 'Oh, George, I thought you might have ...' And she bent low and whispered in his ear.

'Sally, my love, I'm not about to take any chances under the parental roof.' He grinned. 'I respect your parents too much for that.'

'Oh, George, how did you get on – what did Daddy say?'

'Not a lot. He thinks we haven't known each other long enough to be sure – all the things he said to you.' He grinned at her. 'But he says, if that's what we want – who is he to stand in our way? He realizes that you are free to do as you like. I pointed out that we would have liked his blessing, and he said, then I give it to you – and by God, if you let me down, I'll kill you. Or words to that effect!'

'Oh, George!' Sally's eyes were brimming over. She took his hand. 'Let's go for a walk – it's a lovely morning.'

Before lunch, Donald invited them for a glass of champagne in the apartment. 'I know it's not official yet — but, well, let's celebrate anyway.'

He raised his glass. 'I can only hope you two young people know what you're doing.'

Afterwards, Sally urged George to bring out his before and after photographs of the house in Montpelier Street which he had recently finished restoring. Donald was very impressed.

'You know, it seems to me you could do with a pool complex here,' George said, looking about him.

'We have discussed it before, Joanna and I, but wondered if it was justified, with the weather ...'

'No, I meant an indoor pool,' George said. 'Like this.'

With swift strokes he drew an outline, connecting the pool complex with the back of the hotel, a conservatory for extra dining, he said, leading into the pool. It soon took shape with changing rooms and saunas — and Sally saw that her father was engrossed. When he had finished, George handed the sketch to him.

'Perhaps not yet awhile,' he said. 'But for sometime in the future.'

'My word.' Donald said admiringly. 'Ambitious. But I like it. Joanna?'

'Wouldn't it cost an awful lot of money?'

'Of course,' George said. 'But think of the return on your investment.'

'It's certainly a thought for the future,' Donald said, finding himself warming towards this future son-in-law.

He certainly seemed to know his stuff. Perhaps there might be more to George Adams than met the eye. He might be a bit of a rough diamond, but diamonds could always be polished.

Who knew, George might be the best thing that had happened to the family for a long time.

Chapter Sixteen

James Amber stood in his dressing room overlooking the garden, deep in thought. It was, though no one else probably would remember, the anniversary of his wedding day to Amanda, twenty-three years ago. Who would have imagined on that day that he would be standing here, in the house they had bought for themselves, with another wife, a daughter about to be married, and a baby son.

Of course he had not taken silk then, that came after Amanda left him. She had unwittingly been the cause of his enormous successes at the Bar. He had worked and studied, those being the only things in his life worth living for at that time. Even Vanessa had been put to one side — he had no idea what he would have done without his mother.

He looked out on this autumn morning at the two sweet chestnuts, laden with prickly fruit, now some thirty feet high. Alice had given them to him in two small flower pots — seedlings from her own big tree. They had been nine inches high then. And the strawberry tree, Arbutus unedo, which filled the side border where it had been planted as a small sapling, and was now providing shade beneath which they sometimes sat. If he was restricted to one tree alone in a garden, he thought it would be the Arbutus, for there was always something to see: the flowers like transparent lilies of the valley, followed by the fruits which were so brilliant and colourful, while all the year round the foliage was dark green and glossy.

Amanda had had no interest in the garden but Odile had, although she was a city girl who had been brought up in

Paris. She had her herb garden, and was trying even now to grow new French roses, although he had told her that the soil was not kind to them. They were never healthy and strong like Kent or Essex roses or those that grew so well in sooty London soil. But he wouldn't put her off. She was a determined little thing. And there were compensations. Not everyone was able to grow the azaleas and rhododendrons that thrived in this part of Surrey.

He turned from the window and adjusted his tie, looking at himself in the mirror. He saw a man approaching fifty, with prematurely silver hair. He was still slim, tall, with a slightly hawkish nose, a firm chin and very blue eyes which could be kind but more often than not made people feel uneasy, so honest was their gaze, so intense their scrutiny.

He had two problems at the moment; both had been unforseeable. Amanda and Odile, such disparate women. That there was something wrong with his wife just now was all too obvious. She was not happy, and James could not for the life of him put his finger on the reason. It was not as if her moods had started since the news of Amanda's coming, they had begun before that. Soon after the birth of little Edouard, whom she thought the world of, in fact. It was true he had upset her over Phillips, but even now she knew that Nanny was leaving, it seemed to make no difference.

He flatly refused to believe it was jealousy of Amanda — that had simply compounded the problem. If she only knew, he thought, what his life had been like those last two years with Amanda ...

He had never wanted to think about it again, but the prospect of seeing her had brought it all back and he didn't think he could bear it. He could possibly have withstood the confrontation if he and Odile were happy, but now ...

She had been such a liar, Amanda. There was no other word for it. Lied her way through several affairs, lied about so many things. And the rich part of it was that everyone had thought he had made such a wonderful marriage. Well, so he had, he thought wryly, if you looked at it one way. The daughter of a wealthy businessman, Amanda had always had whatever she wanted, her parents had seen to that. Finishing schools, travel, horses — he knew people wondered why she had ever picked him, a struggling barrister, out of the many suitors who hung around her. Had it perhaps been because he didn't show his feelings and fall at her feet that she found him so attractive?

For, of course, he had fallen in love with her. Adored her, couldn't believe in his luck when she agreed to marry him. Her father had been against it, but as usual Amanda got her own way. They had not been married long when he found out about the first affair. Everyone said, how can Amanda possibly live in such a boring place as Surrey? She's a townie, a sophisticate. Well, she was, but strange as it seemed, she was happy about their plans and had gone along with them.

The subsequent visits to Daddy who 'was not well', and to Mummy's charity events, were of course all lies. She was really with Dickie Everest, an ex-boy friend. Then there was 'Chum' Arnold, the polo player — that had been afternoons when she was supposed to be playing tennis. And one had followed the other ...

Why had she married him? It was a mystery James felt he would never solve. Faced with angry accusations, she twisted him around her little finger. At first he had fallen for it, but then, when Vanessa was born — good God, he had even doubted she was his own child! Time had shown him she was her father's daughter; she was like him both to look at and in character.

Amanda had started again when Vanessa was about five — it was as if she just had to have other men around her. Not just to admire her and to flirt with, but to take as lovers — it was unbearable. Not to be borne.

The climax had come when she really fell for Donald Simpson. For the first time in her life, her deepest emotions were involved. Not just excitement as it had been when she'd married James. If asked, James would say that Donald was probably the love of her life. Strange, really. He was not at all the sort of man she usually fell for. A stolid, respectable type, very much in love with his wife — a somewhat boring man, James would have said. But there it was.

He had threatened to divorce her, but then he had so many

times and refrained because of Vanessa. This time had been once too many.

They had rowed, fiercely, and she had gone — fled — much to his surprise. He had never expected that, and the shock had proved greater than he'd thought. He had lost any love he'd ever had for her, but the shame and humiliation of her departure were more than he could bear.

And now, was history repeating itself? Please God, not that! Was there something wrong with him that he couldn't hold a woman for long? Not given to introspection, he found it difficult to blame himself totally.

Since the day he thought he had seen Odile at Rules, that cool profile and the earring were constantly at the forefront of his mind. His memory, he thought, was playing him tricks. It couldn't have been Odile. Several times he was on the point of saying something to her, but of course he couldn't.

Well, another two weeks and Phillips would be gone, and this time he was going to give Odile free rein — whatever she wanted to do. That way, she could never accuse him of being heavy-handed or trying to dominate her. If she wanted a French au pair, much as he disliked the idea, he would let her go ahead. It was sometimes difficult to remember that she was younger than he by some fifteen years. He sighed, and with a last look in the mirror, went downstairs to find her.

She was in the morning room with Edouard in his high chair, his sturdy little legs swinging back and forth, the dark eyes so like his mother's full of mischief and wonder.

James smoothed the baby's head of dark curls, looking down at him with the proud look of a father. Odile was feeding him with cereal, and each time she put a spoonful in his mouth, he followed it with a spoonful of his own.

'Well done, old chap,' James said, looking across at Odile, who was totally immersed in what she was doing. She was a good mother, he thought, seeing her intent face as she concentrated on her son, the way the dark eyes met the child's full of laughter and enjoyment. This was the girl he had married — but nowadays she never looked at him like that.

He bent down and kissed the top of Edouard's head,

then went round to Odile, who lifted her face to his.

'And what are you going to do today?' he asked her.

She shrugged. 'I'm not sure — why?' Her dark eyes looked up at him quizzically. 'Are you going to invite me to lunch?' and he looked slightly guilty.

'My dear, I wish I had the time but until this case is over — however, I won't be late this evening.'

He got as far as the door. 'Don't forget, after the wedding we shall go away somewhere for a few days.' But she was intent on feeding Edouard, her whole attention on the baby.

'I'll see you this evening then.' His voice was swallowed up in a burst of giggling laughter from Edouard who had dropped his spoon on the floor.

James closed the door after him, feeling like an interloper.

Odile put the breakfast dishes in the dishwasher while she waited for Nanny Phillips to come down from the nursery.

It was such a lovely day. The September sun shone over the autumn colours in the garden, the trees already beginning to turn. Odile loved this time of year, and the sun was really warm this morning — she had already been down to the garden to pick the last of the runner beans, and to see how the autumn crocus were coming along under the cedar tree. It was the first time she had ever grown them, having bought some after she had seen them in Alice's garden and been unable to resist growing some of her own. Now, the pale mauve cups brought a splash of spring colour beneath the dark green background of the cedar tree, and she was fascinated. It was so therapeutic to wander round a lovely English garden, and there was no one more surprised than herself to find she had inherited her father's love of horticulture. She had already learned more from the old gardener than she had thought possible in so short a space of time. He had been there in Amanda's time, and she wondered, as she so often did nowadays, had Amanda gone down the garden and talked to him as she did?

Amanda was hardly ever out of her thoughts these days, ever since she'd learned she was coming to the wedding — and, of course, ever since she had discovered that wretched photograph in James's drawer.

She looked up at the sky, blue with puffy white clouds, and made up her mind. She would go for a walk through the park and take Edouard with her. There was nothing she liked more than seeing lovely gardens.

She met Nanny Phillips outside the kitchen door where she had stood Edouard's pram. He was lying down, his legs free to kick in the air, a warm woolly jacket buttoned up, his head uncovered. She had found it difficult to get used to the idea of babies being left out in all weathers, but she had to agree that Edouard was a perfect example of healthy babyhood. Even her mother had accepted the idea that a baby didn't wear a hat all the time. She had been quite horrified at Easter when she had visited them.

'Fresh air all day,' Nanny Phillips had asserted. 'The only time you keep them in is when it is foggy. Of course, we don't get fogs like we used to, and you are too young to remember the old London fogs. Still, heavy mists or fogs are not a good thing — bad for the chest. Rain won't hurt them, even strong winds, providing they are well wrapped up. But fogs — no. Isn't that right, Master Amber?' And he had grinned back at her.

So he'd lain in his pram almost all day, or now that he was older and crawling, sat on a blanket on the lawn or in his nursery.

'I'll take these beans in and get ready to take him for a walk,' said Odile to Nanny Phillips.

'Well, I was just going to — ' she began, but Odile stopped her.

'I'll be down in a moment,' she said, and disappeared into the kitchen, coming back with a cardigan and a scarf.

She pushed the pram down the drive and into the avenue, unaware that subconsciously she was looking, as she always was lately, for an answer to her problem.

Edouard looked about him with interest — at a passing car, at the trees with their overhanging branches — and several times Odile stopped to point out a garden still ablaze with colour or a cat sitting on a wall, which intrigued him enormously. She tilted up the pram for him to see better and he and the cat regarded each other seriously, Edouard's dark eyes round with concentration, the cat with green slits which surveyed him as though recognizing a kindred spirit.

Edouard was fascinated, his eight teeth exposed in a brilliant smile of pleasure. Then a passing car caught his attention and Odile walked on. Green Gables, The Firs, Larch Rise, King's Oak, Queen's Oak, The Limes — how English were all these names, how gracious all the houses, each different, and each standing in its own lovely garden having had almost sixty years of cultivation and loving care, giving so much pleasure to owners and passers by alike.

In the dip where the two great oak trees almost met across the road stood Sheila's house, one of the smallest in the Park but one of the prettiest. After this, the road began to rise again, so that Sheila's house seemed to be set in a hollow, like a picture in a nursery rhyme book. Windrush was gabled, black and white timbered with mullioned windows, almost tumbledown; it would certainly have been Odile's favourite house if she had been a child. At any moment you would have expected the seven dwarfs would appear from nowhere. Instead, it was Sheila, her head covered with an old garden hat, wearing green wellies and an ancient garden coat, coming into view as she stood up from raking leaves, straightening her back.

'Odile! It's you. I heard footsteps and wondered who it was. So few people walk today — everyone is in motor cars.'

'Hello, Sheila.'

She peered over the hedge. 'Oh, you've got the baby with you. Isn't he a poppet?'

She stood the rake against the hedge and came through the gate, smiling at Edouard who chuckled and smiled back.

'Oh, the darling! What a sight for sore eyes on such a morning!'

Her green eyes shone at Edouard, then she looked up at Odile. 'You've got him to yourself today, then?'

'Yes, for once, although Nanny is leaving in a couple of weeks.'

'And you won't be sorry to see her go — she's a bit of a dragon, isn't she?'

'Did you have her, Sheila?'

'Yes, like everyone else, for Gillian anyway. She's the youngest.'

'How is she? Alice said she's engaged.'

'Hmmm.' Sheila nodded, unwilling to talk about it on this lovely day. 'Look — why don't you come in and have coffee with me? I was just going to make some.'

'That's awfully kind of you but I had better keep going. Edouard has an early lunch.' She had a sudden idea. 'Sheila, how about a game of golf? Have you any free time this week? We haven't had a game for ages.'

'Why not? Tomorrow morning, Wednesday?'

'All right, Wednesday. See you up at the club house. Is nine-thirty too early?'

'No, the earlier the better — I shall look forward to that.'

Sheila waved back at Edouard before going in and closing the gate. She couldn't wait until Alison's baby was born and, God willing, she would be able to push her new grandchild around the park.

The idea had come to her suddenly, Odile realized, as she began the steep push up the hill. She would look forward to a game of golf, and perhaps a chat afterwards with Sheila. She was on the beam with Sheila, unlike some of her mother-in-law's older friends. She felt they understood each other. There was no nonsense about Sheila.

She pushed hard then turned right into Chestnut Walk, where the houses were much larger and more impressive, set in enormous gardens. Tucked away among the trees, they enjoyed complete privacy. One of them, like a small palace, was lived in by Ann, one of Alice's friends and a member of the Red Cross sewing circle.

None of them, decided Odile, is as nice as Four Oaks. It has such a dignified, warm and cosy air about it, a real old English house.

But it hadn't always, she thought wryly, been cosy and comfortable inside. First Amanda and now she herself was going through pangs of unhappiness there. If only she could rid herself of these morbid thoughts ...

Nearing the house, Edouard began waving his arms about, and she thought, isn't that wonderful? He knows we are nearly home. Nanny Phillips must have walked him this way many times, and he has come to know where he lives.

'Oh, you are a clever little boy,' she said admiringly. 'Yes, there it is — at the top of the road.'

When she arrived home, she found a letter awaiting her from her mother who always wrote or telephoned once a week. In it she read that her cousin Nicole was staying with her parents on her annual trip to Paris, that they had been busy doing the sights and shopping ...

It gave her the answer. She would fly over to Paris at the weekend, see Nicole and ask her whether she was prepared to come to England for a spell. It was a far better idea to see her personally. After all, there was a difference between a schoolgirl of sixteen and a young woman of eighteen. She might not be at all suitable or adaptable now. Odile would fly out on Friday and stay until Saturday evening. She found herself looking forward immensely to the trip.

She and James were having a drink before dinner when she broached the subject.

'I had a letter this morning from Maman — it seems Nicole, my cousin, is spending a few days in Paris ...'

He had a sudden presentiment.

'I thought it might be a good idea while she is there for me to pop over and see her — with a view to her coming here au pair for a time.'

He forced himself to appear pleased at the idea.

'Yes, well, if you think —'

'I do, James,' Odile said firmly. 'I shall get a flight on Friday and should be back on Saturday. It will be a good opportunity to interview Nicole.'

Was that really what was at the back of her mind, James wondered, or was she going off with someone for a night or two? He cursed himself for his suspicions, but there was an air about her of having planned this and getting her own way, which she was.

He put down his drink. 'I could come with you,' be began, and saw her face fall.

'Oh, no, James.'

'I could do with a break myself,' he said pleasantly. 'In fact, we could stay longer — a few days in Paris.' He hated himself for causing the look of pleasure to die out on her face. So if he went, it meant that it would spoil it for her. If she was going to Paris with someone — like the man she had met on the golf course, or the man she might have been dining with, whom he hadn't forgotten by a long chalk, she ran a risk of him telephoning her family to see how she was. There was no doubt she didn't want him to go with her, which saddened him.

'I thought you couldn't spare any time until after the case,' Odile said.

'That is true, but I could possibly arrange to fly a later plane on Friday, and we could stay until Sunday.'

'Oh, it's not that important,' she said quickly. 'I just thought it seemed a good idea while you were so busy to kill two birds with one stone. I really do want to get an au pair, James, and I think Nicole would be suitable. Better someone you know.'

'Perhaps you are right,' he said. 'You go on your own.' He saw the relief on her face.

So, it has come to this, he thought. Two years and already we're like strangers.

Odile was looking forward to the break. To get away from these ugly thoughts, to get herself straightened out before the wedding.

She and Sheila had an excellent round of golf on Wednesday, and after the game retired to the club house for a snack lunch.

'I really enjoyed that,' Sheila said, the exhilaration and the excercise having whipped some colour into her cheeks. 'We must do it again.'

'Yes, it was wonderful,' said Odile.

'Did you play much in France?'

'When I was younger — with my father, who has a handicap of eight,' she said.

'Whew! Very commendable. And he taught you?'

'No, I had an instructor, but Papa was very good and we played every weekend. Of course, all that stopped when I came to England — but I played the odd game, just to keep my hand in as it were. It is really wonderful to have a golf course so near.'

'Yes, we are lucky.' Sheila said, tucking into her prawn sandwich.

How, Odile wondered, shall I broach the subject of Amanda? And realized deep down that this was what she had planned all along.

'Are you looking forward to the wedding?' Sheila asked. 'I hope it's a day like this, but perhaps it's too much to hope for in October.'

And Odile took the plunge. 'Yes, immensely, although I have to admit, I'm not looking forward to meeting the famous Amanda.'

She saw Sheila's look of embarrassment before she replied.

'Oh, that'll be all right. I was surprised that she wanted to come ...'

'So was I.' And Odile tried to keep the bitterness out of her voice.

Sheila put a hand over hers. 'My dear, she couldn't hold a candle to you. You've nothing to fear — and, in any case, it all happened a long time ago.'

'What was she like?' The words were out now.

Sheila sat back in her chair and looked straight at Odile.

'Quite beautiful,' she said. 'Sexy. But if I'm being honest — and you asked me — a bitch of the first water.'

Odile's dark eyes, almost black in their intensity, were rivetted on her face.

'You mean — ?'

'No man was safe. She was a man eater, devoured them like other people devour food.'

'A nymphomaniac?'

'Could be — but there's another kind, only wanting a man because he belongs to someone else.'

She smiled wryly. 'Oh, yes, my dear. Anybody's husband was fair game — even mine.'

'Oh, Sheila, I'm sorry.'

'Don't give it a thought, Odile, my dear.'

'But James — how did he react to all this? Was it going on right under his nose?'

'Well, he was besotted with her when they got married — any man would have been. After that, I don't know. He had his work, and then Vanessa was born — but it didn't make much difference to her. She was off again. I tell you, he was well rid of her ... But, my dear, what on earth are you worrying about? Meeting her? Don't give it a thought. She may not even mean to turn up. The threat of her coming would be enough to frighten half the men in the Park!' And she laughed out loud, trying to dispel the worry she could see on Odile's face.

'She'd do that, you know. Oh, my dear, she was such a bitch! Poor James, and poor Alice —'

But James, Odile wondered, how did he feel while all this was going on? Did she break his heart? Had he kept in touch with her all this time? Had he forgiven her? Why did he keep her photograph?

Oh, she had heard enough, and nothing that helped her in the slightest. No, she was right to go away, if only to stop herself thinking about it.

'If you ask me,' Sheila went on, 'I don't think she has the slightest interest in seeing Vanessa married — I think she just wants to upset everyone and is also curious about you.'

'Oh, surely not?'

'Well, we shall see,' Sheila said comfortably. 'You've certainly nothing to worry about. You are more than a match for her in every way. It's James I feel sorry for — as if she couldn't have left him in peace. Fancy, after all this time.' And she clucked like an old hen.

She smiled across the table. 'Another glass, Odile?'

'No thanks, Sheila,' Odile said, feeling thoroughly wretched. 'I really must go — I have to get back.'

She drove home in a fury, angry with herself — and with James. Why on earth had she started this up in the first place? It was her own fault. She had no one to blame but herself. She was being ridiculous.

On Friday morning, while Edouard was having his breakfast, Odile began packing. A small overnight bag was all she needed: her makeup, the latest photographs of Edouard, a change of blouse, her pearls, her passport. She moved across the bedroom from one drawer to another and heard rather than saw James come in quietly from the dressing room.

She didn't look up as he stood just inside the door.

'Can I do anything? Take you to the airport?"

'I've booked a taxi for ten-thirty.'

He nodded. 'I see.' He moved towards her and took her arm.

'I'm sorry you're leaving like this,' he said gently.

'Like what? What do you mean?'

'With things so strained between us,' he said. 'They are, aren't they? You're not happy.'

She felt near to tears, she was so strung up. 'Oh, I think I have let things get on top of me. Since Edouard was born, I — '

He went to take her in his arms, but she wriggled free.

'Why don't you want me to hold you?'

'I'm packing.' She shrugged.

'Odile.' He turned her towards him and tilted her face. Meeting those eyes was her downfall.

'Why do you keep a photograph of Amanda in your chest of drawers?' she asked, and could have bitten her tongue out the next moment.

He let her go instantly. 'Photograph of Amanda? What do you mean?'

She brushed past him, rushed into the dressing room, took out the picture from under the drawer lining, and thrust it under his nose.

'There!' She was breathing heavily. 'What's that?'

He glanced down at it briefly, and looked at her. 'This is a photograph of Vanessa — '

Her lip curled. 'Vanessa! It is a picture of Amanda!'

'Taken on Vanessa's tenth birthday in her school uniform — one of the few that I have.'

'You must think me stupid,' Odile said, now quite carried away.

'I could hardly cut Amanda off since they have their arms around each other,' he said reasonably.

She felt a momentary doubt. 'Are you still in love with her?' she demanded, her eyes black now, and suddenly James saw the whole thing clearly, almost wanting to laugh but knowing that he dare not.

'Was it your idea that she should come to the wedding?' Odile demanded furiously.

'Christ!' He pushed her back on to the bed. Odile was shocked more by the expletive than the physical act.

'What on earth has been going on in that head of yours? Is that what all this is about? Amanda?'

Now she felt as if the ground had collapsed beneath her.

He sat down suddenly beside her and buried his face in his hands, shaking his head. 'Odile, if you only knew — '

His reaction had been so unexpected that she was momentarily silenced. She glanced at him covertly and presently he took his hands away and turned to face her.

'I cannot believe that you thought — well, it's fairly obvious that you did otherwise you would not have been so miserable.' He looked drained. 'Is there any way that I can convince you that I have never seen or been in touch with Amanda since she left — until now? And the invitation has gone through Alice — I personally have had nothing to do with her, nor will I have. She is dead to me — has been for many years.'

Odile wavered. James was not a liar. He might gloss over things or say nothing, but he wouldn't lie.

He took her hands, and she didn't pull them away. 'My love for Amanda died long before Vanessa was born. I stayed married to her for our daughter's sake. I won't tell you what hell I went through. If I just say she was an unfaithful wife, you will have to accept that. I never talked about the things she did, not to anyone, and I won't now, not even to you. I do not relish the idea of seeing her again, but this is for Vanessa's sake. It was just bad luck, call it what you will, that she was ever found at all. I personally hoped I would never see her again.'

He looked straight into Odile's eyes.

'When I met you, and you agreed to marry me, I was the happiest man in the world. I love you and would do anything to make you happy. You can have two French au pairs if you want.'

The tears ran down Odile's face — tears of laughter and relief.

'Oh, James!' She put her arms around his neck.

He kissed her, then picked up the photograph. 'Shall I tear this up or will you?'

She smiled at him and shook her head. 'No, but I'm very good with a pair of small scissors.'

'There's something else,' he said. 'You can put my mind at rest. Were you lunching one day at Rules? With a man?'

Her mouthed open, she stared at him. 'Oh, James, you saw me!'

'Indeed I did,' he said, 'although I wasn't sure ... So you had a secret, too?'

'Not really. I went to lunch with Louis — you remember, I met him for a drink at the club house? He asked me, and I was so fed up I said yes.' She looked down. 'He did ask me to go away with him, but I couldn't.'

'Why was that?' he asked. He might have been in court.

'I just couldn't. It wouldn't have been — enjoyable. Not after you, James.'

He eyed her quizzically, and she began to feel her blood stirring and desire rising in her.

'Lock the door,' he said.

'But, James —'

'Do as I say,' he said. 'You can't have everything your own way.'

Later, Odile combed her hair and looked down at her half-packed case.

'The taxi will be here at ten-thirty, and it's —' She looked at her watch.

'Nine forty-two,' he said. 'Well, darling, I suggest you cancel it and wait until this evening when I will come with you. We shall return on Sunday. How does that suit you?'

'Beautifully, James,' she said.

Chapter Seventeen

'Oh, Sally — it's lovely!'

Vanessa looked at the antique ring that adorned Sally's engagement finger. She bent forward and kissed her friend. 'It's beautiful. Old, isn't it?'

Sally, eyes shining with happiness, nodded.

'Yes — it's a "royal" ring, if you can believe me.'

'Goodness, whatever does that mean?'

'Well, there's a story attached to it. It belonged to George's mother, and she gave it to him before she died — for his wife, she said. He offered to buy me a new one, but honestly, after seeing this, would you?'

'No fear!' Vanessa said, looking at the unusual ring with the golden yellow stone surrounded by tiny diamonds. They both sat on the bed in the tiny flat where Sally had gone to tell Vanessa the news and to chat over the wedding which was ten days away.

'Tell about the "royal" bit,' Vanessa urged.

'Well, George's father was a builder, and he was renovating a shop — a jeweller's shop, a small one, but the owner, a man of some taste, it seemed, he collected snuff boxes — went to the sale of some of the late Princess Royal's jewellery — the sister of the Duke of Windsor — got it?'

'Yes, I think so — she was married to the Earl of Harewood.'

'Oh, well done! You do know your history, which is more than I did! Anyway, he was showing these pieces to George's father who just couldn't get this ring out of his mind. It's early-Victorian — Russian, he thought, not one of the expensive ones. Anyway George's father decided to buy it for a silver wedding anniversary present for his wife.'

She took a deep breath. 'Isn't that the most romantic thing you ever heard?'

'I should say,' Vanessa said, looking down at her own solitaire diamond. 'Makes mine look a bit ordinary.'

'Not when you think what Oliver must have paid for it!' And they both laughed.

'Well, I wish you both every happiness,' Vanessa said. 'When's the wedding?'

'Oh, Lord knows — the spring if I have my way. I just can't wait for you to meet George. But you will at the wedding.'

'Sally, I'm so excited. Nervous — you know me, I hate "do's" of any kind — but excited just the same. He's such a dear, Oliver. I expect most people find him a bit boring, but he's awfully kind — '

'Oh, he's a poppet,' Sally rushed in quickly. Too quickly, for she thought him rather dull, and not a patch on George. 'Anyway, the dress is ready, what else do you need to do?'

'I'll show you my "going away" outfit, as Granny Amber puts it so sweetly. Here, what do you think?'

'Love it,' Sally said enthusiastically, eyeing the well-cut slacks in olive green and matching sweater, together with a cream silk blouse.

'But what about this?' And Vanessa took out of its wrappings a soft beige cashmere coat.

'Oh,' Sally breathed.

'Wedding present from Daddy. You know, he's been awfully generous. I expect he was thrilled to bits to win his case.'

'Well, it was an achievement, wasn't it? And a nice write up about him in the *Telegraph*.'

'Yes, I saw it. You know, I'm so glad he has Odile — they're as happy as Larry. Odile has a French girl starting next week, after the wedding — a cousin, I think, from Provence. She says we can always go down there and stay, isn't that useful?'

'Do you think you'll want to start a family right away, Van?'

She made a face. 'Not in this flat, I hope! No, of course

we will, but at the moment I'm staying with Jane — we'll see how things work out.'

'It is a bit twee for the two of you,' Sally said, looking around. 'I mean, Oliver's a tall chap.'

'Yes, isn't he? But, you see, he's always lived in Sussex, commuting every day — don't ask me how he stands it — and I think he needs to be broken in gently to living in town. Working in the city and me here, it makes sense, but it's only temporary. Later on, we'll look around for something bigger.'

'Have you heard any more from your mother?'

'No — only to say she's coming.'

'It's very exciting,' Sally said. 'Weddings always are. I wish it were mine.'

She thought she had never seen Vanessa more relaxed and happy.

'Well, I'd better go. By the way, did you hear that Gillian is engaged?'

'Well, I did. To an Arab — someone from Dubai.'

'She was always mad keen on guys from abroad, you remember that.'

Vanessa coughed discreetly. 'I think we'll gloss over that episode.' And they both giggled.

Sally picked up her handbag and swiftly kissed Vanessa's cheek.

'Well, old thing, all the best — and see you at the wedding. Best of luck and all that — oh, and don't forget. Something borrowed, something blue . . .' And with a wave, she was gone.

Next time I see Sally, Vanessa thought, I will be married.

Now that she had a moment, she could turn some of the drawers out, make room for Oliver and his things. They would have to buy another wardrobe or he could use the one in the spare room, small as it was. This chest of drawers she could empty out. It was rather fun making room for a man, she thought. But it wouldn't be easy for the flat to absorb him, it was so small. Still, they would manage somehow.

She rummaged in a drawer and turfed out her bikinis and shorts. Both she and Oliver had always wanted to go to Corsica and a honeymoon seemed a good time to do it. As long as it was sunny and warm, she didn't mind where it was. Just to be alone with him, to lie in the sun, to make love, to get to know each other ... surely this was the most exciting time in a girl's life?

Oliver was a good lover, she reflected. Of course, their lovemaking had none of the passion of her Indian love affair, as she called it to herself. Then, she had been so young, childish almost, and completely overpowered by the sheer animalism of her lover. Sometimes she thought about him, but rarely nowadays. Just to wonder if he was still in prison.

Humming a little tune, she went into the spare room where on the bed lay an assortment of gift-wrapped parcels. Wedding presents that had been here, although she understood from her grandmother that she too had quite a few lying in wait.

Oliver was spending the weekend at home, the last until the wedding, and she needed the time to prepare anyway.

Later, she made herself some cheese on toast and a salad, followed by freshly picked greengages from Alice's garden.

It was getting dark, around eight, when she heard the doorbell ring. Before opening it, she pushed aside the curtain in the hall. It was Oliver! What a lovely surprise. Swiftly she opened the door to greet him.

'Darling, I thought you were in Sussex!'

She put her arms around his neck and drew him close to her, surprised when he didn't sweep her into his arms as he usually did. Looking up, she saw that he wasn't wearing his accustomed smile, that his dark eyes were preoccupied.

She closed the door behind him and led him in. 'Oliver, darling, what's wrong? You look awful.'

He sat down in the large comfy chair opposite her.

Then she noticed how white he was, his cheeks a greyish colour, and became concerned.

'Darling, you're not ill, are you?'

He took a deep breath. 'Vanessa, I don't know how to say this, to tell you — we can't be married.'

She was struck dumb, her mouth open. Finally she said, 'What?'

'The wedding ... I'm afraid it's off. I can't marry you.'

Her first thought was, My God, he's is ill. There's something wrong with him ...

'Oh, darling — Oliver!' And she was beside him in an instant.

'I know it's an awful thing to do — I feel such a pig — but it's better to tell you now.'

Perhaps he wasn't ill? She frowned. 'I'm sorry, I don't think I understand.'

In a moment she would wake up and find she was dreaming.

'Tell me what?' she persisted.

'That it would be a mistake. To marry you — feeling as I do. I'm desperately sorry.'

'A mistake?' Her voice was dangerously quiet.

He floundered, 'I think you are the dearest girl in the world —'

She stood up suddenly and stood with her back to him at the window, arms folded.

'I think I have always known that my feelings for you were not strong enough for marriage.'

She turned to face him, the awful truth at last dawning on her.

'It's a pity you didn't think of that before we put so many people to so much trouble!'

He bent his head. 'Can you imagine how I feel? How sorry I am?'

'No, actually, I can't,' she said. 'I'm more sorry for me at the moment.'

'You see ...'

She waited. 'Yes?'

'I'm not going to hide the truth from you,' he began.

'Oh, good.'

'It's Rosemary,' he blurted out, and she felt a wave of anger so strong she wanted to lash out and hit him.

'What!'

'Rosemary — I hope you'll understand, Van. She's desperately unhappy — she telephoned me on Friday evening, and, well, I came up to town ... That swine has ill-treated her. He threatened her with physical violence and she was terrified of him, poor little thing. So much so that she left him, with nowhere to go. And, well, to cut a long story short, I − we − she loves me, Vanessa, and I love her. So you see ...'

'Yes, I do see,' Vanessa hissed between her teeth. She was shaking from head to foot, more with anger than anything.

'You'd better go. I think you've said enough.'

He seemed surprised to be let off so easily. 'But, Vanessa, I do realize that you've been put to a great deal of expense and I will see to it that financially −'

She swept open the front door and stood there, waiting.

'But, Vanessa −'

'Please go,' she said, and with a calmness she certainly wasn't feeling, shot the bolt behind him.

Back inside, she flopped into the chair, feeling numb and cold. She couldn't believe it. In the space of a few minutes or so, it was all over. The preparations, the plans, everything, their future − what's more, she couldn't cry. She was as cold as ice. She felt nothing. She couldn't believe that it had just taken place. That he had been and said what he had and gone.

She sat there for what seemed like hours, growing colder and colder, then she got up and went into the kitchen and poured herself a large glass of sweet sherry. Sipping it, she felt the warmth coming back into her limbs, but she was still incapable of feeling any emotion. After the second glass, she crept to bed and lay feeling woozy and slightly dizzy. Each time she surfaced she felt such a fool. It was such a let down, having to tell everyone: 'Sorry to have bothered you, but he had the wrong girl. It wasn't me he loved at all, it was Rosemary.' Bloody Rosemary ... if it wasn't so awful, she could have laughed.

She finally slept, but the awakening was worse, to realize that she hadn't been dreaming, it had really happened. He had gone, forever, to Rosemary. Men were so gullible, she reflected, for she was sure that Rosemary had him on a piece of string. One met girls like her in school and later as adults. There would always be Rosemarys and young men like Oliver to become ensnared. Anyway, perhaps she was being harsh. Perhaps they really did love each other with an overriding passion as she had felt for Karim. But that wouldn't have been right for marriage, she knew that now.

It was strange how she didn't feel broken-hearted. Mortified was a better word. Anyway, you couldn't really feel enduring love for someone who wanted someone else, and what a good thing it had happened now. If they had been married and he and Rosemary had met up again, that would have been worse.

She stretched and sighed. Now it was up to her to do the explaining.

She got up, still dressed, feeling awful, a disgusting taste in her mouth. Looking in the mirror, she turned away from her reflection. She looked ghastly. Strangely enough, she felt no emotion, no sense of loss, of missing him, just plain anger at being let down in the build up of the wedding, at the sheer awfulness of having to cancel everything, for everyone having to know ...

Perhaps later she would feel a sense of love denied of thwarted romance, but not now. What to do first?

She made some coffee and sat and drank it, making plans. Wondering how to deal with it. A telephone call to Jane first to say she would not be in — not for the rest of the week. The wedding was off. Sorry, but the wedding was off ...

She saw herself picking up the telephone, making the first of the awful calls, and steeled herself.

'Darling! You can't be serious!' Jane said, making an effort at a joke, and when Vanessa said nothing realized that it was indeed serious.

'Oh, Van darling! I thought for a moment — where are you? Why? What happened?'

'I can't talk now,' she said wearily. 'Just take my word for it, the wedding is off. I must go. I've so much to do — you can imagine.'

'Vanessa, listen, if there's anything at all I can do — really, I'm here any time. Just call or ring.' She sounded nearly in tears.

'Thanks, Jane,' Vanessa said, and put down the telephone. Now for Granny Amber.

She bit her lip at the thought of the sympathy she would get, the love and affection from dear Granny Amber. She could hardly bear it. Her voice was low and hardly audible when Alice answered the phone.

'Vanessa, my dear! How are you?'

And then she cried, great sobs coming up from deep down in her stomach as she tried to find the words.

'Gran — the wedding's off — it's all off — he — Oliver — ' She could hardly bear to say his name.

There was a moment's silence then Alice's voice, warm and comforting. 'Darling, don't worry. Nothing matters except that you're safe. I thought for a dreadful moment ... Now you must come home at once, straight to me, and tell me all about it. We'll deal with it all, one thing at a time.'

She had packed and was leaving when the call came.

'Vanessa? Are you all right?' It was Oliver.

'Yes, I'm fine!' she said brightly, with an effort at sarcasm.

'I had to ring to see if you were all right — I feel such a dog. I really didn't want to hurt you — you do understand, don't you?'

'Oh, go away!' she said.

She replaced the receiver. How could she ever have imagined that she was in love with him?

Alice was at the station to meet her, her kindly face creased into lines of compassion and sympathy. She put her arms round Vanessa and hugged her.

'I think,' she said, 'you had a lucky escape.'

She let Vanessa talk over supper and during the evening, until she was tired out and ready for bed.

Finally, she told her that she had already rung Joanna and put off the wedding reception.

'Oh!' Vanessa cried. 'What did she say?'

'What could she say? Except that she was sorry, of course — these things happen — and you're not to worry! Now I suggest you go to bed, it's nicely aired, and in the morning we'll let your father know and deal with the cancellation of the wedding invitations.'

'Oh, Gran, I feel awful!'

'Of course you do, darling, but it's not your fault. I'd like to horsewhip that young man!'

When Vanessa had gone to bed, Alice picked up the

telephone and dialed The Bear. Then she asked to speak to Donald.

There was no doubting the relief in his voice when he spoke to her.

'Yes, Joanna told me. God, what a thing to happen! Poor little Vanessa —'

'Yes. I don't think it's quite sunk in yet. Donald, why I rang — do you have Amanda's telephone number?'

'Yes, of course, Alice — I have it right here' And he gave it to her. 'I say, a bit of relief all round, in one way.'

'Yes, Donald,' she said drily. 'I won't keep you now.'

Everyone had their own interests at heart, she thought. It was only natural.

And so the wheels were set in motion — the cancellations, the telephone calls, the letters, the sympathetic messages. James was wonderful; he drove round to pick Vanessa up and took her back to Four Oaks where she helped to bathe little Edouard and later her father took them out to dinner, with Odile listening with sympathy and understanding and James trying very hard to make light of the whole thing.

The next day it had finally sunk in. They had broken up, separated, she had lost him. What had happened to the togetherness they had had, the fun, the laughter, the friendship and understanding? She had thought they were two kindred spirits. How could she have been so wrong? She thought of him, so tall, good-looking, his arms around her, the way he smoothed her hair and kissed her, his touch. She had thought it was a quiet, strong, undemanding love. What did Rosemary have that drew him back to her, time and time again?

In her room, she took out the solitaire ring from its box and slipped it on to her right hand, surprising herself at the hard streak she hadn't known she possessed. 'Sorry, Rosemary,' she said out loud.

'Oh, how awful!' Sheila said, sitting in Alice's kitchen while Vanessa took the dog for a walk through the park. She always took these sort of things very personally. 'What a swine!'

'You know, I'm not sorry,' Alice said. 'I know it's easy to say that after the event — but I never really thought they were right for each other. But who's to know? That little touch of magic or whatever it is seemed to be missing.'

'Well, all I can hope now is that Adbul changes his mind and finds a nice Arab girl,' Sheila began.

'Sheila, you are naughty!' Alice said, chiding her. 'And now for the phone call to Amanda. I bet she'll be jolly disappointed not to be coming.' She could hardly disguise the pleasure she felt.

When Alice told her, there was a long silence. She waited, wondering if they had been cut off. The line was bad and Amanda sounded so far away.

'How is she?' Amanda said at length.

'Bearing up very well,' Alice said. It was so odd to be having a conversation with her at all.

'Will you tell her I am very sorry?' Amanda said. 'Thank you for letting me know, Alice.'

There was no time to ask after her politely, she had rung off.

'Well.' She turned to Sheila. 'That's that. We'll have to get down now to building up Vanessa's self-esteem. She's bound to think she has failed somewhere along the line. I'm going to suggest she goes away somewhere for a while until it all dies down. It won't be easy to face everyone right now.'

'Oh, but people will understand,' Sheila said.

'Yes, but you wouldn't like them to feel sorry for you, would you?'

'Need they know the reason? Can't you say that she changed her mind?'

'I've simply said that the marriage will not take place.'

'Very official,' Sheila said. 'Well, her best friends will know and understand. As for the others, they don't matter.'

Alice thought of the wedding gown she hadn't seen, still hanging probably in Vanessa's little bedroom in the flat; of the wedding presents to be returned.

Then there was the sound of a car outside, and through the open door came Joanna, holding something in her hand.

'Champagne,' she said. 'From both of us. After all, there may not be a wedding but I'm sure you'll find some occasion to celebrate. There's nothing like a glass of champagne to cheer you up!'

Alice looked at her warmly.

'Thank you, dear. Yes, we were just talking about that. Wondering how best to take her out of herself, to put her mind to something.'

'Where is she now?'

'Taken the dog for a walk.'

'How awful for her. I do feel for her,' Joanna said. 'Give her our love. By the way, we're off for the weekend. Isn't it marvellous? Apropos of nothing, Donald said, well, we may not have a wedding to attend but let's go to Paris for the weekend — so you can imagine I jumped at the chance!'

She bent and kissed Alice. 'Stay well, I'll be back on Monday. Cheerio, Sheila.'

'Some people have all the luck,' Sheila said glumly.

'Tell you what,' Alice said. 'When we've sorted this thing out, why don't you and I swan off somewhere — just for a few days?' And Sheila's eyes warmed to the idea.

'Providing it's fairly soon — remember Alison.'

It seemed as if being kept busy enabled Vanessa to keep going, but towards the end of the week, as the wedding day drew near, she flagged, keeping to her room only to emerge when Alice called her. She had dark rings under eyes which, usually so blue, were now lacklustre. She was very pale, and seemed even in this short time to have grown thinner. Alice was getting quite worried about her. She had suggested all sorts of things they might do, but nothing seemed to appeal.

'I'm catching up on my reading,' she said, but Alice didn't believe her. Had she really been madly in love with Oliver?

On Friday afternoon, after a lunch which she had pecked at, Vanessa went into her room. Alice sat looking out of the window and was surprised when a dark limousine, chauffeur-driven, drew up outside the house. She stared as the driver opened the passenger door and helped a woman down, a slight figure, dressed almost outrageously. A hand went to her throat as her heart started to beat fast. It was Amanda! Yes, it must be but ...

The tiny figure tottered up the path, swiftly yet uncertainly. Thin legs in high heels, her hair, masses of hair, streaked with grey, red, black — and a face painted almost to look like a clown's ...

Before she had time to ring Alice opened the door, uncertain yet sure. She saw a face tanned mahogany by the sun, cheekbones standing out, great dark eyes, the lashes heavily mascaraed, garish lipstick applied to make thin lips thicker. The suit she wore had a plunging neckline revealing yards of gold chains. All this Alice took in before realization dawned. She was looking at a dying woman. She had lived long enough to know the signs.

'Come in, Amanda,' she said gently.

'Alice ...' Even her lovely voice was croaky, harsh. 'Where is she?'

'In her bedroom, here.' And Alice closed the front door. She knocked on Vanessa's door and went in. Vanessa was lying on the bed, not reading but with arms above her head, her eyes open. She sat up.

'Darling, you have a visitor — someone to see you. Your mother ...'

She smiled at Amanda, let her in, and closed the door gently behind her.

She sat in the kitchen, tears streaming down her face. From the bedroom came muffled sounds of talking while the car waited outside. Alice dragged herself from her chair to put the kettle on and made a pot of tea. They had been in there now almost an hour. She could hear Amanda's low voice and Vanessa's as they both talked. As she prepared the tray, the door opened and they came in. Shocked yet again at Amanda's appearance, she swallowed hard and forced a smile.

Vanessa, she saw, had come to life. Her eyes were more alive, her movements brisk.

She came over and hugged Alice. 'Thank you for everything, Gran,' she whispered. 'I'm going back to Sardinia for a little holiday with Mother.'

Alice bit her lip and looked at Amanda. Those great dark eyes looked back at her, unflinching. Never, Alice thought, would she forget them. The incongruous make up, that ruined face.

'Aren't you taking anything?'

'Just her passport, Alice,' Amanda said, and held out her hand to say goodbye.

Alice watched the car drive away until it was out of sight, then went back into the kitchen, crying as she hadn't cried for years. It was a relief getting rid of all the pent up emotion. Afterwards she felt drained, empty. Then she went into the dining room and, getting out the patchwork quilt, began to sew the pieces together, finding a kind of relief and therapy in the action. From time to time she looked up and out of the window. It would soon be time to put in bulbs for the spring.

Chapter Eighteen

It was the beginning of December before Vanessa arrived back home from Sardinia. Apart from a few postcards Alice had heard nothing until a few days before her arrival, when a short, cryptic telephone call had told her the news she had been expecting.

'She's gone.'

'Ah ...' The long drawn out expression of sympathy was the only sound Alice could make.

'The funeral is on Wednesday, Gran, and I will wait for that then fly home on Thursday.'

'All right, darling. I'm so sorry, you know that.'

'Of course I do, but it's all right, Gran. I'm so glad I came. See you on Thursday.'

At the airport, Alice looked anxiously for Vanessa's tall slim figure, and when she finally saw her, her throat constricted because she wanted to cry.

Vanessa strode tall, her long mane of hair tied back with a black bow. She was wearing blue jeans and a navy sweater, her face tanned, eyes a vivid blue, and there was a new look about her — a look of composure, Alice decided. She had really grown up. To watch someone die, she thought, is a salutary lesson in human behaviour.

They hugged each other and Alice knew Vanessa was not going to weep. She had probably done all that, she decided, and was now well on the road to recovery.

They didn't speak much on the way home, Alice's capable hands on the wheel of her elderly M.G. Not until they reached Chantry Lodge and Alice had put the kettle on did Vanessa come down after taking her things upstairs and smile at her grandmother.

'It's lovely to be back,' she said. 'And a fire — gorgeous! I left in glorious sunshine. But, you know, Gran, you can have too much of that.'

Alice nodded, warming the teapot.

'And how is Pepi — is that his name?'

'Bereft, I suppose, is the word. Such a nice man, Gran — they'd been together a long time apparently. He adored her and spoiled her. Only natural, I suppose, when you consider.'

'Poor man.'

Alice poured the tea, and they sat down either side of the fire.

'Is it too soon to ask you how you really got on? Did you get to know each other in such a short time?'

'As much as we could, starting from where we left off. Strangely, she bore no relation to the mother I remembered, isn't that odd, Gran? She was not the person I had in mind, and I can't think what she thought about me as a grown woman after knowing a child of ten.'

She stared into the fire, watching the flames.

'Still, we talked and talked, of all sorts of things. I suppose at the end of the day I felt a little sorry for Daddy — she must have been terribly difficult to live with.'

'I think she was, although your father never ever said a word. But I think we knew ... guessed ...'

'Towards the end, in her lucid moments, she said men had always adored her, that they were the cause of her downfall. They all wanted her, she said, and she knew it. She urged me not to place too much dependence on a man. That I was to remember I was a person in my own right, I should be independent, that sort of thing.'

'Doesn't sound like Amanda to me,' Alice said wryly. 'She must have changed.'

'The last few days she was barely conscious for most of the time. She would keep whispering names. James, she said, and Donald — Donald. The tears ran down her face ...'

Alice bit her lip. 'I expect she knew a lot of Donald's,' she said clearly.

'Then she would smile and say: "Pepi — Pepi — my true love." It was so sad ... She died in the night, while we were all asleep, the doctor said, and it was a release, Gran. No one would have wanted her to go on.'

Alice reached out and patted her hand.

'Of course not, my dear.'

'She was awfully good to me. Where she was best of all was about Oliver. She was wonderful, soothed me over the bad days when I first arrived, and in no time I really had almost forgotten him. There was so much to do for her, you see.'

Wisdom, Alice thought, not something she had associated with Amanda, but there you are, you could never tell.

In the days that followed more and more of Amanda's life was revealed. Vanessa seemed to have undergone a kind of therapy. That her visit had made a lasting impression on her in every way was only too obvious.

'I'm not going back to work for Jane, Gran,' she said one morning. 'I'd like to do something useful.' And suddenly she remembered Karim when he'd asked her if she had gone to India to help the starving poor.

'No, just to look,' she had said with the flippancy of youth and the well-to-do. Her feelings if she went now would be very different. Then she had been like a child, greedily absorbing everything she could, taking everything, giving little. She was different now.

'What sort of thing do you want to do?' Alice asked, interested.

'At the moment I feel I want to help with Cancer Research — it's such a dreadful scourge, Gran, and affects so many people — young people, children. It's an awful thing, and you never realize until it hits you or someone you love. After all, Mummy was only forty-four.'

'Yes,' Alice said slowly. 'Well, I'm sure there are lots of things you could do.'

Vanessa would throw herself into something like that, she thought, until she had got it out of her system, before she embarked on another course of her life.

'I suppose I shall have to go up and turf out the flat sometime,' she went on morosely. 'I'm not looking forward to that, Gran. Too many memories. I'll have to think about what to do with the wedding dress. I gave my engagement ring to Cancer Research — I thought that was the best thing to do.'

'That was very good of you, darling.'

'I'm not awfully keen on living in the flat again, but I suppose I shall. It depends.'

She needed time to adjust, Alice thought. 'Well, you always have a home here.'

'I know, Gran. And do you know, I'd forgotten that it's Edouard's first birthday this week. It wasn't until I looked in my diary ...'

So the days passed, with Vanessa meeting people again and picking up where she'd left off. On the last Red Cross sewing morning before the New Year, she joined them for coffee, admiring the finished quilt which was now being backed.

'It's absolutely beautiful, someone will be lucky to win it ... when's the raffle taking place?'

'Sometime before Christmas,' Alice said.

Vanessa pushed back the chair. 'Well, I must fly — I'm going up to town to see Jane and to have lunch with Sally. I'm meeting George this week sometime, I've heard so much about him.'

And she left, a slim figure in scarlet sweater and long navy skirt, she was followed by envious eyes.

'She's a lovely girl, Alice,' Ann said generously.

'Thank you, yes, we think so. She's had a bit of a trial to endure, but at the end of the day, I'm sure it will all be for the best. What we want to hear about is Alison's baby. Any news, Sheila?'

'Well, firstly it's due earlier than I thought. Due around Christmas they say. I just pray everything will be all right.'

'Oh, you mustn't worry,' Alice said comfortingly. 'She'll be fine.'

They were interrupted by Gina coming in to collect the tray of coffee cups. Her large black eyes looked soulful, and she nodded to them silently.

When she had gone, Alice looked up. 'She's been like this ever since the wedding was cancelled.'

'Poor Gina — and she'd bought her outfit.'

'I know,' Alice said. 'I do feel badly about it.'

'So what happened in Sardinia?' Joanna asked. 'It was the most tragic thing, Amanda dying — I couldn't believe it. Sally had said nothing to us about her being ill.'

'She probably saw nothing, but it was obvious to me as soon as I opened the door to her. It was such a shock.'

'How absolutely awful,' Sheila said. 'Only forty-four — it makes you think.'

'The only thing is, she'd crowded such a lot into that short life — and I think she enjoyed it all. The blessing was meeting up with Vanessa again. I'm glad about that, although I was shocked at first.'

The quilt was spread all over the dining table, and now it was clear that just the last few stitches were needed to finish it off.

'You do it, Alice,' they said. And coming round to the other side of the table, she put in the last few stitches of the backing to finish it off. They gave a small cheer and turned it over to the right side, delighted at what they saw.

'If you ask me, it's an achievement,' Sheila said.

'It really is the prettiest thing,' Joanna said, 'and if I may say so, beautifully done. A credit to the Chantry Park Red Cross ladies.'

They all looked down at it: the number of stitches that had gone into its making, the colours carefully blended — mostly light blues, dashes of yellow and white, here and there a pink or heather or brown — the design looking quite professional.

'How much shall we ask for a ticket?' Ann asked, ever the practical one.

'Oh, I think a pound,' Alice said. 'Fifty pence is too cheap, and most of the people here can afford that. Hopefully they'll buy five, or ten, or even twenty pounds worth of tickets — after all, it is for the Red Cross and we all know quite a few people.'

So it was decided. When it was pressed and hung up on the wall in the golf clubhouse, it was much admired. By the second week in December, they had reached three hundred and forty pounds.

This excitement was overtaken by a call for Sheila from

Alison's husband who said that she had gone into hospital to await the birth of the baby.

Full of trepidation, mixed with excitement, elation and foreboding, Sheila set off in the car. She drove straight to the hospital where she found Alison lying in a small room, bright-eyed and very large. Like every mother before her, she wished she could go through the ordeal instead of her daughter.

She kissed her warmly. 'Alison, you look wonderful! Soon be over now.'

'Yes, they're giving me a Caesarian section to be on the safe side.'

'Oh.' Sheila had given birth to the girls quite naturally and disliked the idea of a Caesarian birth, but she smiled warmly. 'Oh, that's good, my dear.'

They stayed talking until Alison's husband arrived when Sheila left and went home to prepare his evening meal. He left again for the hospital at seven with instructions to telephone Sheila whatever the time, even if it was in the middle of the night.

There was no sleep for her. She sat reading magazines, or trying to, put on and turned off the television and the radio. Rearranged flowers, dusted, checked the tiny nursery upstairs, and worried herself through the next six hours.

It was at one o'clock in the morning that the 'phone shrilled through the house. She jumped up, almost knocking over a chair in her haste to reach it.

'Sheila?' She caught the intonation immediately. It was good news! 'We have a son — a seven pound boy.'

'Oh, Ben! Is she all right?'

'She's fine, just fine.'

'And the baby?'

'Absolutely beautiful. And you can come and see them in the morning, the doctor says.'

Sheila flopped into a chair and howled with relief. She was a grandmother and Alison had her baby! How pleased and proud Don would have been. She wept once more. When it was over, she made herself a strong cup of tea, and taking it upstairs to the spare room, sat up in bed and drank it. Then, exhausted, she slept.

She was almost the first visitor, Ben taking a well-earned nap after being up all night.

Alison was radiant though tired, and Sheila kissed her warmly. 'Congratulations, darling — what a clever girl.'

At that moment the nurse came in holding a bundle in her arms which she gave to Alison, who looked down with an expression that changed her from an ordinary into a beautiful woman.

'Let me see him,' Sheila begged.

The nurse pried the blanket away from his chin and Sheila saw a red wrinkled face, a patch of dark hair, a firm little chin. He had a resemblance both to Alison and his father. My little freezer grandson, Sheila thought wonderingly. Without that, he might never have been born.

'Oh, he is the most beautiful baby I have ever seen,' she gulped.

'Six and a half years I've waited for this,' Alison said, 'and he's been worth every minute of it.'

Once Alison was home, Sheila stayed for a few days until she thought her daughter was organized. She arranged the huge bouquet of flowers which had arrived from the Red Cross ladies and, pleased with a job well done, drove herself home to await Gillian's arrival.

Gillian had been overjoyed at the news and announced her intention of flying home to see her new nephew and to shop for her wedding trousseau.

So it was still on, Sheila thought. There was no way now that it could be averted. She would have an Arab son-in-law, and any children of the marriage would not be her grandchildren but would belong totally to Abdul's family. Why couldn't Gillian see the folly of what she was doing?

When Gillian arrived, looking as Sheila told herself like a black crow in her voluminous outer garment, she could hardly conceal her irritation.

'Do you really have to wear that — thing?' she asked after Gillian had kissed her. Her face is wrong, she thought crossly. She just doesn't look right in that thing. She's so English . . .

But Gillian just smiled and hugged her again. 'Better get used to it, Mother,' she said. 'Now tell me about the baby — who's he like? What are they going to call him?'

They found the car in the airport car park, and Sheila began the drive home.

'Thomas,' she said proudly. 'Tom for short — isn't that nice?'

'Perfect,' Gillian said. 'I'm going to enjoy being an auntie.'

'Well, I suggest you don't wear that thing to see him — it's frightening to a baby, so dark.' And she shuddered while Gillian laughed.

'All right, I won't.'

They drove up together to Gloucester where they stayed overnight with Alison, and Sheila thought she had never seen the two girls so close.

She left them together quite a bit while she tidied the garden, and heard them several times discussing the forthcoming wedding, and of course baby Tom's christening.

Pity, she thought, I can't feel as excited about the wedding as I do about the christening.

Once home in Chantry Park, Gillian announced her intention of going up to town for shopping.

'I thought you'd be married in traditional Arab clothes? Don't tell me you're going to have a white wedding dress with all the trimmings.' She was astonished.

'Of course I am! I want to be a real English bride. Just because I'm getting married in Dubai doesn't mean I have to give up everything. I've waited for this for a long time — my wedding day is important to me.'

They searched for a long time, and Sheila had to admit that she enjoyed it all immensely. Seeing Gillian as a bride she was overcome with sentiment, and when her daughter finally decided on a full-skirted creamy gown with lots of pearl embroidery on the bodice, was as pleased as if she had chosen it herself, although it wasn't really to her taste.

'It will have to have some form of embroidery, beading or something, otherwise they won't be impressed,' Gillian explained.

She chose a traditional veil and headdress. Sheila sat watching the salesgirl pin them into place, remembering

Gillian as a rosy-cheeked little girl at her birthday parties — she had always been popular, even at school. What hopes they had had for her when she had turned out to be the brainy one. Winning scholarship after scholarship, excelling at university — the world had been her oyster. Yet she had chosen to work in Dubai after a spell in Kuwait, and now she was, about to embark on marriage so far away from her old life and its customs.

How different it might have been, thought Sheila, as she sat opposite her at the lunch table.

'You will take lots of photographs of the wedding, won't you?' she asked.

Gillian put down her fork.

'I wanted to talk to you about that. Mother, are you sure you won't come over for it? I wish you would.'

Sheila shook her head. 'I'm sorry, Gillian, I can't.'

'But why not? You would find it very interesting — and Abdul's parents and family would make you very welcome.'

'I don't know. Perhaps if your father had been alive ... But I'm not very good on foreign travel — France seems to be my limit — and I wouldn't want to spoil your day.'

'How could you spoil it? It won't be the same if you aren't there.'

But Sheila was adamant.

She left Gillian in town, where she was to finish her English shopping, as she called it, with fine woollies and some presents for Abdul's family. Later she was to meet Sally Simpson after she had finished at the shop.

They packed all the purchases, including the wedding dress in its great box, into Sheila's car and she began the drive home, feeling guilty all the way at her lack of support for Gillian's wedding. By the time she reached home, she knew quite positively that she just couldn't go. For many reasons, mainly that she disapproved of Gillian's marrying Abdul. That being the case, it was better not to go.

Just after five, Gillian and Sally sat having coffee in Way In in Harrods.

'What a fabulous ring!' Gillian said, seeing Sally's left hand adorned.

'Yes, isn't it?' she said, eyeing the girl opposite whom she had more or less grown up with. She had always been an oddity, Sally thought. The one outside the group; the one who did and thought differently from the others. But a brainbox, certainly. And now here she was embarking on a different religion, a different way of life, going to live in the Middle East, speaking the language like a native – it was no surprise really.

'So when are you getting married?' Gillian asked.

'The spring – April, I think. We have lots of things to sort out before then, mainly financial. You don't have that problem, do you?'

'I don't personally. I earn a jolly good salary – enough to keep both of us because, well, I expect you knew, Adbul doesn't have a job.'

'No! I didn't know that. Yet you're getting married just the same?'

'Why not? What's the good of hanging about?'

'That's true, I suppose.'

'The only thing missing is that Mother won't come to the wedding.'

Sally was shocked. 'What do you mean? Not go to your wedding?'

Gillian nodded, and Sally could see that she was really more upset than she showed. Well, she wasn't going to give an opinion, she was fond of Auntie Sheila.

'Couldn't you have another wedding – over here?' she suggested. 'Later. Presumably you will be coming over sometimes?'

'Do you know, we could,' Gillian said. 'I don't know why I didn't think of it ...'

Then the talk centred around Vanessa.

'Awful,' Gillian said. 'Poor old Van – I couldn't believe it when I heard.'

When Gillian arrived home she found Aunt Alice in her mother's kitchen organizing the raffle for the quilt which was to be held the Friday before Christmas.

'You can help us fold the tickets,' Sheila said. 'Do you know, we've sold three hundred and sixty now – isn't that wonderful?'

'Mother, I've had an idea — at least Sally has. Why don't I have a civil wedding here in England when we come over in the spring? You'd like that, wouldn't you?'

'What a good idea!' Alice said.

'Of course,' Sheila said, but without much animation.

It's no good, Gillian thought, she just doesn't like the idea of my marrying Abdul. And she sighed.

'Yes, well,' she said. 'I think that's what we'll do. It's only fair.'

'I put the dress upstairs on your bed,' Sheila said.

'Would you like to see it, Aunt Alice?'

She gave a quick glance across at Sheila.

'Yes please, dear, I would.'

When Gillian emerged half an hour later, Alice drew in her breath. She looked lovely. For the first time Alice understood how Sheila must be feeling. But she would get over it — all sorts of strange things happened in the world today.

On Friday morning, after a fund raising bring and buy sale for the Save the Children fund, coffee was served and a general get together enjoyed by all. The Red Cross sewing bee were all there, even dissident members. The noise of everyone chatting was quite overpowering.

Maggie, who was holding court after being away in Hong Kong, laughed. 'Don't thank me,' she said, 'I had nothing to do with it at all — I'm only visiting.'

She was staying at The Bear over Christmas since the tenants were still in her house.

There was hush when the Secretary of the club clapped her hands for silence, and then the Ladies Club Captain made ready to pick the winning number.

From the hat she withdrew a pink ticket. You could have heard a pin drop.

'Pink ticket number two hundred and forty-nine.' Her stentorian tones reached the back of the hall.

Maggie gave a squeal. 'I don't believe it — I have it!' She waved her ticket as, flushed with excitement, she went forward to receive her prize.

There were many disappointed murmurs.

'Well, she did buy ten tickets,' Alice said.

'You will be pleased to know that the final figure raised for the Red Cross from the sale of raffle tickets was three hundred and eighty-four pounds,' the Captain said, and everyone applauded.

'Well done!'

'That's wonderful, isn't it?' Gillian said. 'You must make another sometime.'

'Not for a while,' Alice said. 'Although, I must say, it was very rewarding seeing the finished garment. Didn't you think so, Sheila?'

'Yes, I did. It was a work of art.'

She stood up to go. 'Well, we must make our farewells. Gillian flies back in the morning, and she has quite a lot of packing to do.'

Gillian shook hands and kissed those she knew well, and was sent off with many good wishes for her future and well-being. She was quite misty-eyed when she left.

In the morning, Sheila drove her to the airport after a difficult journey through heavy traffic, leaving them little time to spare, and accompanied her to the airport lounge with her luggage. It seemed the world and his wife were taking off this morning, and she watched as Gillian put her luggage on the scales and arranged to pay the excess baggage.

Looking up at the board she saw that they were already boarding, and went across to tell Gillian.

She glanced up, tears in her eyes. Suddenly she threw her arms around Sheila and hugged her. 'I do miss you, Mummy,' she said, using the old childish name, and Sheila's heart leapt.

'You don't need me to tell you how much I miss you — how much I am going to miss you,' she said. 'You know you have all my love, and I hope all goes well at the wedding.'

'Thank you. And give my love to Alison and little Tom.' Then her black-gowned figure slipped towards the gate.

'And mine to Abdul,' Sheila called after her, surprising herself.

It was on the way home she decided, and wondered why she had taken so long.

Of course she would go to the wedding! Leave her daughter out there alone in an alien country? Definitely not. What sort of mother was she?

She would telephone Gillian tomorrow and let her know. Suddenly she felt more lighthearted than she had for months. She certainly had a duty as a mother to meet her future-in-laws, and somehow she felt Don would have been pleased at the decision.

She had put the car away and was locking the garage door when she heard another car draw up behind her. She turned in time to see Maggie get out.

'Hello, Maggie, I've just got back. Come in and have some coffee.'

'Love to, she said, delving into the car, her elegant legs stretched out, bracelets jangling, gingery hair gleaming, long pointed nails around a large Harrods bag.

She followed Sheila into the house.

'I brought this,' she said. 'I hope you don't mind — it's not exactly looking a gift horse in the mouth, is it? I'd like to give it to your new grandson, Tom.

And she drew out the patchwork quilt.

Sheila stood speechless then took it, eyes brimming.

'How kind of you. Thank you, Maggie.'

'My pleasure,' she said. 'Now — tell me all the news.'